THE
JURY

Books by Fern Michaels

Betrayal
Southern Comfort
To Taste the Wine
Sins of the Flesh
Sins of Omission
Return to Sender
Mr. and Miss Anonymous
Up Close and Personal
Fool Me Once
Picture Perfect
About Face
The Future Scrolls
Kentucky Sunrise
Kentucky Heat
Kentucky Rich
Plain Jane
Charming Lily
What You Wish For
The Guest List
Listen to Your Heart
Celebration
Yesterday
Finders Keepers
Annie's Rainbow
Sara's Song
Vegas Sunrise
Vegas Heat
Vegas Rich
Whitefire
Wish List
Dear Emily
Christmas at Timberwoods

The Godmothers Series

Deadline
Late Edition
Exclusive
The Scoop

The Sisterhood Novels

Home Free
Déjà Vu
Cross Roads
Game Over
Deadly Deals
Vanishing Act
Razor Sharp
Under the Radar
Final Justice
Collateral Damage
Fast Track
Hokus Pokus
Hide and Seek
Free Fall
Lethal Justice
Sweet Revenge
The Jury
Vendetta
Payback
Weekend Warriors

Anthologies

Making Spirits Bright
Holiday Magic
Snow Angels
Silver Bells
Comfort and Joy
Sugar and Spice
Let It Snow
A Gift of Joy
Five Golden Rings
Deck the Halls
Jingle All the Way

Published by Kensington Publishing Corporation

FERN MICHAELS

THE JURY

ZEBRA BOOKS
KENSINGTON PUBLISHING CORP.
http://www.kensingtonbooks.com

ZEBRA BOOKS are published by

Kensington Publishing Corp.
119 West 40th Street
New York, NY 10018

Copyright © 2006 by Fern Michaels
Copyright © 2012 by MRK Productions
Published by arrangement with Severn House Publishers, Ltd.
Fern Michaels is a registered trademark of First Draft, Inc.

All Kensington titles, imprints and distributed lines are available at special quantity discounts for bulk purchases for sales promotion, premiums, fund-raising, educational or institutional use.

Special book excerpts or customized printings can also be created to fit specific needs. For details, write or phone the office of the Kensington Special Sales Manager: Attn. Special Sales Department. Kensington Publishing Corp., 119 West 40th Street, New York, NY 10018. Phone: 1-800-221-2647.

Zebra and the Z logo Reg. U.S. Pat. & TM Off.

ISBN-13: 978-1-4201-2574-0
ISBN-10: 1-4201-2574-5

First Printing: June 2006

10

Printed in the United States of America

THE
JURY

Prologue

Nikki Quinn opened her eyes and groaned at the bright sunlight shining through her bedroom window. Normally she closed the blinds before getting into bed, but last night she'd consumed way too much wine. Couple that with her frenzied state of mind and she was down for the count. If you added Jack Emery to the mix, she was nothing short of a basket case.

She rolled over and squeezed her eyes shut. Her cheek touched the damp pillow. Damn, she'd cried in her sleep *again*. What was wrong with her? She was tougher than this. She shouldn't be falling apart emotionally like she was.

Temples throbbing, Nikki swung her legs over the side of the bed. She gripped the edge of the mattress before she got up to make her way to the shower. A nice hot shower, then a laser-like cold one and she should be up and running. Coffee and juice would add the final touch so she could get on with the day.

Get on with the day? Just what the hell did that mean lately? She'd lost her teaching job at Georgetown University. Her twelve-member all-female law firm, which she'd started up years ago with Myra Rutledge's help, was thriving but these days, with things going as they were, she didn't spend much time at the firm. Madeline Barrows did a wonderful job of managing everything in her absence. Still she missed the routine, missed court, missed her colleagues.

As the hot, steamy spray pelted her body, Nikki's thoughts took her back in time to when Myra Rutledge, her adoptive mother and heiress to a Fortune 500 candy company, had come up with the brilliant idea of forming the Sisterhood so that she could avenge her other daughter's death . . .

Water cascaded over Nikki's head like a waterfall. Once, a long time ago, she and Jack had picnicked at a wonderful spot in Pennsylvania where there was a waterfall. They'd frolicked like little kids and then made love behind the sheer curtain of water . . .

All she had now were those memories, because Jack Emery was determined to put her and the other members of the Sisterhood in prison. So far, though, she and the sisters had remained one step ahead of the former assistant district attorney. Lost love was so very painful.

Nikki stepped out of the shower, toweled herself dry and then brushed her teeth.

It was June. A month for weddings. She and Jack were supposed to get married a year ago in June. But that had never happened and probably never would happen now. She thought about the wedding gown hanging in her closet and how beautiful it was. Tears gathered in her eyes.

Memory Lane was not a good road for her to travel these days. She needed to move on. In fact, she thought she had until recently, when the Sisterhood had convened and her name had been chosen for their next revenge mission. She'd been so startled that she hadn't said a word. When they formed the Sisterhood it had been her understanding that she was there for legal counsel. While she belonged, she wasn't a true sister—she hadn't been wronged by the judicial system. And now she had to come up with a wrong that needed to be made right. The only problem was, the only wrong thing in her life was Jack Emery. There was no way she could turn Jack over to the Sisterhood. Because . . . because . . . she still loved him.

Nikki felt lower than a snake's belly as she dressed in a lime-green sundress with appliquéd sunflowers on the oversized patch pockets. Matching sandals completed her outfit. Her mind raced as she struggled to come up with a solution to her immediate problem.

Was she a member of the Sisterhood or not? Yes and no. She'd taken part in Kathryn's, Julia's and Myra's missions. She'd been an active participant each time. That alone proved she was a true sister. And now it was her turn to exact a revenge on her own behalf. If she didn't go along with Jack being her mission, she would betray the others.

She knew they would show her no mercy if she balked.

Nikki locked the door of her town house and walked to the parking lot and her BMW. She needed to talk to Myra and Charles and she needed to do it now before she drove herself insane. She had her cell phone in her hand even before she drove out of the parking lot.

"Madeline, it's Nikki. I'm on my way to Pinewood. Is everything OK? How's our new lawyer working out?"

"It's only been ten days, Nikki. She's had a few walk-ins but no cases that need to be litigated."

"I hear a 'but' coming. Spit it out, Maddie. Do you think I made a mistake hiring her?"

"No. But she's very aggressive, Nikki. Exceptionally so. She's stepped on a few toes, but has apologized. I explained the pecking order to her. She didn't take it well. I think she'll do fine but she needs to be watched. When are you coming in?"

"I don't know, Maddie. I have some things to take care of. I turned two of my cases over to Janice. I've got a clean plate for the time being. I'm thinking about taking a vacation. I need to get away."

"Nikki, why don't you just patch it up with Jack?" Maddie asked in a motherly tone.

"Easier said than done. Keep your eye on Allison. If it starts to look sticky, call me and I'll fire her. I don't want anything to upset the harmony we have in the office."

"Will do, kiddo. Have a nice day."

Nikki clicked off her cell phone. Had she made a mistake hiring Allison Banks? With so much on her mind it was entirely possible. She gave a mental shrug as she steered the BMW by rote.

Fifty minutes later, after filling her gas tank and getting a cup of coffee, Nikki barreled through the gates of Pinewood. By the time she parked the car and got out, she could see Myra leaning over the terrace railing.

"Darling, how wonderful to see you! Charles and I are having a late breakfast here on the terrace. Join us."

Nikki entered the house, walked down two hallways to a set of French doors and then out to the terrace. It felt good to be hugged, to be kissed by someone who cared about her. She bit down on her lip as she fought to keep her tears in check.

"Sit down, dear. Orange juice?"

Nikki nodded as Charles poured coffee from an elaborate silver coffeepot. A plate of croissants and melon sat in the middle of the table. If she had to eat either one, Nikki knew she'd choke.

Charles sat down, his eyes full of concern. "Tell us what's bothering you, Nikki. You look like you're carrying the weight of the world on your shoulders."

Nikki looked from one to the other. How dear they were to her. She blinked. "I feel like . . . like I'm in the Sisterhood under false pretenses. When we started the organization I thought I was just to be legal counsel and help in whatever way I could. I didn't have a wrong that needed to be made right, other than losing Barbara, and we already avenged her death. Now it's my turn and I really don't have a mission. I know the others are expecting me to choose Jack and I simply can't do that. I can't, Myra. That doesn't mean I want to leave the Sisterhood. I don't. I just want a pass."

Myra frowned. How she loved this young woman who was sitting across from her. She was so tortured, so driven. "That's doable, dear. Why don't you go away for a while? Take a nice, really long vacation. Go to the islands, soak in the sun, splash in the water, eat and sleep when you feel like it. The main reason I'm suggesting this is that we will not be reconvening at the end of June, when we were expecting Julia to return. Her doctor called last night and said her last blood test wasn't as good as they would have liked. It seems he wants to keep her a little longer. It's all still very positive, though. Her departure has been moved back till the end of August. Julia is disappointed but her health is the main concern. We called the others early this morning and all the girls are OK with moving our next mission back to September or even October. I called you, too, dear, but you had already left. So, you see, you're free to take a nice long vacation. Charles can arrange everything."

Nikki digested the information. She felt a sense of relief, but it was short-lived. Taking a vacation was fine but she would have to return eventually and deal with the problem of Jack Emery. You couldn't put a Band-Aid on a severed artery. But as a short-term reprieve, the idea appealed to her.

"Jack?" Nikki said flatly.

Myra looked out across the newly mowed lawn and all the colorful flower beds. "Your revenge is yours, dear. If you want to, as you say, take a pass, then that has to be your decision. I think you need some private time to get things clear in your head. What do you think?"

"There's the firm. I don't know, Myra. Maybe a few days, but there's so much going on I'm not sure I can take an extended vacation."

"Darling girl, you told me yourself Maddie runs the firm with a strong hand. You also told me you turned your pending cases over to Janice. There's nothing standing in your way to prevent you from taking an extended vacation—unless it's Jack."

Charles fiddled with the collar of his shirt. "Might I take this moment to tell you how tired and drawn you look, Nikki? You've been burning the candle at both ends and dealing with Mr. Emery at the same time. That alone would take a toll on anyone. I agree with Myra; a vacation is a good idea, my dear."

Nikki clenched her teeth. "Is that an order?"

Myra leaned across the table to take Nikki's hands in hers. "Actually, dear, it is."

A blue jay swooped down on the terrace before he settled on the iron railing to squawk his displeasure over something. Charles shredded a croissant and dropped it over the railing. The blue jay flew off, still squawking.

They were right and Nikki knew it. "All right, make the arrangements."

Myra and Charles smiled. In spite of herself, Nikki laughed.

"What shall it be, the islands or the mountains?"

"The islands. I'll leave the day after tomorrow. I need to go shopping. I think I'll leave now and get a head start."

"What about Mr. Emery, dear?" Myra asked.

"I doubt he'll be joining me, Myra. He's allergic to sun and sand. Will you call and keep me updated on the others, especially Julia?"

"Yes, of course. Myra and I decided a little while ago to take a road trip. We also have the Truckers' Ball to look forward to. I think taking the summer off is a good thing for all of us. Alexis is getting settled back into her little house and enjoying the company of her dog. Isabelle has a few new clients to take care of and this is Yoko's busy time at the nursery. Kathryn said she has several West Coast deliveries to make. We'll reconvene on the first of September," Charles said.

"Then it's settled. I'm off."

A round of hugs and kisses followed.

Myra played with her hands as she watched her adopted daughter drive through the gates. "I'm worried about Nikki, Charles. Young love is so . . . sad sometimes. She'll be all right, won't she?"

"Nikki will be fine. Everything came down on her shoulders at once, but she can handle it. Right now she needs to fall back and regroup . . . I have an idea, Myra. Let's go riding. I saw something the other day at the Barringtons' farm that I didn't understand. I'd like to check out their horses. Are you up for a morning ride? And how about a picnic?"

"That's a wonderful idea, Charles. Let me change while you make the picnic food."

"Now, how did I know you were going to say that?"

Myra looked up and twinkled. "Because you know me better than any other person in the whole world. You're right about the Barringtons' horses, too."

"Scat. Whatever it is, we'll make it right."

"I love you, dear."

"You're just saying that so I won't make egg salad for our picnic."

Myra laughed as she sashayed her way into the house. "That too," she said, laughing.

One

The smoky scent of burning leaves hung in the autumn air as Myra paced back and forth. The day was cool, the way the last days of September usually were in Virginia. She hugged her arms to her chest, her pace picking up each time she circled the terrace. She stopped twice to pluck yellowing leaves from the clay pots of crimson chrysanthemums that lined the terrace. Charles watched Myra from his position in his favorite Adirondack chair. He couldn't remember the last time he'd seen his lady love so agitated, so frustrated.

"We should have called Nikki when all of this first happened. She *is* the president of the Virginia Equestrian Society. She may never forgive us, Charles. She's as headstrong as Barbara was. Surely you remember what that was like. You know how

Nikki feels about animals, especially horses. Sending her off to that private island in the middle of nowhere, virtually incommunicado, might not have been such a good idea after all. I know, I know, she was on the verge of a breakdown and needed to get her head straight. But how are we going to tell her what's going on? We need to bring her back home. Better yet, have the plane readied and I'll go personally to fetch her."

Myra plopped down in a matching chair, her arms and legs at all angles, proof that she was so upset she didn't care how unladylike she appeared.

"Myra, listen to me," Charles said soothingly. "Nikki was in a bad emotional state when we sent her off to the island and she knew it. She was more than willing to go, to take time off so that she could get back on an even keel. She understood the rules—no contact with the office, no contact with Jack Emery and contact with us only once a month. She also understood our phone calls would deal only with pleasantries. She *agreed*, Myra, to take time off, to go away. It was her idea in the first place. I don't want you blaming yourself for any of this. Nikki knew back in May that she was teetering on the edge and she knew we only wanted what was best for her. If she'd been here when all of *this* happened, she would have teetered off that shaky ledge she was standing on. She's healthy and strong now. She'll be able to handle this."

Myra's voice rose shrilly. "This, this, this! Why don't we give *this* a name, Charles?"

Charles's voice was still soothing and calm.

"Because talking about *this* upsets you. You're screaming at me, Myra. I'm going down to the war room to call my people and arrange Nikki's return home. She's ready to return; she told us so on Sunday when we spoke to her."

"I want to be the one to bring her back, Charles. No matter what you say, I still feel like this is all my fault."

Charles stood up and clicked his tongue. "It is not your fault, Myra. In fact, the equestrian world has you to thank for bringing the situation to light. And, no, Nikki does not need her mommy to bring her home. She left on her own because she's a big girl, and she's going to return the same way: a big girl."

"Those are just words, Charles. We live next door to the Barringtons and we had no clue that they were starving those beautiful horses. I still can't believe seven of those magnificent animals died because we didn't get to them in time. What kind of people allow animals to starve to death? And the miserable court system, which failed me after Barbara's death, failed me again when the judge ruled the horses should remain under the Barringtons' care. Those people are monsters and they're walking around as free as the air they breathe. All thanks to that . . . that . . . twit from Nikki's firm who represented them in court. Nikki would never have allowed that to happen if she had been here. Maddie must have been asleep at the switch."

"Myra, don't do this to yourself. You're obsessing. Nikki will handle it all when she gets back. I want you to sit here in the sun and think about how wonderful it will be when Nikki gets back. Why don't you call the girls and arrange a meeting for the end of the week? Maybe the weekend. Whatever works best for all of them. I may be an hour or so as I also have to arrange for Julia's return. She is hale and hearty so we do have something to be thankful for. I want your promise, Myra."

Myra offered up an elaborate sigh. "Very well, Charles. I'll sit here and count the leaves on all these flowers until you get back." She couldn't resist one last parting shot. "In the old days, they hanged horse thieves. What those high-priced lawyers did was worse than thievery. I say we hang 'em high, as soon as I can figure out how to do it . . . I think I'm going to call Cornelia Easter and invite her out here for supper. I should have called her when all of this started. I'm sorry now that I didn't. She is a judge, Charles, so she'll have the inside details."

Charles frowned. "Myra, I don't . . ."

Myra held up her hand. "Don't go there, Charles. Nellie and I have been friends for fifty years. Good friends. Actually, we're more than good friends; I'm her daughter's godmother. Our husbands died within months of each other. We've laughed together, cried together, applauded each other and our daughters were best friends, too. That alone makes us closer than close. Nellie's more like a sister than a friend. The way Nikki and Barbara were like sisters."

"Myra . . ."

The soft warning in Myra's voice was something Charles had never heard before. "I told you, Charles, do not go there. I'm calling Nellie to come out for dinner. And I want you to . . . to stay out of sight. I'll call ahead and have her pick up some of our favorite Chinese from the Imperial Dragon." Myra's voice softened. "It's all right, Charles, I know what I'm doing. I know you don't always think I do, but this time I really do know what I'm doing."

Charles chuckled at her words, but he sobered almost instantly when he saw the sudden bitterness in her eyes that didn't match the soft tone in her voice. He felt a chill ricochet down his back when he realized Myra meant what she said about hanging horse thieves and people who abused animals. Just the way she'd meant it when she said she wanted to take on the justice system to correct their mistakes by forming the Sisterhood years ago. She'd acted on that thought, too. The chill stayed with him as he made his way to the war room where all missions of the Sisterhood were planned, plotted and executed.

Charles looked around his domain. It was so state of the art that it sometimes boggled even his mind. If only they'd had half of what was in this room years ago when he was in Her Majesty's Service, his cover might not have been blown. He'd been the best operative at MI6 and was on first-name terms with the Queen. It had been the Queen's decision to send him to America with a new identity when his cover was blown, to ensure his safety. He hadn't come empty-handed, though. He'd brought a list of contacts from across the world—old friends, operatives still in the intelligence business, as well as retired operatives who were only too glad to offer assistance when he requested it, just to keep their hands in.

In his youth, before going into Her Majesty's Service, he'd had an intense relationship with Myra when she was living in England with her parents. Because of her youth, Myra had had no say when it was time to return to the States. She'd gone back to America, her heart broken as was his, only to find out when she got there that she was pregnant. At her parents' insistence she'd married William Rutledge, who died ten years later.

Charles had had no knowledge of her pregnancy or the birth of his child until he started to work as the chief of security for Myra's candy company—a post arranged by MI6. And the rest was history. To this day, he had no idea if the Queen knew of his relationship with Myra or not. He rather thought she did.

How he'd loved Barbara and Nikki. Myra had wanted to tell Barbara that Charles was her real father, but he'd been against the idea. She had loved William Rutledge and Charles saw no reason to add to her grief by telling her that he wasn't her biological father. But then Barbara had died not knowing that Charles was her real father. How he regretted that decision now.

His shoulders heavy, Charles finished his glass of iced tea. Wool-gathering was for other people who lived and dwelled in the past. He needed to get his thoughts together and get on with the business at hand. Myra would do whatever she wanted to do, regardless of what he said.

* * *

Federal judge Cornelia Easter arrived in a luxurious chauffeured town car complete with two female security guards. Myra winced at this new development. Nellie had told her that not a day went by when she didn't receive a death threat. She was philosophical about it, saying it's just the world we live in today.

The whistle in her hand, Myra blew two sharp blasts. The silent guard dogs that had been circling her feet raced off to the barn. Myra nodded at the driver to show it was safe to get out of the car.

Judge Easter was a buxom, round little woman with springy curls and twinkling eyes behind wire-rimmed glasses. Her voice was raspy from too many cigarettes and her fondness for good whiskey, but only after hours, as she always said.

After the obligatory hug and peck on the cheek, the judge looked around in the late-afternoon sunshine and said, "God Almighty, Myra, when did you turn this place into such a fortress?" She pointed to the razor wire atop the electrified fence, the new state-of-the-art security gates and, of course, the pack of guard dogs.

Myra's expression grew vague. "A while ago. We had a few spots of trouble a while back. It's more a precaution than anything else. How are you, Nellie?"

"I'm fine, Myra, but I'll be a lot better once you serve me some refreshments. Make it a double." She turned to the security guards and their shopping bags full of Chinese food. "Girls, go in the house and watch television. I'll be on the terrace. That goes for you, too, Malcolm. This is my down time. If I need you, I'll call. Go along now. We discussed this exact situation on the ride out here. As you can see, there's all kinds of security here. Do as I say," Nellie said in her best courtroom voice, which had cowed many a lawyer. The security detail was no different; they scattered.

"We have a year's worth of catching up to do, Myra, so let's get to it. I can't believe it's been a whole year since I've been out here to the farm."

Nellie plopped down on one of the more comfortable chairs, her eyes sharp and keen as she watched Myra pour whiskey into a cut-glass tumbler. "Skip the ice and the water. Today I need it straight up." She took a healthy gulp before she set the glass back on the table. "Talk to me, Myra."

"I thought we'd go for a ride after you finish your drink. You have riding clothes upstairs in a closet and we still have two hours of daylight."

"That sounds like a plan. How's Nikki?"

"She's coming home tomorrow," Myra said as she fiddled with the glass in her hand.

Nellie sighed. "Jennifer was really worried Nikki wouldn't be here when she has the baby. Four more days, Myra, and I'll be a grandmother. Then the christening will be in two weeks, with Nikki being the godmother. Jennifer wants Jack Emery to be the godfather. I know, I know, but these young people have minds of their own. Then, six months later, I retire and kiss that black robe goodbye.

"They've been friends since high school. The

four of them went through college and law school together. The girls stuck together when Nikki decided to open her all-female law firm, and Jack went to the District Attorney's office. When Barbara was alive you couldn't find a closer group of girls. I have to tell you, Myra, Jennifer has kept me apprised of the goings-on in that firm since Nikki went off to . . . to . . . recover. She's on maternity leave now, but she keeps her hand in. What in the world was Nikki thinking when she hired that troublesome woman? It's just my opinion, but she would have been better off to leave Barbara's position open."

Myra chewed on her lower lip. "I don't know, Nellie. Nikki doesn't even know what happened. Charles and I will tell her when she gets home tomorrow."

"She doesn't know? Myra, for God's sake, why didn't you tell her? Nikki's a trooper. She would have kicked that young woman's ass right out of the firm the minute she got wind of what was going on."

Myra took a sip of her drink. "That happened later, Nellie, after she was gone. Don't think Charles and I haven't agonized over this. We have, night and day. Our primary concern was Nikki's physical and mental health. Don't think I'm not dreading the moment I have to tell her what happened with the Barringtons. Aren't you finished with that drink yet, Nellie? It's not like you to be so slow."

Nellie's eyes narrowed. "I'm done. See?" she said, upending the squat glass. "It will take me five minutes to change. Leave the bottle right there on the table. I have a feeling I'm going to need a triple when we get back. Am I spending the night, Myra?"

"I think that might be wise if you plan on drinking your dinner."

The round little judge walked over to Myra. "I'm not going to like this, am I?"

"Nellie, I . . . No, you aren't going to like it."

Nellie reached up to put her hands on Myra's shoulders. "For some reason, Myra, you always seem to underestimate me. Having said that, don't be so sure. Five minutes and I'll be ready to go riding."

Myra sighed. "You're a good friend, Nellie. What is it, fifty years?"

Nellie laughed, a robust sound. "Fifty-one and a half years. We met in Miss Dupré's dance class. Neither one of us could dance worth a damn back then. We were ten years old. Time does fly, doesn't it?"

"Sometimes, Nellie," Myra said sadly, "time crawls by."

Two

Nikki was ready to pull her hair out by the roots when a small boy of ten or so came running down the path to her bungalow.

"Telephone, Missy. Come quick."

Nikki tossed the magazine she'd already read twice onto the floor of the porch and raced after the little dark-haired boy. She handed him a dollar bill and smiled. He grinned as he scampered off to play show-and-tell with his friends. She was breathless when she picked up the phone.

"Hello?"

"Nikki, it's Charles. I'm sending the Gulfstream for you, so pack your bags. Someone will drive you to the airstrip at first light. I hope you're ready to come home."

Nikki sighed with happiness. "Charles, I am *so* ready you cannot believe. I've read fifty-six books since I've been here. I will probably never read another work of fiction for the rest of my life. I've watched over a hundred videos, some of them two or three times. I have snorkeled so much I've grown fins. I'm totally sick of sunshine. I long for a gloomy, wet, rainy day, the kind you used to have in England. I can't wait for a thunderstorm! I've been sleeping twelve hours a night and take naps in the afternoon. But despite all that activity, I'm bored out of my mind. Are the leaves starting to turn back home?"

Charles smiled at the wistful tone in Nikki's voice. He knew all about homesickness. "The leaves are just starting to turn. The evenings this past week have been cool. One of the neighboring farms has been burning leaves so the scent is in the air. The weather people are predicting a hard frost by the weekend. The produce stands are full of pumpkins. Myra insisted I buy two the other day. We carved one and put it on the porch to welcome you home. I made two pies with the other one."

Charles heard Nikki suck in her breath before she asked her next question.

"Has Jack given you any trouble?"

"No. If he still has us all under surveillance, he must also be bored out of his mind. Nothing has gone on at Pinewood since you left. Myra and I did take a road trip, and we attended the Truckers' Ball because Myra insisted. But this time we did not leave the house and grounds unattended. Alexis and Isabelle stayed here and kept an eye on things. I'm hoping Mr. Emery gave up on us."

"No such luck. He's out there. He's just waiting. Trust me when I tell you he knows everything you and Myra have been doing. How is Julia and when is she coming back?"

"Julia's progressing well and will be staying at Pinewood on her return. She will arrive home the day after tomorrow. You might find this of interest. Julia treated herself to some plastic surgery six weeks ago. Just enough to alter her appearance so she doesn't look like the old Julia. And she dyed her hair blonde. She e-mailed a picture and, I must say, I had to look twice to realize it really was Julia. She's quite beautiful."

Nikki's voice turned wistful again. "Good for her! How's her plant doing?"

Charles knew Nikki was trying to keep him on the phone as long as she could. "Myra repotted the plant and it's thriving. It has three trailing vines so Myra clipped them and rooted them in the center of the pot. I think it looks lush, and I know Julia will be more than pleased."

"Is everyone OK? What about Alexis's new boyfriend?"

Charles laughed. "As it turned out, the new boyfriend was allergic to dogs, so Alexis bid him adieu. She didn't seem too brokenhearted at the breakup. She said it wasn't hard to make a decision because she does love that animal. And before you ask, Isabelle has managed to get several small jobs with her reinstated license. Yoko and Kathryn are keeping busy with their lives, doing what they do to earn a living."

"I've missed you all so much. I can't wait to get

home. Did you put a candle in the pumpkin, Charles?"

"We did but we haven't lighted it yet. Now, I suggest we curtail this phone call so you can pack. Myra sends her love. By the way, the girls will all be here tomorrow to welcome you home. Julia, of course, won't arrive until the next day. I'll say goodbye for now."

Nikki wiped at the tears trickling from the corners of her eyes as she hung up the phone. Her step was light as she made her way down the path bordered with crimson bougainvillea and fragrant gardenia bushes. She sprinted toward the lagoon where four white swans moved gracefully back and forth. She raced across the bridge that would take her back to the cottage she'd called home for almost four months.

The small, private island was a place to come to on a honeymoon or with a lover. A place of beauty, a place of peace and contentment. A place to lick one's wounds. A place to heal. How wise Charles and Myra were to send her here, even though she hadn't thought so on her arrival. Back then, she'd thought of it as a punishment. Now she realized how close she'd come to a complete mental breakdown. But that was all behind her now.

She was going home. Back to her town house, back to Charles and Myra at Pinewood, back to her law firm and to all her new friends in the Sisterhood.

Home.

The best place in the whole world.

* * *

Nikki ran across the tarmac, dragging her oversize duffel bag on wheels toward the town car that waited for her. She was breathless as she watched the driver pop the trunk to toss her bags inside.

She was almost home. She felt giddy at the thought.

The driver was an older man with white hair and a bristly white mustache. He held the door for her, nodding curtly. Inside, before he started the engine, he leaned over to say, "Mr. Martin said I was to take you either to Georgetown or to McLean. If you opt for Georgetown, I am to call him."

Nikki leaned back into the softness of the plush seat. She closed her eyes. "I'd like to go to Georgetown. Do you have the address?"

"Yes, miss, I do. Georgetown it is."

Nikki snuggled into the corner of the car, wishing she'd worn a long-sleeved sweater. She estimated the temperature to be in the low sixties. By tomorrow or the following day her dark tan would disappear. Not that she cared. Hugging her arms to her chest, she watched the landscape go by, recognizing this and that as the town car took short cuts to avoid the rush-hour traffic.

Forty minutes later, Nikki exited the town car to a mass of swirling leaves. The sudden gust of wind made her laugh, her hair blowing in all directions. She tipped the driver twenty dollars when he set her bags in the small foyer inside the door. The town house smelled musty and stale. Still, it was her home no matter what it smelled like.

Nikki ran around the rooms, rolling up blinds and opening windows. Within minutes she'd stripped her bed and was headed toward her compact laundry room on the first floor.

The refrigerator beckoned. She snorted at the contents. A bottle of wine, two bottles of beer, a six pack of Evian water and an unopened can of coffee. Since she'd be going to Pinewood tomorrow there was no need to go grocery shopping. She could hardly wait to order a pizza with the works. She knew she'd scoff it down in a heartbeat. It was going to be a very, very long time before she ate mangoes, pineapples, bananas, fish and island vegetables again. Ditto for the fruity drinks that had been part of her diet for four long months.

Nikki lugged her two duffel bags into the laundry room and dumped them. Since they were full of summer attire, there was no need to hurry with the laundry process. She did, however, remove her cosmetic bag and carried it back upstairs where she made up her bed with fresh linens from a zippered bag in her linen closet. The sheets smelled like lavender, her favorite bedroom scent. Jack had always liked the way her bed smelled. It was going to be a pleasure to slip between the sheets tonight. Her gaze dropped to her nightstand where there was a picture of herself and Jack sitting on the steps of the Lincoln Memorial. She should put the picture away. Maybe she should *throw* it away. She'd wanted to, many times, but for some reason she couldn't bring herself to do it.

Now she didn't stop to think. She picked up

the picture, snapped the back into place and then pushed it as far back in the nightstand drawer as it would go. Don't think about Jack, she cautioned herself. She sat down on the edge of the bed and dropped her head into her hands.

"Copping out, eh, Nik?"

Nikki's head jerked upright. "Now you show up! Where were you when I needed you on that damn island, Barb?"

"I was there but you didn't need me. You did just fine on your own. That was the purpose of the whole exile thing, Nik."

"Oh, yeah, sure, easy for you to say. Do you have any idea how hard that exile was?"

"Now that's a really dumb question to be asking me. Of course I know how hard it was. I'm not exactly among the living, you know. Do you really think putting Jack's picture in a drawer is going to change anything?"

"No, I guess not. It just makes it easier if I don't have to look at it. I don't need any pep talks where Jack is concerned. I've got my emotions under control. I don't know what happened to me to make me . . . cave in like that."

"Every single person walking the earth has a breaking point, Nik. You met yours head-on. It won't happen again. I think Mom just hit hers."

Nikki's voice turned shrill. "What does that mean? Is something wrong with Myra?"

"No . . . Well, yes, in a manner of speaking. But she has a handle on it. She did what she had to do. You took the easy way and caved in. There's no shame in that, Nik. That's what's really bothering you. You're worried at how the others will perceive you. Don't worry about it."

"Don't preach to me, Barb, and don't evade the question. Tell me about Myra."

"There's nothing to tell. Mom's her own person, you know that. All I said was she's smart enough to seek out help if she needs it. You kept it all bottled in. You didn't even share with me. Shame on you, Nik."

"What could you have done, Barb? I had to work through it on my own. For God's sake, I drugged the man I thought I was going to spend the rest of my life with. He was so sick and I did it anyway. I tricked him and then I drugged him. I helped skin a man to within an inch of his life. I lost my teaching job. I assigned my caseload to other lawyers in the firm because I couldn't get a handle on my life. What the hell does that say about me?"

"That you're human. Get over the guilt already. There's no turning back now. You have to play it through to the end. If things go awry, you'll deal with it at the time. For now, you take it one day at a time. C'mon, Nik, you're tough and resilient. Put the picture back where it was and go take a shower. Order a pizza and skip the anchovies. Have a couple of beers and then go to bed. If you want, I'll stay and watch over you."

It was a comforting thought. "I'm fine, Barb. I don't need a spirit-sitter. I'm not going to wig out. See?" Nikki said as she opened the drawer and put Jack's picture back on the nightstand. Her voice turned cool and firm. "Just so you know, Barb, I will always love Jack."

Nikki smiled at Barbara's tinkling laughter. *"I know that. Jack will never love anyone but you, either. True love is so wonderful."*

The tinkling laughter came again as Nikki headed for the shower. At last, she'd finally said the words out loud. Words from her heart. Words that lifted the heaviness from her shoulders and her chest. Barbara was right, she needed to take it one day at a time.

"OK, Jack, from here on in, the only time I'm going to see you is in my dreams."

Tomorrow was another day. Tomorrow she would take charge of her life and get back on track.

Nikki woke, stunned to see that it was mid-morning—ten o'clock to be exact. She must still be on island time. She showered, dressed, made coffee and was ready to leave by eleven o'clock. She was on her way out when she stopped, turned around and retrieved her cell phone that had been charging during the night. Now she was ready to head out to McLean, to Myra and Charles. But first, she wanted to call her once-a-week cleaning lady to let her know she was back and then she wanted to have a picnic lunch all by herself in Rock Creek Park. It was no coincidence that she chose Rock Creek Park. She'd picnicked there hundreds of times with Jack. There was something about big, leafy trees with picnic tables underneath and patches of mossy grass that had appealed to them both. She wondered if Jack ever went there these days.

Nikki called ahead to her favorite deli to order two pastrami on rye sandwiches with spicy brown mustard, two apples and two bottles of iced tea.

She didn't realize she'd ordered two of everything the way she used to do for her and Jack until she paid the bill. Old habits were hard to break. She made a promise to herself to eat and drink it all.

Twenty minutes later, paper sack in hand, Nikki climbed out of her car, locked it and headed for a large flat rock a few feet from the running track where she spread her lunch. Joggers and runners alike waved half-heartedly as they whizzed by. Nikki barely noticed them. It was time for her to get back into some physical fitness routine, too. Maybe next week.

As she munched and chewed, Nikki let her gaze travel farther into the park where she and Jack used to sit. No one was at the picnic table. She could have spread her lunch there, but sitting there would have been like pouring salt on an open wound. She'd tortured herself enough these past months. Like the song said, breaking up is hard to do.

Nikki felt her shoulders slump inside the flannel-lined windbreaker as she finished her sandwich and the last of the iced tea. She'd crunch on the apple during the drive to McLean. Damn, she wished she'd never come here. What in the world had possessed her to come to the park that was so full of memories? "Well, maybe this was my farewell to the park because I'm not coming back," she muttered as she headed for the trash bin to deposit the empty bottle and the waxed paper from her sandwich. She was too frugal to throw away the extra sandwich. She'd divide it up and give it to the dogs when she got to the farm. Her decision made, she turned around and that's when she saw Jack sitting at the picnic table, his eyes glued to her. He offered no greeting. Nikki felt her heart kick up a beat at the sight of him. He was wearing a Redskins cap and a dark-blue windbreaker similar to hers with a white tee shirt underneath. She couldn't see them but she knew he was also wearing jeans and Docksiders, his favorite outfit.

Should she wave? Should she walk away? Should she offer up a greeting? *You knew this might happen. That's why you came here. You were hoping to see Jack,* a niggling voice inside her head told her.

Nikki's legs felt rubbery and the knuckles clutching the paper sack were white as she walked over to the picnic table. She stopped a foot away.

"Hi, Jack. Want some lunch? Out of habit, I ordered two of everything." She stepped closer and slid the bag across the table.

Jack looked at the bag as though it were a coiled snake. "I wouldn't eat anything you gave me even if I was starving. What are you doing here anyway? Spying?"

Nikki felt her heart beating extra fast. She tried for a light tone. "Isn't that my line? I think it's pretty safe to eat. I bought it at Hyman's Deli, pastrami on rye with spicy brown mustard, an apple and some iced tea. I didn't know you'd be here, Jack. If I had known, I would have stayed away."

Jack tossed some popcorn toward a group of bright-eyed squirrels. Overhead in the maple trees, birds squawked and screeched. Jack's tone was so bitter, so challenging that Nikki flinched. "No one is stopping you from leaving. Just for the record, you ruined my day by showing up here. I guess I'll have to find a new spot to go for peace and quiet. You're the last person I wanted to see today. Gee, you must have been really working hard this summer to get a tan like that," he sniped.

"I've . . . I've been away, Jack. I've been gone for four months. Actually, I just got home last night. I was on my way to Pinewood and I was hungry. I didn't think you'd be here. It wasn't a vacation, Jack. I had a breakdown of sorts. Myra and Charles sent me away to . . . to . . . to get myself together."

"You look fine to me. Guess it worked. I had a breakdown of sorts myself. My mother died the beginning of August. I tried calling you but just got your answering machine. Your cell phone said you were out of the area."

"I'm sorry, Jack. I'm really sorry. I didn't know."

A blue jay swooped down out of the tree overhead to perch on the end of the picnic table. Jack rolled a few kernels of popcorn in the bird's direction. The bird flew off without touching the popcorn. Jack picked it up and tossed it to the waiting squirrels.

"I needed a friend. Just a friend, Nik. My sister had her husband and the kids. Mark was with me, but it was still hard. In some ways, it was a relief for all of us, especially Mom."

"It's never easy, Jack. I was just a little kid when my parents died, but I still remember it, and you know what, it still hurts like hell. I still miss them. In time the grief fades a little but it never goes away. Is there anything I can do for you now?"

"Yeah. Get some guts and tell me the truth about what's going on out there at ye olde farmhouse. Why'd you *almost* have a nervous breakdown? Don't tell me it was because of me either, because that won't fly. I think whatever you're doing out there is getting to you. If you're even telling me the truth, which I doubt."

Right then Nikki wanted to sit down across from Jack and pour out her heart. She actually took a step forward but stopped when the blue jay and one of his feisty companions flew onto the table and started to peck at Jack's hand.

"Blue jays are mean birds, Jack. Throw the damn popcorn on the ground and get up. They'll go for your eyes next," Nikki said as she threw the bag of food on the table. The birds squawked some more and then flew off. The squirrels scampered forward and feasted.

"Why, Nikki Quinn, I didn't know you cared. For a minute there you sounded like the old Nik," Jack said, sarcasm ringing in his voice.

Nikki looked up at the trees before she gingerly sat down on the edge of the bench. "It was partly because of you. Partly because of personal . . . issues. I didn't have my own phone where I was this summer."

"And that's supposed to impress me, I guess. Excuse me if I find that hard to believe."

"Jack, I'm just trying to explain why you couldn't get hold of me. By the way, what are you doing here?"

"I come here every day hoping to get some

insight on what the hell happened to you. So far, no luck. Don't even try telling me you're not involved up to your neck in what's going on out there at Pinewood. If you really did *almost* have a nervous breakdown, it wasn't because of me; it's because of what you're doing. You're breaking the goddamn law and we both know it. I'm gonna catch you, too. It's just a matter of time.

"In case you're interested, my leave is almost up and I'm going back to the DA's office. This private-eye business is too taxing. Mark loves it and we're actually making some money. When I catch you it will be legally, with the DA's office behind me, not with a private eye's license. And there is one other little thing that you need to be aware of, Miss Smart Ass. I now have a new best friend, Marcey Watts. I'm sure you've seen her byline in the *Post*. The woman lives to see her name in print. She's better than a hound dog. She's agreed to sub for me with Mark's private-eye business. You know how those news hounds are. Don't say I didn't warn you."

Nikki felt something clutching at her heart. Hot tears pricked at her eyes. "Bye, Jack. It was nice seeing you again here in this beautiful spot. Are you sure you don't want this sandwich?"

"Kiss my ass, Nik."

"Your loss. It was a very good sandwich." Nikki, shoulders stiff, hands clenched, marched off. She made a production of dropping the paper sack in the trash bin.

"I can handle this. I can really handle this. I know I can handle this," Nikki muttered over and over as she drove out to McLean.

Three

Nikki tapped the horn lightly to announce her arrival as she zipped through the open security gates of Pinewood. She swerved into her designated parking space, wondering whose car she was parking next to. It looked familiar but she couldn't quite place it. Maybe Myra had invited an old friend for lunch.

Nikki was no sooner out of the car than Myra and Charles were running to her, arms outstretched. Nikki closed her eyes, savoring the warm comfort of their arms. It had been a long time since she felt such comfort and she allowed herself to bask in the feeling for a minute or so.

"Darling girl, you look wonderful! Doesn't she look wonderful, Charles?"

"She certainly does," Charles said as he winked at Nikki. "We missed you terribly."

"Charles has been cooking all day. Yesterday, too. I think he's made every single thing you ever said in passing that you liked. Come in, dear, it's getting chilly out here. Charles even made a fire in the kitchen fireplace. It's cozy and warm and we have hot chocolate with loads and loads of marshmallows," Myra gushed happily.

Nikki linked arms with Myra and Charles. "I can't tell you how good it is to be home. I missed you all so much. Do you have company?"

Myra's step faltered but she just said, "These darn new shoes. Just Maddie, dear. She drove out here to welcome you home."

Drove out here to welcome her home. Madeline Barrows had never been *out here* in her life.

Barbara's words of the previous evening rang in her ears. Something was wrong.

"Well, hi there, boss!" Maddie said, getting up from the chair she was sitting on. "I thought I'd come out here to welcome you home. We sure did miss you and your grouchy ways."

Something was definitely wrong. Nikki could feel it, sense it, even smell it. She offered up her cheek for Maddie's brief peck and then said, "Tell me what's wrong. Don't leave anything out, either. Don't look at me like that. I can read it in your expressions. Somebody say something. What?" She threw her hands up in the air in exasperation.

"Sit down, Nikki," Charles said firmly. He turned to Myra. "Never mind the hot chocolate. Pour Nikki some brandy." To Nikki he said, "I want you to hear me out before you explode."

Nikki sighed. "I knew it! I knew something was

wrong!" She fixed her gaze on Maddie. "Is someone suing the firm? Did the new girl screw up?"

Charles set the brandy snifter in front of Nikki. "I'd like to do this in chronological order if you don't mind. This way you'll get a clearer picture of what happened and everyone's role in it."

Aware of Charles's love of storytelling, Nikki grimaced. "Can you just cut to the chase and give me the highlights?"

Charles frowned. He'd rehearsed this speech a dozen times at Myra's insistence. Now he had to deviate. "All right. Right after you left, Myra and I went riding because both of us thought there was something strange about the Barringtons' horses. As you know, their property borders Pinewood. At any given time there are usually thirty to forty horses in their pastures. Recently they sold off the prize horses. Those that were not top of the line breeds were left without food or shelter. Barrington kept only those that would turn a profit. The sixteen remaining horses were in desperate need of medical attention. They would all be dead by now if Myra and I hadn't gone riding that day. We called the authorities and, out of the sixteen, only one horse died. However, we found the bodies of seven other horses that had died earlier. The Barringtons were away but were tracked down by the authorities. Their defense was that they left the horses in the care of some man whose name they couldn't even remember, according to the police. The state filed charges. The Barringtons sued the state and Myra.

"The attorney the Barringtons hired to defend them was the young woman, Allison Banks, whom you hired to fill Barbara's position at your firm. She successfully defended the Barringtons and won the case. Myra was ordered to make restitution to the tune of ten million dollars for the horses we took to safety. Add to that unlawful trespassing and a few other things they managed to add to the indictment.

"Now, the Barringtons are back home and in the horse business again, buying and selling to top bidders. Your firm has gone downhill since the verdict came in at the beginning of the month. Several of your colleagues quit, not wanting to be associated with such people. Ms. Banks is sitting on top of the legal world and, at the moment, weighing her options. It seems all the prestigious firms in the District are vying for her expertise."

"They were acquitted?" was all Nikki could say.

Maddie spoke for the first time. "Nikki, I told Allison not to take the case. The others in the firm agreed. We said it was a conflict of interest and she said, and this is a direct quote, 'Tough shit!' That mousy little thing you hired turned into a monster. She threw away those thick glasses and got contact lenses. She highlighted her hair, got a makeover, bought herself Armani suits, a different one for every day of the week, all with miniskirts. She looked like a sexy movie star when she strolled into court. Even the judge was smitten with her. She's hard as nails, Nikki. She could chew a nickel and spit rust. I would have fired her but you gave her a year's contract so there was nothing I could do.

"Jack Emery, your old boyfriend, was in court every day watching the proceedings. So was I. Every single day he asked me if you knew what was going on. Every single day I had to say no. He couldn't believe the state lost the case. They are appealing. Myra is appealing, too.

"There was some talk, and it was just talk, Nikki, that after the verdict came in, the Barringtons settled a hefty sum of money on Ms. Banks for winning their case. Like I said, it was just talk, but talk has to start somewhere.

"There's one other thing, Nikki. I don't know if you're interested in this or not, but I happen to know it's true because one of our lawyers is dating an ADA in Jack's old office. Jack's old boss approached him to come back to the DA's office to try the case, but he turned it down when he saw Myra's name on the lawsuit. Think what you will about Jack, but he did turn it down. They're after him hot and heavy. Scuttlebutt says he is going to go back when his leave is up. No more Assistant District Attorney, either. He's got the two initials if he wants them. But *if* is the operative word here.

"Last, but not least, the firm's business is down fifty percent. There are no new clients walking through the doors. No one in this part of horse country wants to be associated with lawyers who defend people like the Barringtons. Some of our old clients bailed on us, too."

Nikki gulped the fiery liquid in the snifter that Charles had handed her. Her eyes started to water as she tried to come to terms with what she'd just heard. When she could finally get the words out she said, "And none of you saw fit to tell me any of this? How could you keep all this from me? How, Myra?"

"Nikki, dear, we never thought it would escalate to this. In the beginning the horses were all that was important. Yes, we did trespass, but the Equestrian Society backed me up when they found out what was going on at the Barringtons' place. If that . . . that twit you hired to replace my daughter hadn't stepped in, none of this would have happened."

"But it did happen, Myra. Now my firm is a shambles, you owe ten million dollars, and that *twit* is sitting on top of the world. I would have come back and figured out a way to chop her off at the knees. I never would have allowed this to happen. I would have shut down the firm first and taken my lumps. Who was the stupid judge who let this go to trial?"

"The Honorable Robert Krackhoff. The one who likes a pretty face and a nice show of leg. Kracker himself," Maddie said, referring to the judge's courthouse nickname. "He plays golf with the Barringtons. He should have recused himself, but he didn't. There are grounds for appeal all the way around."

"And the Barringtons are back in business, is what you're telling me," Nikki said.

"Yes, they are back in business, Nikki. Myra and I think they will relocate as soon as they can find a suitable horse farm. They've become pariahs here in town. As far as I know, the only person who will associate with them is their attorney. There are rumors circulating that the farm is up for sale, but no realtor will handle the sale so they'll have to do it privately. They'll be squeezed out sooner or later," Charles said.

Nikki compressed her lips into a grim line. "That isn't good enough for me. How many horses do the Barringtons have now?"

"Twelve. Five are serious contenders for the Derby. If you want a price on the horseflesh, I'd say he's got over twenty million dollars tied up in those horses. I don't think he's going to have an easy time selling them at this stage. He might have been acquitted, but the right people have been spreading the word in the circles he and his wife travel in. You know the rule, Nikki, mistreat a horse and you're down for the count. Pictures don't lie."

"Then how the hell were they acquitted?" Nikki snarled.

"They blamed it on their foreman. A foreman with no name who vanished into thin air. We saved all the newspaper articles for you," Myra said quietly.

Nikki slipped her arms into her windbreaker as she stalked over to the door. "You'll see me when you see me," she called over her shoulder.

"Follow her, Maddie. She's going to the office. I've never seen her so angry. Please don't let her do anything she'll come to regret later," Myra pleaded.

Maddie rushed out the door but by the time

she got to her car, Nikki was blasting through the gates and flying down the long drive to the main road.

It took all of fifty minutes for Nikki to drive back to the District, park her car in the lot and storm her way into the law firm she'd started with her own blood and sweat. The four lawyers clustered around her, welcoming her back.

"Where is she?" was all Nikki said. The women pointed to a closed door in the middle of a long carpeted hallway. "Go! You don't want to see this. Later, I don't want you to have to lie for me." The women scurried and were out the door in seconds.

Nikki stomped her way to her office and was surprised to see a pot of colorful chrysanthemums sitting on her desk. A small card said WELCOME HOME. She unlocked and yanked at the drawer of the file cabinet behind her desk, then rifled through the folders looking for Allison Banks's résumé and employment application. When she couldn't find them, she cursed under her breath. She turned to see Maddie with the folder in her hand. Nikki grabbed it. "You need to leave too, Maddie."

"Nah. Why don't you let me beat the shit out of her? The Bar Association can't disbar me."

"I'll take my chances, Maddie. Go! I don't want any witnesses to this."

"See, that's where you're wrong. You *do* need a witness. I'll just sit out here in the reception area. Leave the door open."

Nikki knew when she was up against a brick wall. "What do you suppose she's doing in there?"

Maddie snorted as she finger-combed her short curly hair. "Reading *Vogue*."

Nikki walked down the hallway and opened the door quietly. What she really wanted to do was rip it off by the hinges. She gaped at the young woman sitting behind the shiny, glass-topped desk. She looked nothing like the woman she'd hired five months ago. Maddie was right, she was definitely what Jack would call "a looker" and she had good taste in clothes, too. Nikki walked over to the desk, delighted when the young lawyer looked up with a sheepish as well as guilty expression on her face.

"Well, hi there, Nikki. Welcome back."

"You're fired. I want you out of here in the next two minutes. You take nothing but your purse when you leave. Do we understand each other?" Nikki reached down and grabbed Allison's arm to drag her out of the chair. Allison squealed her displeasure as Nikki gave her a shove that sent her sprawling across the carpeted floor.

"What are you doing? Are you insane? I have a contract! You can't fire me, but you can buy out my contract."

"Ha! That will be the day! If you're referring to this," Nikki said, holding up Allison's contract, "it doesn't exist. You were a temp and now it's time for you to leave."

"Wait just a damn minute. I billed mega hours for this firm with the Barrington case. Which I won, in case no one told you."

Nikki continued the moment she shredded the employment contract. "You were told by Maddie and the other members of this firm that the Barrington case was a conflict of interest. You took it anyway. That's not how this firm does business. Myra Rutledge is my mother. Get your ass out of here now."

"Look, I didn't know that when I took the case."

"I don't want to hear it. I told you, you're fired. Leave now before you really make me angry." To make her point, Nikki's foot snaked out. An instant later, Allison was looking up at her from the floor.

"I'll sue you and this damn firm. I'll sue every lawyer until they bleed for money and I'll sue you for assault and battery. I'll ruin you. I'll own this firm when I'm done!" Allison screeched.

Nikki laughed. She watched as the young lawyer managed to get to her feet. Allison took a moment to straighten her designer suit before she moved right up to Nikki's face. "Read my lips, Nicole Quinn. I will ruin you!"

Nikki laughed again. "How about this?" Her clenched fist shot out and landed square on Allison's nose. Blood spurted all over the pale-blue Armani suit. Nikki pushed her toward the door and made sure blood smeared the doorframe. "I'm one person you don't ever want to mess with, Miss Hotshot. Now, get your ass out of here and don't ever come back."

"You broke my nose! I'll have you disbarred for this. Give me my files."

"Maddie, show Ms. Banks to the door and then lock it. You're on a slippery slope, Ms. Banks. If I ever find out you took a kickback from the

Barringtons, it will be you who will be disbarred. You think about that for a while."

"You!" she screamed at Maddie. "You were here all this time and you didn't do a thing! I'm suing you, too. You heard and saw everything, so that makes you an eyewitness."

"I didn't see or hear anything. I was in the bathroom. You're bleeding on the carpet. We'll have to send you a bill for that. Blood is hard to get out," Maddie said quietly.

"Oh, shut up! I'm leaving and I'm coming back with the police! I want my files and my corre-spondence."

Nikki and Maddie both laughed, but stopped the minute Maddie locked the door.

"I'll switch her computer with one she used from time to time in the library. You take the files. It will be our word against hers. Hurry, Nikki. She might really bring the police back."

"No, she'll go to the hospital first so she has something to add to the lawsuit she's going to file. Then she'll go to the cops. She'll get a free nose job out of it."

"You don't look worried, Nikki. This firm doesn't need a lawsuit. None of us needs a law-suit. Do you know something I don't know?"

"Nope. Doesn't it feel good that she's gone? You know, Maddie, she really snowed me, and she had such an exemplary résumé. I thought she would be an asset to the firm. Well, this isn't the first time I've made a mistake. My gut feel-ing is she isn't going to do anything. I'm think-ing the Barringtons promised her money but she couldn't accept it as long as she was still working here. I may have done her a favor by firing her. Time will take care of everything. By the way, how is Jennifer doing?"

"She's been on bed rest for the past three weeks. The baby is due in a few days. Her mother is staying with her. She's fine otherwise. She had more than one run-in with Allison."

Nikki clicked on the replacement computer and booted it up. "It's ready to go, Maddie. You better download a few files in case she comes back. Wait a minute. No, no, don't download anything. I'll say she took it and her files with her. You realize this makes you an accessory, don't you, Maddie?"

Maddie's chin jutted outward. "I think I can live with that. I'll bring everything out to the farm on the weekend. For now, I'm going to take everything over to Josh Appleman's office and stash it there. He's out of town till next Tuesday. I'll use the rear door. Go back to Pinewood, Nikki. I have it under control."

"Maddie . . ."

"Nikki, everyone in this firm is solidly behind you. Sometimes drastic measures are called for."

Nikki hugged her office manager. "Whatever would I do without you?"

"You'd have to make your own coffee and pick up your dry-cleaning," Maddie said and laughed. "I haven't forgotten all you've done for me. The others feel the same way. Now go on, get out of here."

"Yes, ma'am."

Four

Nikki sat in her car, her thoughts chaotic. What in the hell had gotten into her back there in the office? She wasn't a brawler. She looked down at her clenched fist and saw blood on her knuckles. Allison's blood. She had nothing to clean her hands with unless she wanted to go back into the office, which she didn't.

She slid the key into the ignition but she didn't turn it. Instead, she picked up her cell phone, looking at it for a whole thirty seconds before punching in the number she knew by heart. She continued to stare out the windshield. It puzzled her that a small brown bird would settle on the hood of her car. The phone at her ear was still ringing as she eyeballed the little bird. Six rings, seven, and then finally there was a connection.

"Jack . . ."

"Yeah?"

"Jack . . ."

"Yeah, yeah, this is Jack."

"Jack . . ."

"Where are you, Nik?"

"Jack . . ."

"Nik, where *are* you?"

"I'm in the parking lot at the office . . ."

"I'm on my way, Nik. Stay put. Wait for me. Will you do that?"

"Jack . . ."

"I'll be there in ten minutes. I'm in town. Ten minutes, Nik. Wait for me."

"Jack . . ."

This time Jack shouted into the phone. "Nik, I'm on my way. Listen to me. Just sit there and wait for me. Will you do that?"

Jolted by Jack's tone of voice, Nik reared backward. "Yes, I'll wait. You don't have to shout."

"Don't hang up, Nik. Keep the line open. I'm almost there. Just a few more minutes."

Nikki didn't respond. She tilted her head to watch the small bird, which now had three companions and they were all prancing around on the hood of the car. From time to time they stopped to peer at her through the windshield. She wiggled a finger in their direction and didn't feel silly at all.

She knew when Jack arrived because the birds squawked and flew off in all directions. The squeal of his tires would have been her second clue. Her hand found the door handle and then she was standing in the bright sunshine.

How wonderful he looked in his jeans and tee shirt, his out-of-office uniform. His sandy hair was tousled with the whipping wind as he loped toward her, his arms outstretched. Nikki fell into them. She closed her eyes at his scent, at the smoothness of his freshly shaven cheeks. He didn't kiss her; he just held her. What seemed like a long time later, a swirl of orange and yellow leaves whipped past them and only then did they move.

"What's wrong, Nik? Talk to me. Let's be Nik and Jack again, OK?"

Nikki turned and stared into Jack's dark brown eyes. "Nik and Jack. Can we ever be just Nik and Jack again?"

Jack held her tight. "If we both want it bad enough, we can. Do you want me to take you back to Georgetown? I can leave my car here and pick it up later. Does that work for you?"

Nikki looked toward the hood of the car. The birds were back pecking at their reflections. "Yes, let's go back to my place. Can you take the time off?"

"Well, sure. This is my last week of being self-employed. I go back to work on Monday. Things are slow right now. I just came into the District to tidy up some last-minute details. That's how I was able to get here so quick. Get in, Nik. I'll drive."

Nikki obediently climbed into the passenger side of the car, buckled up and then handed over the keys. She pretended not to see Jack looking at the blood on her knuckles.

The birds flew off when the car's engine turned over.

They made the ten-minute drive to Georgetown in silence, although Jack reached over to hold Nikki's hand. He squeezed it from time to time. Nikki returned the pressure.

When the cell phone on the console rang, both Nikki and Jack looked at the display number. Pinewood. Nikki turned and looked out the window. Jack said nothing but his mind raced in all directions as he remembered times when Nikki would drop whatever she was doing to take a call from Myra. He wished he knew what was going on in Nikki's mind. He squeezed her hand again. She returned the pressure and even smiled. Jack's spirits soared as he imagined all kinds of wonderful things that could happen between them.

The minutes ticked by as Jack maneuvered Nikki's car up and down the cobblestone roads. "We're here, Nik. I guess I have a question. Am I dropping you off or am I invited inside?" He wiggled his hand free of Nikki's to set the handbrake the moment he'd backed into a parking spot.

Nikki looked puzzled for a moment. "Come in. I'll make some coffee unless you want something stronger or unless you have someplace to go. I really don't have much of anything since I've been away."

"Coffee will do. Do you need to take anything in the house? Anything in the trunk?"

Nikki crossed her arms over her chest as she looked up and down the street. "Just my briefcase. It's really chilly out here. We can make a fire if you like."

If he liked. Well, hell yes, he liked. For a moment Jack thought he'd died and gone to heaven. The only thing that bothered him was the flat tone in Nikki's voice. Ever hopeful, he bounded out of the car and ran around the side to open the passenger door. Together they walked up the steps to her town house.

Once inside, Jack smacked his hands together. "Tell you what, you make the coffee and I'll make the fire. Then we can talk. By the way, you left your cell phone in the car. Do you want me to get it?"

"No. I left it in the car on purpose."

Well, hot damn! Jack didn't break his stride as he made his way to the living room and the stack of birch logs that were nestled in the wood box at the corner of the fireplace. The dry wood caught fire immediately, sparks shooting upward as it crackled and spit. Satisfied, he sat back on his haunches and looked around at the scene he'd just created. All it needed was Nikki at his side, and a glossy golden retriever. Back when they were together, they'd had a dream of owning a golden retriever, but not until they returned from their honeymoon. Their mutual love of animals was one of his and Nikki's strongest bonds.

When his calf muscles started to protest at the position he was in, he gingerly lowered himself to the floor and wrapped his arms around his legs. Was he getting ahead of himself here? His thoughts of happier times had carried him away. He was so lost in his memories he didn't hear Nikki until she was standing right next to him. He reached up to take the tray out of her hands. She sat down next to him while he poured the coffee.

"Talk, Nikki. I've always been a good listener. If I can help you, I will."

Nikki chewed on her lower lip. "First, give me a dollar. Attorney-client privilege. If you don't want to do that, then we just sit here and drink the coffee. It's your call, Jack."

Jack didn't hesitate. He fished out a crumpled dollar bill and handed it over. Nikki smoothed it out and stuck it in her pocket. She pointed to the coffee cups. Jack shook his head. She didn't want coffee, either.

Nikki cleared her throat. "That blood you saw on my hands earlier . . . I assaulted Allison Banks, the lawyer who defended the Barringtons in the horse abuse trial. I shredded her employment application and Maddie confiscated her computer. I broke her nose. She was bleeding all over the damn place. She said she was going to sue me, the firm, and each lawyer individually. Maddie, too. She went ahead and tried the case even after Maddie told her it was a conflict of interest. There is a rumor out there that the Barringtons are going to pay her a kickback of some sort. It's just a rumor. She claims she didn't know Myra is my adoptive mother. By the way, Jack, I heard your old boss wanted you to try the case but you refused because Myra was involved. I want to thank you for that, but I think if you had tried it, you would have won. Maddie said you were in court every day of the trial."

"That's because I was pissed to the teeth.

Kracker stacked the deck. The DA is appealing the verdict. That bastard fined Donna Abrams three different times. I have to tell you, Nik, Donna is damn good, almost as good as me in a courtroom. Kracker drooled, even lusted after your gal. Hell, the whole courtroom could see it. She played it like a pro. The media had a field day bashing your firm. Every day the press wanted to know where you were. That horse set you belong to think you bailed out for the money and the high profile case it turned into."

Nikki snorted. "And ruin my firm? Where's the logic in that?"

"Nothing else was going on in the news so the reporters ran with what they had. Myra wouldn't give any interviews. Your firm just kept saying 'no comment.' Banks gave out interviews every day after court. Hey, she made good copy and she showed up well on the six o'clock news. The press loved her. Well, most of them loved her. My old buddy, Ted Robinson at the *Post*, blasted her every chance he got. He saw what was happening in the courtroom. He told me something he can't prove and he tried his damnedest. Seems a friend's sister's aunt claims she saw Judge Krackhoff and Allison Banks at a little hideaway inn in Fredericksburg one weekend toward the end of the trial. Unfortunately for Ted, he can't nail it down. As you know, a reporter needs two sources and his one source is iffy at best. Ted's like a dog with a bone and he won't give up, but that's about the only thing that might help. Kracker should have recused himself but he didn't. His peers didn't like that, but they aren't going to turn on one of their own. It's like the cops with their blue wall."

Nikki continued to chew on her lower lip as she listened to Jack. She hated Judge Robert Krackhoff. Every case she'd ever tried before him, she'd lost because he hated Myra.

"What are the chances on appeal, Jack?"

"Damn good, in my opinion. Tell me why Kracker hates Myra."

"Because Myra blocked his application to join the Equestrian Society the same way she blocked the Barringtons' application. They don't care about the horses. They just buy and sell them. Kracker boarded two of his horses at the Barringtons' farm, and they were among those that were starved to death. So, you see, he had his own agenda. Having said that, you would think he would have been on the prosecution's side. But he owed the Barringtons a lot of money for board."

"According to Ted, there is no paper trail; this is all speculation on his part. Kracker doesn't come from money. All he has is his bench salary. He linked up early on with the Barringtons, but as Ted said, he backed the wrong horse since the equestrian set didn't take to them socially. Speculation, Nik. Ted is on it, and that's the best I can tell you."

Nikki jumped when one of the logs in the fireplace toppled, sending a shower of sparks upward. "That's a really good fire, Jack."

"It's the Boy Scout in me."

Nikki smiled. "Myra told me there's a new herd of horses in the Barringtons' pasture. I want to know who in their right mind would sell those people more animals after what they did. You know what, Jack, the judicial system sucks."

Aha! "The state didn't prove its case. It all comes down to dollars, supply and demand. The Barringtons were out of town. The blame falls on their manager, who hightailed it out of town. He's the one who left the animals to starve. The law's the law. You know that."

"Yeah, well, it still sucks."

Jack jiggled around, propping his elbow against the hearth. His eyes narrowed slightly. "Well, until things change, it's all we have."

"Are you looking forward to going back to the DA's office?" Nikki asked abruptly.

"Yes and no. It's a nice promotion. Is that all you wanted to talk to me about?"

Nikki wiggled around and propped herself on her elbow so that they were facing one another. She responded in kind. "Yes and no. I needed to tell someone what I did back there in the office. For some crazy reason I thought you would understand. Sometimes I don't know myself, Jack. Sometimes I do things I don't think I'm capable of doing, and yet I do them. Sometimes I think I made a mistake going to law school. Sometimes I hate the law."

Jack listened to her words. For some reason everything Nikki said sounded more like questions than statements. "Is that why you and the others took the law into your own hands, Nik?" he asked quietly.

Nikki closed her eyes. Her response was little more than a hushed whisper. "Yes."

"Is that what this *talk* is all about?"

"Yes. But it's more about us." Nikki fished in her pocket for the dollar Jack had given her. "Do you want it back?"

Stunned, Jack fell back on the floor. This was what he wanted. He'd just heard the words he'd hungered for these last couple of years. If he took the dollar back, he would have to make decisions. If he didn't take it back, Nikki's secrets were locked inside his head and heart forever and ever. No matter what she told him, no matter what she confessed to, he would have to respect the attorney-client privilege. She was giving him a choice, knowing the consequences that would follow.

Jack sat up, the love he felt for her written all over his face. Her gaze was clear and bright as she stared into his eyes, knowing full well what she'd just done. He grinned.

"Not much you can do with a dollar these days. Put it back in your pocket, Nik."

"Do you mean it, Jack?"

"Yeah."

"Oh, Jack."

"Now can we talk, Nik?"

"Yes, now we can talk.'

Five

Myra Rutledge paced the fragrant kitchen, oblivious to the fact that she was getting in Charles's way as he tried to prepare one of his famous gourmet meals for their guests. Normally a patient man, Charles finally swung around, a pair of tongs in his hand, and said, "Enough, Myra. Please, dear, sit down. Let me fix you a cup of tea."

Myra looked down at what was left of a square of paper towel in her hands. She'd shredded it to thin strips and was now picking at the edges. "I don't want any tea, Charles. Sometimes tea is not the answer to life's problems. And don't give me a lecture on how many cups of tea the Queen Mum drank in a day. I'm worried about our girl, Charles. I don't understand how you can be so . . . so . . . calm about it. All you're doing is cooking! Nikki isn't answering her phone. She *always* answers her phone. It's been a day and a half and she hasn't returned one of my messages. Something must have happened to her. I think one of us should drive into the District and see if she's all right. She is all right, isn't she, Charles?"

"Of course Nikki is all right. Otherwise we would have heard something to the contrary. I'm sure she had a lot of things to catch up on. After all, she was gone for over three months. I grant you, it is unlike her not to respond to your phone messages, but she isn't a child anymore, Myra. She's all grown up and in charge of her own life. She'll call, and she'll be here to greet the girls. Now, if you don't want tea, how about a little snort of brandy? You could use some color in those beautiful cheeks of yours."

Myra looked around the kitchen. "If it will make you happy to pour me some brandy then by all means pour me a . . . snort. Julia is going to be so pleased when she sees her plant. It's growing better than a weed, and you know how fast weeds grow."

"Myra, please stop agonizing over this. Take a deep breath and relax. Nikki is fine. When she's ready to come out here to the farm, she'll come out here and not one minute before, no matter how much you wish for it."

Myra wiped at her eyes. "I know, Charles. It's the mother in me. It's a mother's lot in life to worry about her children, you know that. I worry that something . . . I lost Barbara and I don't want . . . All right, Charles, I'll put on my happy face. I'm even going to drink this brandy. Now, tell me again what you're making for dinner."

"Everyone's favorites. Rack of lamb with mint jelly for Kathryn; buttered parsley potatoes for Alexis; yeast rolls for Yoko; baby carrots in a brown sugar and honey sauce for Isabelle; artichokes stuffed with crabmeat for Nikki; and pecan cream praline pie for Julia. For you, dear, a garden salad. As you know, I can eat anything."

"It sounds wonderful. The dear girls just love your cooking. I can't wait to see them. Oh, look, Charles," Myra said, pointing to the security monitor positioned over the kitchen door. "It's Alexis, and it looks like Isabelle is right behind her. Our chicks are returning."

The phone on the kitchen counter rang. Charles reached for it before Myra could cross the kitchen. His greeting was quiet. When he heard the voice on the other end of the phone, he shook his head at Myra to indicate that it wasn't Nikki on the other end. Myra barely listened as she rushed to the kitchen door. Grady, Alexis's dog, rushed toward her. Myra hugged him as he lathered her with affectionate kisses.

The women's greetings were exuberant as always. Inside, with the door closed against the brisk, chilly wind, Myra let her gaze go to Charles, who was now sitting down with the phone still in his hand.

Panic ricocheted among the women. "What's wrong, Charles?" Myra shrilled, her hands going to her heart. Alexis and Isabelle clutched at each other, their eyes full of fear. Grady whined at Alexis's feet. "Say something, Charles!"

Charles looked at the phone in his hand. "That was Julia's doctor. Julia . . . Julia suffered a stroke. She's resting comfortably."

The kitchen door opened to admit Kathryn and her dog Murphy. Kathryn looked around at the stunned expressions on everyone's faces. Her jaw clenched but somehow she managed to ask what was wrong.

Still clutching her chest, Myra told Kathryn what had happened.

"How can that be? She was doing so well. She was supposed to arrive tomorrow, or was it tonight? Look at her plant. It's thriving! We can't let her go through this alone. We have to go there to be with her. What do they mean, she's resting comfortably? Is she going to die? I thought you said those doctors over there were the best of the best. Well?" she demanded tearfully.

Charles stood up and squared his shoulders. His words were cool and clipped. "Resting comfortably means just that. The doctors *are* the best of the best. It's the treatment that is experimental. Obviously, Julia will not be joining us tomorrow. We will soldier on because that's what Julia would want. No, we are not going to Switzerland. To do so would only alarm Julia. She's getting the best care possible. Will she die? I don't know. I certainly hope not. As to Julia's plant, there are some things beyond explanation and this is one of those things. Julia's doctor has promised to call hourly to keep us updated. For what it's worth, he sounded optimistic."

Kathryn bristled. Her words spewed out like

shards of ice. "Don't talk to me about optimistic doctors, Charles. Been there, done that. When that doctor calls back, will you please ask him for explicit details? One more thing. Don't tell me I can or can't go to Switzerland to see Julia. She has no one but us. She needs us. If you can't understand that, then I'm outta here."

The kitchen door blew open to admit Yoko. Grady and Murphy barked half-heartedly as she removed her coat and took a moment to pet each of them. "What's wrong?"

Kathryn explained the situation in the same cold voice. Yoko started to cry. The dogs whined. Myra paced and Charles fussed at the stove.

"Where's Nikki?" Isabelle asked.

"We don't know where Nikki is at the moment. We expect her shortly," Myra said as she continued to pace around the kitchen table.

Murphy and Grady moved to the kitchen door and barked. Alexis opened the door and both dogs rushed outside. When she closed the door, she leaned against it as her gaze swept around the kitchen to settle on her fellow sisters. She tilted her head to the side, a signal that they should all go upstairs. Myra watched them, a troubled look on her face.

"I seriously doubt if anyone is going to eat anything tonight," Charles said.

"I agree, but you prepared it so we'll serve it. It looks delicious, dear. I think I might have just a tad more of that brandy."

"I'll join you, Myra. I wasn't expecting this," Charles said quietly as he poured brandy into two heirloom snifters. "I don't know what to think. Let's go out on the terrace. Do you need a sweater?"

"I'm fine," Myra said, pointing to the long sleeves of her plum-colored knit dress. "Yes, let's go outside."

Myra and Charles both leaned against the railing on the terrace, their eyes on the dogs racing about the lawn. The guard dogs stayed in the barn and didn't bother them. From time to time they sipped on the fiery brandy. "Kathryn was drawn to Julia from the beginning. She means it when she says she will go to Switzerland. When Julia came here at the start of her mission with that straggly plant, Kathryn literally breathed life into it. Right or wrong, Kathryn equates the plant's health with Julia's health. Julia feels the same way."

"Yes, I know."

Myra touched Charles's arm. He turned to face her. "I think Nikki is with Jack," she said.

"Yes, I know."

"You know! Why didn't you say something?"

"It was just a thought, Myra, nothing more. If I shared every thought that runs through my head, I would drive you insane. Our girl has been through a lot these past months, and she's going to go through a lot more. It's natural for her to seek out . . . comfort. The kind of comfort only Jack can give her. Her love for him has never waned. We can't blame her if that's what she needs."

Myra drained the rest of the brandy and set

the empty glass on the railing. "It's not Nikki I'm worried about. It's *him*."

"What's that American saying that gamblers use in Las Vegas?"

Myra smiled wanly. "You play the cards you're dealt. Something like that."

Charles changed the subject, hoping to drive the look of worry off Myra's face. "We should call the hospital to see if Jenny had her baby."

"Cornelia said she would call the moment Jenny delivers. I do so hope it's a little girl. They make the prettiest things for little girls. Nikki is going to be the godmother. I wonder if she knows she has to provide the christening outfit."

"Didn't you tell me Jack is to be the god-father?"

"Yes, that was the original plan. I don't know if that's going to happen now, though. Jenny, Nikki and Barbara were such good friends. I would hate to see that friendship disintegrate. Cornelia adores Jack. She said he gives the law a whole new meaning. She called him an *entertaining* prosecutor."

"We should probably go back inside so I can check on our dinner. I didn't mean for us to harp on about Jack."

"He's front and center, dear. We can't ignore what's right in front of our noses, now can we?"

"No, dear, we can't," Charles said as he opened the kitchen door. The dogs raced inside and then bounded upstairs.

* * *

Nikki rolled over and stretched her arms and legs at the same time. A long, contented sigh escaped her lips. She didn't open her eyes until Jack spoke to her, even though she was aware of his body pressed against hers.

"I didn't think you were ever going to wake up," he said, his voice husky with emotion.

Nikki rolled back over. She reached up to touch Jack's face. "I missed you," she whispered.

"Not as much as I missed you. Where do we go from here, Nik? I don't think I can bear to lose you again. I don't know about the—"

"Jack, I told you everything because I love you. I didn't ask you to join the Sisterhood. I just couldn't lie to you anymore. I know it's wrong. I know I'm breaking the law, but I can't stop. The truth is, I don't want to stop. But I can't juggle everything anymore with you breathing down my neck. You gave us all a run for our money, I can tell you that."

Jack made a sound that resembled a laugh. "You didn't tell me anything I didn't know. I just couldn't prove it. All you did was fill in the details. Just think, I might never have known Senator Webster has the American flag tattooed on his ass if you hadn't fessed up. Imagine going through life not knowing a detail like that."

In spite of herself, Nikki laughed as she tweaked Jack's nose.

Jack's voice turned solemn. "You're all going to get caught sooner or later. How's Myra going to handle jail time?"

"I know. *Déjà vu* and all that. Myra says she is OK with it, so I have to believe her. She's never lied to me. We all knew—*know* there's a possibility we'll slip up along the way, make a fatal mistake and get caught. We're all willing to take that chance. From here on in, I'll console myself with the fact that if we do get caught, Aunt Cornelia will be the presiding judge and you'll prosecute us and do a lousy job."

Jack's head snapped upward. "Judge Nellie is going to retire soon—six months or so. I heard that last week. I assume it's true. She wants to spend time with her new grandchild. I meant to call Jenny and ask, but I forgot. She did call me a few weeks ago to see if I was still willing to be the baby's godfather. I said yes."

"No, I didn't know that. The part about Aunt Cornelia retiring. Myra didn't see fit to tell me. Oh well, she's not without influence. I can't worry about it. I committed to the Sisterhood and have to see it through to its conclusion. I'm glad you agreed to be the godfather. I mean that, Jack."

Jack worked his fingers through Nikki's curly hair. "How are we going to handle this? Are you going to tell them you confessed to me? I need to know, Nik. Aren't they going to be suspicious when I stop dogging all of you? I can't tell Mark. However, I did confide in Ted Robinson, so he's going to be snooping around. He and Mark will eventually team up at some point along the way. I can't do anything about that now except plead overload at the DA's office. The whole world knows we're overworked and underpaid. They'll buy it for a while but there are no guarantees. You need to know that, Nik."

"I do know it. I'll deal with it. You didn't catch

us and I consider you to be the best. I want the truth—would you have turned me and the others in if you had come up with your proof?"

Jack didn't stop to think about his response. "Back then, yes. I couldn't believe you turned on me like that. I felt like you ripped my heart out and all I wanted to do was get back at you for hurting me. Every hour of every day I asked myself how I could have loved someone like you. I blamed myself for being so damn stupid.

"Last week I drove Jenny to her prenatal class and stood in for Brad because he worked late. It was an experience. When the class was over, Jenny insisted we go to the nursery to see the new babies. I watched the new parents with their brand-new babies. I heard those same parents make promises to those babies about safeguarding them always, loving them with all their hearts. I . . . I had a hard time with what I was seeing. I got a better understanding of what Myra must have felt when Barb died and why she couldn't let it go.

"When Mom died, I wanted to lash out and kill something. But how do you kill a disease? I fixated on the doctors. They didn't know what they were doing; they didn't give Mom the right medicine. I blamed everyone and everything, especially you because you weren't there for me to lean on. I was a mess, but there wasn't a damn thing I could do about it."

"I'm so sorry, Jack. Did the doctors really mistreat your mother? If they did, we can go after them."

"No, they didn't. It was me. I wanted to blame

someone. You know how it goes when someone passes away. You can't accept it so you try to place blame. Like I said, how could I kill a disease?"

"Does that mean you're really going to leave us alone? You won't interfere with what we're doing? I want your word, Jack."

Jack reached for her. "You have my word, Nikki. I will not interfere. Jesus, did you really help to skin that guy? Damn, I would have paid to see that."

Nikki snuggled into the crook of Jack's arm. "Yes, we did that. It's what pushed me over the edge. Every time I think of Barbara—remember her laugh, how tough and yet how gentle she was, the baby she was carrying—I know I'd do it all over again if I had to. We avenged her death, but we didn't kill anyone . . . I need to know why, Jack."

Jack didn't pretend he didn't understand the question. "Because I love you. I don't want anything to happen to you. I finally realize you aren't going to stop so you need someone to cover your butt. I'm that someone."

"Jack . . ."

"Shhh."

Six

Nikki came out of the bathroom wrapped in towels from head to toe. Jack leered at her.

"I do like sarongs."

"Don't go there. I have to run, Jack. I really do, so don't start something neither one of us can stop. Are you going back to McLean today?" she asked, hoping to divert Jack's lascivious thoughts.

"No. I have to scrounge around and find an apartment between now and Monday. I also have to pick up my car at your office. Do you think you can drop me off before you head out to the farm?"

"Sure, no problem . . . Stay here, Jack. I won't even charge you rent."

Jack backed up a step. His expression seemed to turn inward. "Do you mean stay here as in stay here, or do you mean move in as in move in?"

Nikki did a little wiggle as she settled her jeans more firmly over her hips before she pulled up the zipper. "As in move in. Like you put your stuff next to mine in the closet, you get half the vanity and half the drawer space. We take turns grocery shopping, I do the cooking, you do the cleanup. We each do our own laundry."

Jack rubbed at the stubble on his cheeks. "I thought this was all supposed to be a secret. Did I miss something?"

Nikki pulled a thin-knit cherry-red sweater over her wet head. She laughed, but it was a nervous laugh. "I never said it was supposed to be a secret, Jack. Are you saying you're having second thoughts, or is it that you'll have to grocery shop? I'll make you a list so all you have to do is go into the store and pick it up."

"I assumed . . . Are you sure you know what you're doing? Are you going to tell the others what we agreed on?"

Nikki ran a brush through her hair before she slid her feet into a pair of clogs. "I wasn't planning on announcing it if that's what you mean. Now, if someone should ask me outright, I'll decide at that time. My personal life is my personal life, just like my secrets are my secrets."

Jack looked befuddled. "But what about Myra?"

"Myra is my mother. She loves me and wants what's best for me. You are what's best for me. Myra is the one person I will not lie to. I will not bail out on you if that's what you're worried about. I love you, Jack. Hurry up and shower, I have to get to the farm."

"OK, boss. When am I going to see you again?" he called over his shoulder.

Nikki poked her head in the door of the blue and white bathroom. "I don't know, Jack. I'll call you. Do you want some coffee?"

"Yeah, make it to go." As an afterthought, he added, "Please."

Nikki laughed all the way to the kitchen. She made the coffee by rote, her mind on the past hours with Jack. For some crazy reason she felt like singing.

He came up behind her and nuzzled her neck. He smelled good. She turned and melted into his arms. "You really are OK with this, aren't you, Jack?" she whispered against his chest.

"I'm OK with it," he whispered back. "What about your ring?"

"I can't wear it on my finger just yet. But I am wearing it. See?" Nikki said as she pulled out her slim gold chain with its sparkling diamond from under her sweater. "Come on, Jack, we have to get moving."

Together, hand in hand, they ran from the town house, their coffee sloshing over the sides of the cups. Neither cared.

In the parking lot of her office, Nikki squeezed Jack's hand before he hopped out of the car. The moment he was clear of the passenger door, she peeled out of the parking lot. Her destination: Pinewood.

As always, the women greeted Nikki with exuberance. She felt guilty at the relief on Myra's and Charles's faces. She should have called. Well, she couldn't change that now. "Where's Julia?" she asked, her eye going to the luscious green plant sitting under the skylight.

Myra brought Nikki up to date. "We last heard around dawn. Julia is resting comfortably. It was a minor stroke. The doctors expect a full recovery—if Julia cooperates. She wants to come home but the doctors don't think that's advisable at this time. A few more weeks and we'll know more. She sends her love and her regrets."

Something good happens: Jack. Something bad happens: Julia. Life was just too damn short not to live it to the fullest. Nikki knew right then that she hadn't made a mistake where Jack was concerned. She didn't trust herself to speak so she simply nodded. Later, when she was alone, she'd pray for Julia.

"Would you like some breakfast, Nikki?" Charles asked. "I still have some pancake batter left. I'm sorry to say that Grady and Murphy finished the bacon."

"Coffee's fine. I'm sorry I'm late and I know I should have called. I'll tell you all about it when we go downstairs to the war room." She waved her arm about to indicate someone on the outside might be listening.

"We can clean the kitchen later," Myra said. "Since we're off schedule by twenty-four hours, I suggest we get right to it."

It was an admonishment directed at her. Nikki knew it and accepted it as she fell into line behind Myra and Charles as they led their way to the living room and the secret opening that would take them down to the high-tech room that they all referred to as the war room.

Charles bent over and pressed a small rosette in the molding before he stepped aside, allowing the wall to move on its well-oiled track.

The women's chatter ceased as they went to their assigned chairs at the round wooden table. In front of each chair was a bright-red folder with Nikki's name emblazoned on the cover. They seated themselves as Charles walked up the two steps to his station in front of a bank of computers that would have put the White House to shame. He pressed a switch and three large monitors came to life with the scales of justice spread across the screens. Charles pressed the remote control a second time and three major twenty-four-hour news networks came to life, the sound muted.

Myra called the meeting to order and then deferred to Nikki, her gaze expectant.

For some reason, Nikki felt more relaxed than she had in months. She didn't bother to stand, but instead spoke from her seated position. "I know you all more or less expect my mission to be about Jack Emery. It isn't. We've handled Jack for our last three missions and there's no reason to think we can't continue to outwit him. He's not going to do us in by an end run at this stage. If he attempts it, we'll cut him off at the knees.

"My mission is the Barringtons and the horses at their farm. The main reason I was late getting out here was because of Allison Banks, an attorney I hired before I left in the spring. I made a mistake hiring her. I admit that. Against my office manager's instructions, she accepted the Barringtons as clients. I fired her and then I pretty much assaulted her. I even broke her nose and she bled all over her brand-new pale-blue Armani suit. She's going to sue me, the firm and each of my colleagues, plus my office manager. I can handle that, and I'm only telling you as it's background.

"Allison billed astronomical hours, something any other law firm would be grateful for. I am not grateful. The Barringtons paid their bill in full. There appears to be a rumor going around that Allison Banks was either given or promised a large sum of money if there was an acquittal. While in my employ, she could not accept it legally. Now that I've fired her, she can, if the offer was ever on the table to begin with. As I said, it is a rumor. Most rumors usually have a seed of truth to them. Just for the record, the Armani suit set her back around four thousand bucks. Unless she has a trust fund, she couldn't afford Armani on what the firm was paying her. According to my office manager, Allison had eleven such suits and she wore one to court each day. Her shoes were Bally, her handbags Chanel. Do the math.

"Supposedly, Ms. Banks was seen at a little hideaway inn in Fredericksburg with Judge Robert Krackhoff, who presided over the Barringtons' trial. At the moment, that rumor can't be nailed down. I'm hopeful that eventually it will be confirmed.

"Kracker, as we call him, should have recused himself from sitting on the bench but he didn't.

He has horses he boards, or did board, with the Barringtons. They are friendly and that's why he should have recused himself.

"McLean is horse country. I'm the president of the Virginia Equestrian Society. I'm not sure about this, but I think I'm in the process of being impeached because my firm represented the Barringtons. Our clients have fled our offices like we have the plague. There are no new clients walking through our doors. Had I been here, my firm would never have agreed to represent the Barringtons. In case you're interested, I've heard that Allison Banks can pretty much name her price in the District now. It's my understanding that legal firms, some of the biggest in Washington, are standing in line to hire her.

"Now, somehow, some way, the Barringtons have a new herd of horses. What they do is buy two or three high-priced horses that will turn them a profit in the right market. They drive down that high price by taking on other horses whose bloodlines aren't up to their standards and then let them starve to death."

Nikki felt breathless. She looked over at Myra. "If I left anything out, tell me now. My mission is this: I want those horses moved to safety and I want the Barringtons to pay for what they've done to all those defenseless animals. They have to pay for that. I want Myra's and my reputation restored. And I want Allison Banks to lose her license to practice law."

Kathryn's eyes popped. "This is a pretty hefty mission, Nikki. How many horses are there? Do you mean for us to steal them? I think it's going to be pretty hard to steal a horse, let alone a herd. Horses are big! What do you want for the Barringtons?"

"I don't have the answers. I said it was what I want. The six of us should be able to come up with a solution with Charles's help. As for the Barringtons, if I had a wish it would be that they spend the rest of their lives shoveling horse shit from pile to pile. A never ending pile. Help me out here, girls."

"How much are the horses worth?" Alexis asked.

Nikki shrugged. "There's no way for me to know. You can ask Myra, she might have heard something. Remember, I just got back so I'm not up on the details."

"I really don't know, dear. I can try and find out. Charles is still trying to find out who sold them these particular horses. What I do know is there are nine horses in the pasture and, if I remember correctly, there are three high-priced animals in another pasture. So, to answer your question, there are at least twelve. However, I haven't seen all of them. For all I know, they could have been sold off already."

"Are we going to have to ride horses? I do not think I can do that," Yoko said in a jittery voice.

"Get over it, kiddo. You thought you couldn't ride a motorcycle but you did. Just think of a horse as a cycle with four wheels. Instead of turning a key, you say giddyup and the horse moves," Kathryn said and grinned.

Charles cleared his throat. "It's time for me to show you who the Barringtons are. If you look at the monitor, you'll see the aerial photos we took of the Barrington farm. There are pictures of piles of bones of other horses that were starved to death. It isn't a pretty sight and the pictures were taken by the local police. The bones you will be seeing have since been buried by local volunteers."

Picture after picture appeared on the over-sized monitor. The women all wiped their eyes from time to time. Nikki sat quietly, her body rigid, her face grim. Suddenly, she jumped out of her chair and bellowed, "I want that scummy judge who was bought off to pay, too!"

"Whoa!" Kathryn said, holding up both hands to stop whatever else Nikki was about to say. "I know this is your mission, Nikki, but it's a three-parter. How can we do all that? Hell, I'm up for it, but we could be spreading ourselves pretty thin here. Remember Julia isn't here, so there's only six of us. Seven, if Charles goes active."

"Then Charles is going to go active. It's what I want," Nikki snapped. "How about if we offer to buy the nine horses through a third party?"

"We already thought of that, dear," Myra said. "The Barringtons don't answer their phone or their door. The property is covered with No Trespassing signs. We've left letters in the mailbox at night. There's been no response from the Barringtons. I don't see any other way except to steal the horses. I'm sure Charles will come up with a plan. He's been in contact with many people these last few weeks."

"Maybe we could get them out through the tunnels," Nikki suggested. "There must be an opening in their barn just like the opening in our barn. Do you know, Myra?"

"How strange that you should bring that up, Nikki. Just last week, at the meeting of the Historical Society, Marion Cunningham and I were discussing our ancestors. My ancestors never owned slaves. We had paid workers, as did the Cunninghams. Both of our families aided the runaways via the tunnels. I thought the tunnels ended at the Barringtons' place, but Marion said they went all the way to their farm. Her section of the tunnels was added at a later date because they made it easier to get the slaves to the underground railroad. She did say the tunnels were never shored up and she herself never explored them, nor did her children. She doesn't know how they work or where the Barringtons' tunnels connect to hers."

Nikki looked up at Charles. Her eyes were full of questions.

"The steps are too steep, Nikki," was Charles's response.

"Maybe Isabelle could design a ramp of sorts. One going down, one going up. We just need two. There has to be a way. Possibly concrete to hold their weight. I don't know, Charles, I'm grasping at straws. All I know is I don't want those horses to starve."

"They aren't going to starve. Myra and I have been feeding and watering them at the fence line. Soon as the horses see us, they come to the fence. I don't know where the foreman is. We haven't seen a sign of him in the three weeks we've been feeding and watering the horses."

Nikki and the others were outraged. "Did you report the neglect?"

"Of course we reported it, but with no results. The police don't want to leave themselves open to a lawsuit. The Barringtons won their case, remember? We even took the police out to the pasture and showed them how we fed and watered the horses. Do you know what they said? They said that the horses didn't look neglected and looked healthy as a matter of fact. We wanted them to get a search warrant but they refused that, too. No probable cause. The horses looked fine. Thanks to Myra and myself."

"Where does that leave us?"

"Right where we were when we entered this room. I'm working on things. It's ten thirty now. We can reconvene at three this afternoon. At that time, I hope to have some news for all of you. Before you leave, I want to see a show of hands as to whether or not we proceed with Nikki's mission, all three parts of it."

Six hands shot in the air.

"Good. Be back here promptly at three o'clock."

The women filed out of the room, mumbling among themselves. Nikki's mission was now on the front burner.

Seven

Jack Emery looked at his belongings. A huge pile of stuff, half of which could be thrown away if he was so inclined. He wasn't. It had taken him three trips, loading his car to the top, to get all his stuff here. Now, he had to put it all away. No way was all this stuff going to fit in his half of the closet, his half of the dresser and his half of the vanity. Probably what he should have done was rent a storage locker somewhere. He shook his head. Storing his stuff would mean that when he wanted something, he'd have to scramble and drive all the way to the storage place to get it. There was a basement of sorts and a crawl space overhead. That would have to do for the time being. Maybe Nikki would assign him some more space later on.

Nikki. God, how he loved her. But that love

was going to cause him some mega trouble. He could already feel that trouble starting to sprout. Mark had looked at him with questions in his eyes although he didn't voice them. Mark had known for weeks now that he was going back to the DA's office, but what he didn't know was Jack's plan to move back to the District. All things considered, Mark had taken the move in his stride, especially when he'd ponied up his half of the rent for two months until Mark could find a new roommate. All he'd offered by way of explanation was that he was moving in with a friend.

He'd no sooner squared that part of the deal away than his reporter friend, Ted Robinson, called to invite him for a drink at Squire's Pub, the *Post*'s watering hole. An army of ants went on the march in his stomach when he let himself think about the *why* of the invitation. Well, he still had an hour. With any luck he could stash most of his stuff and still have time to take a shower and run to the pub. There was no sense giving Ted anything to worry about, at least not yet.

Jack moved like lightning, shuffling his belongings to the crawl space, to the basement, and the two hall closets, making sure he didn't take up more than his allotted space. He took a minute to view his pitiful wardrobe next to Nikki's when he hung his three off-the-rack suits and two sport coats on the rod. A laundry basket held his jeans, tee shirts, various windbreakers, underwear and socks. Heavy-duty sweatshirts and sweatpants were in a trash bag. He wouldn't be needing them for another month or so. He pushed the bag as far back in the closet as he could. His three pairs of good shoes went under his suits. His ties and white dress shirts, fresh from the laundry, went into one of the dresser drawers.

He placed his shaving kit and toiletries on his half of the vanity. Now he felt like he belonged here. He turned on the exhaust fan and the shower and waited for the hot water to spew out before he stripped down. Under the steaming spray, he wilted for the first time in twenty-four hours. His shoulders slumped and he felt like crying. He'd sold out everything he believed in—everything he'd worked for all his adult life—for love.

Jack struggled to rationalize things in his head as he soaped his body. Yeah, now he had the proof he'd searched for. But the attorney-client privilege was in place. Well, hell, when you sold your soul to the Devil, what was breaking a little thing like attorney-client privilege? He knew he wouldn't do it because he loved Nikki and wanted to be part of her life again. And because of that love, he was prepared to look the other way or close his eyes entirely to what Nikki and the ladies of Pinewood were doing.

There was no turning back now. He'd committed.

Forty minutes later Jack was shouldering his way through the mob of yuppies that clogged the pub. He worked his way toward the end of the bar, high-fiving friends and winking at the blondes holding white-wine spritzers. The blondes winked in return as he continued his struggle to the end of the bar where Ted Robinson had just taken possession of two Heinekens. Jack hoisted his bottle and drank thirstily.

Ted Robinson was tall and gangly with a shock of black, unkempt hair and a face full of freckles. His brown eyes were the sharpest, the shrewdest Jack had ever seen. Not a week went by that he didn't have a byline, above the fold, in the *Post*. It was said that Ted lived at the paper, that he slept on a couch and showered at a gas station. It wasn't true, but he spent so many hours a day there that it might as well have been.

"So, Big Foot," Jack said, referring to Ted's size fourteen sneakers, "what's going on? You got a big scoop or something?"

The brown eyes were so penetrating that Jack was unnerved. He brought the green bottle to his lips so he didn't have to look into those eyes.

Ted reached for a handful of pretzels and crunched down. Instead of answering the question, he asked one of his own. "You ready to get back in the saddle to fight crime? The criminals out there are probably shuddering in their boots as they wait for Monday morning."

Jack laughed. "I'm ready. I liked being a private dick with Mark, but the DA's office knocked on my door and I opened it. I got my suits cleaned, my shirts laundered, and my shoes polished. I'm good to go. Is this a slow news day or something? By the way, you're picking up the tab, right?"

"You moving back to the District?"

"Yeah, as soon as I can find something I can

afford. Until that happens, I'll bunk in with a friend. You wanna order a hot dog or something?" Squire's was known for its Dollar Dogs that came loaded. Jack was known to put four away at one sitting; Ted could outeat him by two.

Ted banged his beer bottle on the bar to get the bartender's attention. "Ten dogs, Charlie, and two more beers." He turned to Jack. "I got a nibble on that mess you were working on out at Pinewood. By the way, what are you going to do about all of that if you go back to the DA's office?"

Here it was, the purpose of the meeting. Jack shrugged. "Look, you were right, Mark was right. I was obsessed with the whole thing. I went over the edge when Nikki dumped me." He stared into the penetrating brown eyes and hoped his own were guileless. "I'm not giving up, but will pursue it on my own time, after hours. Don't tell me you were lucky enough to come up with something."

Ted swung his stool around. Jack did the same thing. They could see each other in the bar mirror.

"Jack, you spent three hours spinning your story to me, and I bought into it. What about that beating you took from the guys with the gold shields? By the way, I was able to confirm that there is such an elite little group. I have sources," the reporter said smugly.

"That's your scoop?" Jack scoffed. "Hey, I knew it was for real. I was the one who got the beating. And don't forget Mark witnessed the whole thing. Damn, for a minute there I thought you had some *real* news."

The Dollar Dogs arrived and both men dived in. Within minutes, they'd devoured all ten hot dogs and had drained their beers. "Now, that's what I call a sterling dinner," Ted said happily.

Jack grinned. "Did you hear our arteries snapping shut? Good thing we do this only once or twice a year." The army of ants in his stomach were on the march again. He waited, knowing he wasn't going to like whatever it was that Ted was about to tell him.

Ted leaned closer to be heard over the high-pitched conversations surrounding them. "I managed to get copies of Myra Rutledge's bank records. The last couple of years she's been moving money around and spending it like she was printing it herself. It goes in, then goes out to some very, very strange places. Millions and millions, Jack. Lots of it going offshore. I'm only telling you this now because you aren't in the DA's office yet."

Jack blinked. "No shit! Well, everyone knows Myra is filthy rich. A few million here or there would hardly be missed. So, what did she buy? Do you know?"

"Well, she bought three motorcycles a while back. Maybe it was four, I can't remember and I didn't bring my notes with me. The fuel bill for her Gulfstream is incredibly high. I was able to nose around and there was no candy business going on. That means she used the jet for private purposes. Now, if she charges all that to her candy company, she could be in trouble with the IRS if someone wanted to snitch on her. Big-time criminals usually get caught by some pissy-assed detail like this."

"That's it? Jet fuel and three or four motorcycles?" Jack scoffed. "What in the hell are we going to do with that information?"

The brown eyes narrowed. "There was an extremely large expenditure on some high-tech equipment several years ago. Some of the stuff that Ms. Rutledge bought hasn't arrived in the marketplace. Even the FBI doesn't have it."

Jack's heart raced. "What did she do with it? Where is it?"

Ted held up his bottle for a refill. He shrugged. "No paper trail for delivery. Maybe it was picked up. It sure as hell wasn't delivered. Cold trail. Three million was the cost. I haven't been able to get much of anything on that guy Martin. It wasn't for lack of trying, I can tell you that. Mark shared his files, but if I pursue any of those then I know I can expect a visit from those gold shields."

Jack's jaw dropped. "Listen, I'm sorry I got you involved in this. Let it drop, go back to the paper and forget you know me. Those guys . . . They'll show you no mercy. I don't want to see you get hurt. So just drop it, OK?"

"Can't do that, old buddy. I already stuck my nose into it. I never backed off before and I'm not going to back off now. If I crack this, it could be a Pulitzer for me. What do you want me to do if I do crack it and Nikki is in it up to her eyeballs?"

The ants were now eating their way up to

Jack's chest. He wished there was a way for him to kick his own rear end for involving Ted in this mess. "Just let me know. *Before* you break the story, OK?"

"You got it. Right, they need me back at the paper. Call me." Ted threw some bills on the bar and stalked off. Jack turned around and ordered another beer.

His chickens were coming home to roost. How the hell was he going to tell Nikki all of this?

Ted Robinson pushed his chair away from his desk and then rubbed his gritty eyes. Time to go home to his cats, Minnie and Mickey, who were probably hissing at the door in frustration. His thoughts were on Jack Emery as he shut down his computer, gathered up his backpack with his Blackberry, his scrawled notes and his laptop. He slipped his arms through the straps and headed for the door. There was no one to wave to; no one cared if he worked eighteen hours a day or two hours a day.

Ted lived in a six-floor walk-up eight blocks away. He hunkered into his flannel-lined jacket as he walked into the windy, rainy night. He hated the rain. Jack had seemed nervous tonight. Maybe nervous was the wrong word. Jittery was more like it. All of a sudden he was giving off indifferent vibes. Six months ago he'd practically gotten on his knees and begged Ted to look into what was going on at Pinewood. Ted had reluctantly agreed and putzed around with the mess just to keep Jack happy. Now *he* was the one who was obsessed, to his boss's horror. The old man's words rang in his ears every time he thought of Jack Emery and the women of Pinewood. "This paper is not interested in learning anything about Madam Rutledge. Keep poking your nose into things that aren't of interest to this paper and you'll be on the unemployment line."

That was all Ted Robinson had needed to hear. His hound-dog instincts had kicked in and he'd hit the ground running. Suddenly, everything else paled in comparison. Jack had dropped the gauntlet and Ted had picked it up.

A cab raced by, kicking up a spray of rainwater that drenched Ted's legs. He cursed as he picked up his feet and jogged the rest of the way to his apartment.

On any other night he might have noticed the black car parked in front of his building, but with the falling rain and his wet jeans cleaving to his legs, he was intent only on getting home to change his clothes.

"Screw you, Jack. You get me all excited and then you bail out on me. See if I give you credit when I finally write this damn story!"

Ted's long legs took the concrete steps two at a time to the secure door that led into the vestibule of his apartment building. Inside, he checked his mail but found nothing of interest, so he dropped the whole bundle into the trash basket before heading upstairs. As he rounded the corner he saw the three men lounging against the wall outside his door. He could hear Minnie and Mickey meowing inside. Something clutched at his gut. He sucked in his breath, knowing something bad was about to happen. He'd skirted the edges of trouble too many times not to recognize it.

"Mr. Robinson?"

Ted decided being flip might get him points. "That's what my mama named me. I hope you aren't selling something. If you are, I already have it. Excuse me," he said, bending down to put his key in the lock. Mickey and Minnie had stopped meowing and were hissing now. He loved the sound; it convinced him he wasn't having a bad dream.

"Actually, what we sell is safety and security. Invite us in, please."

It wasn't an invitation, it was an order, and Ted recognized it as such. Since he had never experienced real fear in his life, he took a second to wonder if that was what he was feeling now.

"Well, sure, come on in. I bet you're Harry, Mike and Moe, and you each have a gold shield. How'm I doing so far, boys?"

"He's a wiseass, too," one of the men said as he flashed his gold shield. The two remaining men held up their matching shields.

Mickey and Minnie were streaks of black fur as they raced to hide. Ted wished there was a place for him to hide, too, but the one-room studio didn't exactly have many hidey-holes.

"Are you still tailing Jack Emery?" he asked bravely.

"Tsk, tsk," the tallest of the three said, clucking his tongue. "We ask the questions, we don't answer them."

"Is that what you said to Jack Emery before you beat the shit out of him?"

"As a matter of fact, it is," said the third man, the one who hadn't spoken so far.

Ted was about to respond when his head suddenly felt like it was going to explode. He went down onto his knees and was struggling to get up when he saw a foot coming his way. He closed his eyes and let it happen.

Eight

The war room crackled with sound, all three twenty-four-hour news stations announcing the current news as it happened. Charles's printers spit out reams of paper while Charles himself tapped out messages to his fellow retired operatives all over the world.

The women seated themselves, talking in hushed voices so as not to distract Charles. The conversation mostly pertained to the weather and how cool it was so early into the fall. Winter, they said, was probably going to be as brutal as it was last year. While no one actually said the word "horse," they were all thinking about the cold and how the animals would fare at the Barringtons' unless something was done before winter set in.

Suddenly the giant TV monitors went black. The printers pinged, signaling that whatever

Charles was printing had come to an end. The women watched as Charles separated the papers into seven separate piles, then stapled them. He walked over to one of the monitors and looked down over the railing at the women. They waited expectantly.

"I have an announcement to make before we get under way. In case any of you don't already know this, our main adversary, Jack Emery, will no longer be a freelance threat to us. Do not take that announcement to mean he's through with us. I suspect he isn't. On Monday, he will take up his duties as a full-fledged District Attorney. Having said that, I want you all to know that Mr. Emery appears to have passed his torch along to a *Post* reporter named Ted Robinson. The matter is being taken care of as we speak."

Nikki stared at Charles with unblinking intensity, aware that all eyes were watching her to gauge her reaction to this news. She was glad no one could see the tight knot inside her stomach. She shrugged, indifference in her expression, and waited, saying nothing. If the matter was *being taken care of*, then it was already too late to call Jack to alert Ted.

Charles descended the two steps to the round table where all the women were seated. He handed out the stapled dossiers on Myra's neighbors, the Barringtons, and then returned to his position behind the computer bank. He pressed a button on his remote control. The scales of justice appeared on all three monitors. The women stared overhead, their expressions somber and serious.

Charles pressed the remote again. A picture of the Barrington farm appeared. It was an old picture, the buildings pristine white, the lawns manicured with exquisite shrubbery and brilliant flowers. A second picture appeared, taken just weeks ago. It showed buildings in disrepair, the lawns and flowers replaced with gravel and tufts of grass and weeds. A third picture appeared, showing dilapidated barns and sheds. All looked ready to tumble down. The fencing around the pastures was spindly at best.

"I'm sorry to report that the information I've been able to gather on the Barringtons is rather sketchy. Originally, Myra and I thought that Amelia Barrington, a very distant cousin of the elder Barringtons, was married. It appears that isn't the case.

"The Barrington farm was neglected for many, many years. Fifteen, to be exact. The original family died off and the property passed from one to another until Amelia Barrington decided to take it over. This is a picture of Miss Barrington."

A picture of a stunning redheaded woman appeared on the screen. "This picture was taken before Miss Barrington fell on hard times. What that means is she frittered away her rather small inheritance on the jet-set life. At some point, she teamed up with Jacques Duquesne, a playboy she met on the Riviera. He made the mistake of thinking she was a rich heiress. She, in turn, thought he was a rich playboy. When the truth came out between them, they put their heads together and proceeded to hit up their jet-setter friends for what they called 'seed money' to start up a five-star racing stable here in the States. They returned here to McLean and started buying and selling horses. And, if you are interested, they haven't repaid any of that 'seed money' to their rich friends abroad."

Nikki's eyes bulged. "Five-star racing stable!"

Charles nodded. "It's obvious no one lives on the farm. Miss Barrington and her friend have an apartment in the District at the Watergate. I just found that out this morning. If you look inside your folder you'll see a handsome brochure that Miss Barrington handed out to her rich friends. As you can see, it is not the Barrington farm. It is, however, a racing stable. It's in Kentucky and it's called Blue Diamond Farms and was owned and operated by Nealy Coleman. Nealy Coleman was the first woman to own, train and then ride her horse to a Triple Crown. Miss Barrington's friends were none the wiser and couldn't wait to put up their money in hopes there would be a horse to ride to a Triple Crown."

"Then she must have some really stupid friends," Kathryn snapped.

Charles pursed his lips. "Not stupid, just bored and way too rich. They wanted to be part of something and couldn't wait to donate to the cause. Both Amelia and Jacques are very persuasive people. In other words, superb con artists."

"But the lawsuit was brought against both Barringtons. Who is the other Barrington?"

"Amelia's brother Conway, who, by the way, is a decent chap. His name is on the deed to the farm along with Amelia's. He had nothing to do with anything. The state was overzealous in prosecuting him. He lives and works as an insurance broker in Washington. He has a family and lives in Falls Church. Every day of the trial he had heated words with his sister, whom he claims to despise. He had his own attorney and the trial bankrupted him. The man and his family are not very happy with Miss Barrington. He is now suing his sister and the state. It's one rather messy affair."

Alexis leaned across the table to get a better view of Charles. "Aside from Nikki and Myra, the rest of us know very little about the horse business. What kind of money are we talking about? What exactly did they do? And how? I don't think any of us has a clear picture of what happened."

"Of course. I apologize. Let me run through it from the beginning. From what I have been able to gather, Amelia and Jacques secured over seven million dollars in seed money. They used it to set up a bogus racing stable to impress their jet-setting friends in Europe. Amelia and Jacques came back here and set themselves up in a luxurious apartment in Washington. They started buying up top-bred horses. They also went to auctions. They cut deals with horse owners to buy a particular horse with a top bloodline by agreeing to buy other less impressive horses that they didn't really want. It costs a great deal of time and money to care for a horse. They then turned around and sold the prize horses for double the money they paid for them. The others were left to fend for themselves. They literally

starved to death. As far as I've been able to de-
termine, no vet has ever visited the Barrington
farm. At least, no vet from this area. This has been
done four times that I'm aware of. That's all I've
been able to trace up to this point, but I'm not
giving up since this has been going on for five
years."

"And the foreman?" Isabelle asked.

"According to the police, he left in the middle of the night. He left no trail to follow. I doubt
the name that Amelia Barrington gave to the
police is the foreman's real name, since there is
no trace of him to be found."

"It is most sad that animals died because of
starvation," Yoko said, tears in her eyes. "This is
America with food for all, including animals. I
wonder how Miss Barrington would handle starvation."

Kathryn sat straight up in her chair, her eyes
spewing sparks. "Yoko is right, there is no excuse for what those people did. That's what we
should do, we should starve that bitch! I'm never
going to get those pictures of those poor animals out of my head. On second thought, starving is too good for her. We should do something
more drastic," she said, venom dripping from
her lips.

Nikki clenched her teeth. "That works for
me. All we have to do is come up with a plan
and make it work."

"Then let's put our heads together and come
up with a plan while Charles continues to do
what he does best," Myra said.

Nikki locked her gaze with Myra's. "Doesn't Judge Easter live at the Watergate?"

"Why, yes, dear, she does live there. Ah, I see where your thoughts are taking you. With Jenny about to give birth any second, Nellie will be staying with her for a little while, which means her apartment will be empty. Well, that's one problem solved. We'll have easy access to Miss Barrington."

Alexis frowned. "Are we just going to go there and say, 'We're going to starve you to death'?"

"If that's what we have to do, then, yes, that's what we do. There are other things we could do. We can let their jet-setting friends know that they were ripped off. They will then be persona non grata in that social scene, which is obviously important to Barrington and Duquesne. We need to know how Duquesne got here and has been able to stay so long. Maybe we can have him deported so he goes back in disgrace. He might actually have to work for a living. There are all kinds of possibilities open to us if we care to pursue them. Most important, we can't forget about Judge Krackhoff and Allison Banks," Nikki said.

Myra reached inside the shoe box sitting in the middle of the table. She handed out pencils. "All right, let's get to it!"

Mark Lane turned off his computer, uncapped a beer and then propped his feet up on his desk. He looked around and was suddenly aware of the silence. When Jack was here he was forever whistling, snapping his fingers or muttering about something or other. Mark realized that he missed his partner. He knew the business would survive without him, but it was nice to have someone at arm's length to hash things over with. But Jack belonged in the DA's office—always had, always would.

Mark liked being his own boss, liked being the one who issued the orders and then followed them up. Not like when he was at the FBI, where he had to march to orders, like it or not. He liked making his own hours, liked the fact that he helped people and actually got to see the results of his operatives' work.

He looked around again at the cluttered office. The only neat spot was Jack's old desk. Maybe he should give some thought to hiring a replacement for Jack. Then again, maybe he should hire a temporary secretary instead. A secretary would make noise, make coffee, run errands and water plants once he bought some. The idea was so pleasing, he jotted down a reminder to himself to call an employment agency in the morning.

Time to go home, back to his empty apartment. He was going to miss Jack and his clutter. Maybe he'd get a cat. A big old cat who meowed when he came in and hissed when he wasn't fed on time. A cat and a secretary. It sounded like a plan. Then he laughed. He couldn't wait to tell Jack he'd replaced him with a secretary and a big old cat. He was still laughing when he locked the office and headed for his car. It was raining, which meant he'd have to fight traffic with a bunch of asshole drivers who did eighty miles an hour in a twenty-five-mile zone. He jogged to his car and was turning over the ignition when his cell phone rang. He picked it up on the third ring; then a red light appeared, which meant his battery was either dying or already dead. The moment he said hello, the battery died. Now, if he had a secretary, she would be responsible for charging the battery. He shrugged. Whoever it was would call back or else they'd leave a message on his landline. He shrugged a second time. Rarely in the private-eye business was there a true emergency.

In no hurry to go home to his apartment, Mark stopped to pick up some Chinese food and a six pack of Miller Lite. It was ten o'clock when he finally unlocked his door. He was disappointed that there was no cat to greet him. He decided to make the cat a priority.

Inside, he shed his jacket and kicked off his sneakers before he even hit the kitchen. That's when the phone rang. He muttered a greeting as he spooned shrimp chow mein onto a plate. He stopped what he was doing when he heard Jack's angry, agitated voice. "Whoa, whoa, Jack. Slow down. What happened?"

"Never mind what happened. Meet me at the emergency room of George Washington Hospital. Like *now*, Mark."

Mark looked down at the chow mein on his plate. Suddenly, he wasn't hungry. He scooped everything back into the carton and shoved it in the refrigerator. He scrounged around inside his closet, found his deck shoes and a dry light-weight jacket, then headed back out to his car, his mind going a thousand miles an hour. What the hell had Jack done now?

An hour later, when Mark pulled up to the emergency entrance, he was stunned to see Jack pacing up and down, the bright light from inside ricocheting off his back. He watched for a second as his old partner smacked his clenched fist into the palm of his hand. Jack Emery was pissed off. Big-time.

Mark maneuvered his SUV out of the ambulance lane. Jack hopped in before Mark could even shift into park.

"What the hell is going on, Jack? Do you know what time it is? What are you doing here?"

"Those goddamn gold shields got to Ted Robinson. That's what's going on. Those bastards didn't give up; they've been following us ever since they beat the crap out of me. They worked Ted over worse than they worked me over. He managed to call nine-one-one after they left and the hospital called me. He's in surgery right now having his spleen removed. Now you can say something."

"Oh, shit!"

Nine

Nikki tossed and turned in the narrow bed, the same bed she'd slept in as a child. Back then, she and Barbara had whispered long into the night, sharing secrets, giggling and laughing. At times they would stretch their arms across the space between the beds and hold hands. Even though they weren't related by blood, they were still sisters.

Nikki knew there wasn't going to be any more sleep for her, so she might as well get up. Something was wrong. She could sense it, literally feel it. Her gut instinct told her that whatever it was had something to do with Jack. Did she dare call him to find out if her instincts were on target?

"This might be a good time for you to make an appearance, Barb. Help me out here," she said into the darkness.

"*It's the middle of the night, Nik. Go back to sleep. I'll sit here and rock with Willie.*"

"I can't sleep. Something is wrong, I can sense it. Do you know what it is?"

"*I'm a spirit, Nik. I don't have anyone's ear. You really need to learn to relax. Going on all cylinders is not good. Things will work out. You're happy about the thing with Jack?*"

"Well, sure, I'm happy. I wish I were there right now. I'm telling you, something is wrong and I'm sure it involves Jack. I want to call him."

"*Then for heaven's sake, call him. If that's what you have to do to get some sleep, then you should do it. Curl up in the bed and whisper sweet nothings in his ear. I promise not to listen.*"

It was all Nikki needed; permission to call the man she loved. If Myra or Charles had a way of listening in, so be it. Her fingers moved at the speed of light as she tapped out Jack's number. She was stunned when he picked up on the first ring. Her eyes flew to the digital clock on the nightstand.

"Did I wake you?" she whispered.

"No. I haven't gone to bed yet. I'm at the hospital with Mark."

Nikki's heartbeat raced. "What's wrong with him? Is he OK?"

Jack's voice came over the wire tired, weary, angry and cool. "It's not Mark, it's Robinson. He had to have his spleen removed. He's in the recovery room right now. Mark and I are waiting to see if he's OK. Before you ask, those gold shields got to him and beat the living shit out of him."

"Oh, God! Is there anything I can do?" Nikki asked in a choked voice.

Jack's voice was so cool that Nikki shivered inside her flannel pajamas. "Not unless you can give him back his spleen. I guess those goons have been following all of us. For some crazy reason, I thought they backed off after they beat the crap out of me. It appears I was wrong."

"I'm sorry, Jack. I don't know what else to say."

"Yeah. You know, Nik, right now I feel like I made a pact with the Devil. I don't want to say anything else that I might regret later. I don't think you do, either. Let's hang up so I can wait to hear how my friend is doing. Call me tomorrow."

Nikki licked her dry lips as she clicked off her cell phone. She looked over at the rocking chair. "Well, hearing *that* isn't going to let me go to sleep."

"*Shift into neutral, Nik. Sleep will come if you let it. Here, Willie will keep you company.*"

The next thing Nikki saw was the stuffed bear sailing through the air. She caught it and snuggled beneath the blankets. "Night, Barb."

"*Everything will work out, Nik.*"

Nikki wasn't sure, but she thought she felt something soft and feathery touch her cheek. A smile settled on her lips as she drifted off to sleep.

Nikki wasn't the only one who was having difficulty sleeping.

Myra's arm snaked out only to touch Charles's pillow. She moved her hand up and down the place where her man should have been sleeping. She sighed as she swung her legs over the side of the bed. Four o'clock in the morning was too early to start the day. She found herself muttering as she made her way downstairs. She was almost to the bottom when she was joined by the dogs, Murphy and Grady.

The dogs settled themselves under the kitchen table while Myra made coffee. While the coffee dripped into the pot, Myra handed out treats, which both dogs ignored. Perplexed, she opened the refrigerator and took out two slices of roast beef, which she dangled in front of them. Both dogs gobbled the unexpected treat and then went back to sleep just as the coffee finished dripping into the pot. When the last popping sound was heard, Myra fixed a tray with two cups and carried it to the secret entrance that led to the tunnels.

Charles looked up when the door to the war room opened soundlessly. His eyes were bright and alert, his smile warm and welcoming. So warm and welcoming, Myra felt good all over. There were times when Charles didn't want company down here in the bowels of the farmhouse, but his smile told her that today he was grateful for her company at this early hour of the morning.

"Ah, coffee. I think you're getting more and more tuned into my thoughts, old girl. I was just thinking how good a cup of coffee would be right now. Couldn't you sleep?"

"I missed you," Myra said simply. "How are things going, dear?"

Charles eyed his true love over the rim of the bone-china cup. "I regret to say, not as good as I would like. I've been working on dossiers of all our key players who are involved in our next mission. What's that expression Nikki uses all the time? Oh, yes, *slam dunk*. It is not a slam dunk the way I thought it would be. I have calls and encrypted e-mails going out to all my old colleagues, who will in turn call in favors from some of our own people who are still in the game."

Myra sipped at her hot coffee. "Is there any one thing in particular that is bothering you, dear?"

Charles slouched back in the swivel chair, something he never did. His posture was always the same, sitting or standing: ramrod-stiff.

"Yes and no. It would appear no one involved is really who they seem to be. Take Conway Barrington, Amelia Barrington's brother. Imagine this, Myra. Amelia Barrington doesn't have a brother. Conway Barrington isn't married and Conway Barrington doesn't have children. That was all a facade. I don't know who he is. He is not Amelia Barrington's husband, either. There are no records anywhere to back up the story that the courts and the press put out. I have my people on it, my dear."

"Are you saying Mr. Barrington . . . *borrowed* a family and passed them off as his own? Once a lawsuit is under way, don't the authorities check the backgrounds of the individuals involved?"

"One would think so. Obviously, that didn't happen. Then there is Judge Robert Krackhoff. The man is also a bit of a mystery at this moment. I've been able to track his financials. He has a very robust brokerage account. At first glance there is nothing suspicious about that; many people dabble in the stock market. But if you factor in his income, living expenses and so on, you have to wonder how he could have such a high balance in his account. Even if he were a super-duper wizard he couldn't have racked up that much money in four years. He's had some help from somewhere in regard to his paper trail."

"Do you think the man has been taking bribes?"

"That's one explanation. I have a colleague going back over every case he's ever presided over to see if any of his brokerage transactions coincide with those trials. It's going to take a little time to get it all together. I don't want you to fret about it. My man is the best of the best. He'll sort through it all. For a judge, Krackhoff does have some questionable friends and acquaintances."

"I wonder if Nellie knows anything about the judge. She would be in an excellent position to hear gossip. Judges are not above a little gossip, Charles, so don't look at me like that. Everyone likes to gossip. I can ask her, if that won't upset things with your people."

"It might come to that, dear, but not right now. Let me muddle along here with my people. I don't like involving outsiders unless it's a dire emergency."

"Did you run any checks on that . . . that twit Nikki hired, the one who defended the Barringtons?"

"I certainly did. Miss Allison Banks isn't really Miss Allison Banks. I don't know who she is. Obviously, she is an attorney, but with an alias. The real Allison Banks died in a car accident three months after she took the bar exam. The real Allison Banks went to New York University Law School and lived in Manhattan. She has a sister who lives somewhere in the Midwest. I haven't been able to locate her at this time. Based on what I've found out so far, I think the . . . ah . . . twit assumed Miss Banks's identity. I have a picture of the real Allison and, while there is a resemblance—blonde hair, brown eyes, more or less the same height—our twit isn't the same person. If you place both photos side by side, you can tell the difference between the two women. I used one of the pictures I saved from the newspapers for a comparison."

"Then that means . . . that means this is all a big conspiracy. Is that what you're saying, Charles?"

"Yes, dear. We have five players here. Barrington, Duquesne, the bogus brother, Judge Krackhoff and Allison Banks. It's entirely possible the bogus brother was born on the wrong side of the blanket. I just don't know yet, Myra."

Myra looked down into her empty coffee cup as though she thought more coffee would materialize just by her looking. "It sounds so complicated. Nikki's revenge was to be Amelia Barrington and her neglect of the horses. Now . . . now it has grown legs. Are we up to this, dear?"

Charles's eyes twinkled. "Let me put it this way. It will definitely be a challenge, but I do think we're up to it. At the end of the day, it will be Nikki's decision and her mission. If she wants to go all the way, then that's what we'll do. If she just wants to punish the Barringtons, then that's what we'll do."

"I have a wonderful idea. Let's go upstairs so you can cook breakfast. The girls will be up soon. The dogs need to go outside, too. We can make decisions later this morning."

Charles got up and then picked up the tray. "You do have a way of diverting me, don't you? How do waffles and fresh berries sound?"

"They sound wonderful. I so wish I were half the cook you are, Charles. It's still a mystery to me why my mother never taught me to cook." Myra shrugged as she followed Charles from the war room and up the steps to the main part of the house. Both dogs were sitting at attention when the secret door opened. They whined softly and then raced to the kitchen door.

"My dear, cooking is not something you should worry about. You have so many other talents, your lack of culinary expertise is hardly noticeable."

Myra tapped Charles on the arm. "Fine, name me one. Just one, Charles."

Charles whispered in her ear. She blushed a bright pink and then laughed. "Oh, yes, *that*!"

The sun was creeping over the horizon when Jack Emery and Mark Lane exited the hospital.

Both were gritty-eyed and tired as they trudged to the parking lot to pick up their cars.

"Want to get some breakfast?" Mark asked.

"No. I just want to go home to take a shower. I'll make some toast. Look, Mark, thanks for coming and hanging out with me. I need to do some real hard thinking, and I need to be alone to do that. I also want to go by Ted's place and feed his cats. I took his clothes and keys," he said, pointing to the plastic bag he was carrying.

"Then I guess I'll go home and eat last night's Chinese. It sucks the next day, but what the hell. We can talk later. Call me."

"Yeah . . . Mark?"

"What?"

"What do you think about the owner of the paper showing up to see Ted?"

"Well, hell, Jack, the guy got the shit beat out of him on his watch. Taking out someone's spleen isn't like getting your tonsils out. I think I'd be pretty damn upset if he *didn't* show up."

"Aside from that. I think he's gonna get behind Ted if Ted pursues this. Or he's going to call him off totally. Papers are all for scoops. Can't you just see the headlines if Ted defies these guys and goes all out? If the paper gets behind Ted, Myra and her gang are dead in the water and I don't think it will make one bit of difference if Myra knows the governor or not."

Mark stared at his friend with narrowed eyes. "If my vote counts, I say we forget we ever heard the names of Myra Rutledge and Charles Martin. I'll meet you back here later this afternoon. I want to hear with my own ears what Ted has to say."

"Yeah, OK. See ya."

Mark sat in his SUV for a long time after Jack peeled out of the parking lot. His original intention was to follow his friend, but Jack would have picked up the tail in a heartbeat. He knew in his gut where he was going: Nikki Quinn's house in Georgetown. He threw his hands in the air. "The hell with it!" he muttered.

Jack spent half the drive to Georgetown looking in his rearview mirror. He fully expected to see Mark following him. His shoulders slumped when he made it all the way to Nikki's house without a tail.

Inside, he showered, changed, dressed in clean clothes and cleaned up after himself before he made toast and coffee. He swilled down the coffee and gobbled the toast before he grabbed the plastic bag to head to Ted's apartment. There he fed the two hissing, snarling cats, cleaned out the litter boxes, carried the contents to the trash, locked up and was back in Nikki's house in ninety minutes. The first thing he did was dial Nikki's cell phone. He smiled at her sleepy voice that turned instantly alert when she heard him.

"Can you come into the District and meet me in Rock Creek Park, Nik? If you can't manage that, how about if I head out to McLean? We can meet by the monument."

"I'll call you back, Jack. I just woke up. Off the top of my head, if I can swing it, it will have to be late in the afternoon. I'll do my best."

"If that's the best you can do it will have to do.

I want to go back to the hospital. I promised to meet Mark later this afternoon. Call me and let me know what works for you. My day's pretty much open with the exception of going to the hospital. I love you, Nik. With all my heart."

"I love you too, Jack. With the whole of my heart."

Jack felt like he was walking on pure air for all of sixty seconds before he came back down to earth with a hard thump. All he could think about was Ted Robinson and how white and still he'd looked in the hospital bed. Ted was going to be all right, although his recovery wouldn't happen overnight. Nor would Ted be running any marathons for a long time, something he loved to do. Someone had to pay for what was done to his friend. If he was the only one willing to step up to the plate, well, tough shit. If it took him the rest of his life, he was going to find a way to shove a red-hot poker up those gold shields' asses, but not until he ripped their arms out of their sockets. All three of them.

Jack felt like his brain was on fire as idea after idea invaded his head. Revenge had to be the sweetest aphrodisiac of all. He stopped in his tracks and blinked, his eyes rolling back in his head. So, this was what that little band of gutsy women felt like when they took on the bad guys. Well, hot damn!

Ten

"Girls! Girls! Come inside," Myra called from the kitchen door. "Julia is on the phone. I'll put her on the speaker and we can all talk to her."

The women on the terrace raced down the steps and over to the kitchen door, pushing and shoving each other in excitement. As one they babbled a greeting.

"How are you all? I am so sorry I'm not there, but my doctors are telling me I can possibly travel in as little as two weeks. I'm fine, don't go worrying about me now. I want to hear all about you, one at a time. I'll be able to read between the lines, but be careful just the same. First things first, how is my plant?"

The relief on the women's faces, even Myra's,

was comical. Julia was dear to them all. As one, they shouted, "The plant is thriving!"

One by one, they brought Julia up to date on the mundane things in their lives. No mention was made of Nikki's mission or anything else pertaining to the Sisterhood.

Nikki brought the conversation to an end by saying, "Charles promised to make pecan-crusted salmon this evening with shoestring sweet potatoes. Myra brought in the last of the peas from the greenhouse and Yoko and I shelled them. Alexis is going to make cheese biscuits, her specialty. Oh, one other thing. We have a huge pumpkin on the front porch that Myra and Charles carved. We light the candle inside every night. If you make it home in a few weeks, we'll get a fresh pumpkin and carve your initials in it to welcome you home. We're all up for a Halloween party, how about you, Julia?"

Julia laughed. "I'm up for anything at this point. I guess I better hang up. My love to you all, and hug Charles for me. Kathryn, give Murphy an extra biscuit and don't forget Grady. Bye, all."

They started to babble again, their comments running into each other.

"She sounds good. I thought she was upbeat. Did you hear her laugh? Two weeks and she might be here. We really need a very *large* pumpkin!"

Nikki sneaked a look at her watch. She had to leave now if she was going to meet Jack. What excuse could she possibly give? She clenched her teeth. Why did she have to give anyone an excuse? She could offer up an explanation if she wanted to, but that was it.

Nikki looked around at the sisters. "Since this is free time, I think I'll go into town. I need to pick up a few things. Can I bring anything back for any of you?" Before she knew it, requests were coming in fast and she had to get a pencil and paper to write down the list because she didn't trust her memory.

"Anything for you, Myra?" Nikki asked cheerfully.

Myra fingered the pearls around her neck. "I don't think so, dear, but thank you for asking. Oh, wait, I think Charles might need some shaving cream. Noxzema is what he uses."

"Got it. If you think of anything else, call me on my cell phone. Listen, I have an idea. Two weeks isn't that long. Let's all go out to the farm stand and get a scarecrow and decorate the porch for Julia's arrival." Nikki looked over at Myra and smiled. "Myra always did it for Barb and me when we were little. We'd jump off the school bus and race up to see the Halloween display. She did the same thing at Christmas. It always smelled so good. Isabelle, you're the architect, measure the front porch and draw us a diagram and we'll do the rest."

"OK. It will give me something to do. Do you want to include the steps and the doorway?"

"Well sure, the whole nine yards. Lots and lots of pumpkins," Nikki said.

"You got it. I'll get right on it. I'm open to suggestions if you have any."

The girls started to offer their input. Nikki reached for her button-down sweatshirt that was hanging on the coat rack by the back door.

"If I'm not back by dinnertime, go ahead without me. Depending on traffic, I might go to see Jenny. Bye!"

My darling girl is up to something, Myra thought. She turned away, puzzled at Nikki's high mood. Then the blood rushed to her neck when she heard Kathryn say, "Nikki isn't one of us in the true sense of the word. She's our mouthpiece. I wish it were otherwise. She worries me."

Myra whirled around. In a voice that was so stern, so sharp that the others winced, she said, "I don't ever want to hear anything like that again from any of you. Is that understood? None of you would be here if it weren't for Nikki, and don't you ever forget it. I'm disappointed, Kathryn, that you feel the way you do."

Kathryn didn't back down. "It's how I feel, Myra. Would you rather I whispered among the others? That's not my style. If I feel the need to say something, I'll say it. I hope I'm wrong, but I don't think I am. Nikki's heart is not in this the way our hearts are in it. It's that simple. You could take a vote, Myra," Kathryn challenged.

Myra was about to respond when Charles entered the kitchen, saving her from saying something she might come to regret later.

The women scattered because Charles's first rule was that no one clutters his kitchen while he cooks. Myra winked at him as she made her way to the second floor via the kitchen staircase, but only after she brought him up to date on Julia's phone call. She was tempted to say something about Nikki, but decided to keep her thoughts to herself. Because they were just thoughts, nothing more. Nikki would never compromise the group in any way. She was so certain, she didn't give Kathryn's words another thought.

With time to spare, Nikki entered Santelli's drugstore and bought everything on her list plus a bag full of stuff for herself that she didn't need. She returned to her car to wait for Jack. She knew she had a good forty minutes to wait so she called Jenny to see how she was feeling.

"You know, Jenny, I was going to drive into town to see you, but it's getting late and I know how tired you get at the end of the day. How are you feeling? Is there anything I can do for you?"

The voice on the other end of the phone sounded tired and weary. "Thanks, Nik, but no. Brad waits on me hand and foot. Mom is staying with us and she just keeps saying I'm not the first woman to have a baby and to stop whining. It's hard not to whine when you have to pee every two minutes. You're right about one thing, though. At this time of day, all I want to do is sleep. My feet and ankles are swollen so badly I can barely walk and I have heartburn twenty-four-seven. I'm thinking of just moving into the bathroom and sleeping in the tub. My doctor told me if I don't deliver in the next two days he will induce labor . . . But let's not talk about me, it's too depressing. How are you? What's going on? What about the firm?"

Nikki leaned back in the driver's seat and drew a deep breath. "I'm fine. My suntan is about

gone. Nothing is really going on. The firm . . .
Well, I fired Allison Banks and then I got a little
physical and broke her nose. She said she's going
to sue all the members of the firm and will own
it when she's done. How's that for news?"

"Wow! You actually broke that cute little rhino-
plasty nose of hers! Now, I would have paid to see
that! What got into you, Nik? That's something
Barb would have done. You were always the level-
headed peacemaker."

Nikki sighed. "That was then; this is now. She
gave me some lip and I didn't like it. I want
someone to tell me where she got the money to
buy eleven Armani suits. I know that sounds like
a petty thing, but it is important. No new clients
have walked through the doors according to
Maddie. We have very little business. I'm glad
you're taking off the entire six weeks because I
can't afford to pay you. I'm hoping it's not too
late to build the firm back up. I'm having a hard
time believing some of our oldest clients de-
serted us."

"There was something out of sync with Allison.
We all felt it. She wasn't a team player. No one
liked her. I hate to ask this, Nik, but just how
worried are you?"

Nikki closed her eyes. "I'm worried. I know
the others will stay on, but what's the point if we
don't have clients? If she brings a suit against us,
we'll lose the few clients we have left. I'm going
to go out aggressively and start giving interviews
to the papers if they want them."

"I'm behind you all the way; so is Maddie. No
one is going to leave you, Nikki, even if you can't

pay them. They'll hunker down and stick it out. It's called loyalty."

Nikki choked up. "Thanks, Jenny. Let's hope it doesn't come to that. So, have you picked a definite name for the baby yet?"

"Sort of. Brad gets to pick the name if it's a boy; I get to pick the name if we have a girl. Brad wants Joshua Adam. If it's a girl, it's going to be Barbara Caroline. We didn't tell Myra yet. Do you think that will please her?"

"Jenny, she will be over the moon. You'll probably have to fight her and your mother off with sticks, as they'll want to babysit all the time. Isn't your mom going to retire soon?"

"She was. In fact she was so wired up I was actually starting to dread the day she walked away from the courthouse. Then she switched and said she wasn't ready to step down from the bench. I'm glad because she isn't the type to retire so she can putter around in the garden. She'd go nuts in two weeks. Listen, Nik, as much as I love talking to you, I have to hang up now. Time for my trek to the bathroom. Make sure you come to the hospital to see me. My doctor said I can stay two days! Two! Mom said when she had me, she stayed in the hospital for ten whole days."

"Times have changed. I don't have anything else to say anyway. I'll call you tomorrow. Have a good night. Bye, Jenny."

Nikki fiddled with the dial on the radio until she found a station that played soothing music— if Frank Sinatra music could be called soothing. Her eyes closed and she was mouthing the words to a song when she felt a tap on the window. She jolted upright to look into Jack's angry face. Her heart started to thump inside her chest. She got out of the car and stood uncertainly, her eyes full of questions, until Jack reached for her.

"Let's leave our cars here and walk over to the Sweet Grass Café," Jack suggested.

"How's your friend?"

"I just called. He's doing OK. Not good, but OK. Mark is there now. I'll stop to see him when I get back. Who is Charles Martin, Nik?"

"He's Myra's longtime lover. He's also Barbara's biological father. They don't know I know that. Barbara knew, too, but never let on that she did. That story has nothing to do with our present circumstances and I don't feel right talking to you about their personal lives. Charles used to be an MI6 operative in Her Majesty's Service. He and the Queen were personal friends. She knighted him. When he was compromised, they spirited him out of the country for his own safety. He went to work for Myra's candy company as head of security. He has friends all over the world who are helping him with . . . with our . . . situation. Even in retirement, Charles is a very powerful man."

Jack digested the information as a frown appeared between his brows. He held the door to the café open for Nikki. He squeezed her arm to show her he appreciated that she was telling him the truth.

Seated, they ordered coffee, burgers and fries. They held hands across the table. "Look at me, Nik. They have too much power. They could have killed Ted."

"I know. I'm sorry, Jack. Look, you opened the can of worms. Why in God's name did you involve someone else?"

Jack leaned across the table, his voice a low hiss. "Because you were all breaking the goddamn law, that's why. You're still breaking the law, but I'm pretending I don't know that because I am hopelessly in love with you. I needed help and Ted listened to me. Now he's minus a spleen and in the hospital. I can't ignore that, Nikki, and I don't think you expect me to."

Nikki chewed on her lower lip. "Get him to back off, Jack. I don't care how you do it, just do it."

"Listen to me, and read my lips: it's too late. The paper is going to get behind Ted. That's a given. It's all going to blow up in your face and there's nothing I can do. Oh, yeah, I can tell Ted to blow it off, but he isn't going to listen. Someone has to pay for Ted losing his spleen."

Nikki continued to nibble on her bottom lip. She was still holding Jack's hand. She squeezed it. "There's nothing I can do, Jack."

"I know that. I'm going to do what needs to be done, but . . . I need you to do something for me. I want you to tell Charles Martin that the paper is getting behind Ted, and that when Ted is out of the hospital, he's going to pick up where he left off. Scare the crap out of him, Nik. I want to flush those gold shields out into the open one more time. That's all you need to know. Will you do it?"

Nikki didn't hesitate. "Yes, I'll do it. They won't go easy on you this time. You know that, right?"

"Yep. Our food is here. It's like old times, eh, Nik? Burgers, fries, coffee. Holding hands across the table. How are you going to do it?"

Nikki poured ketchup all over her fries. "I'll say you called me on my way home from town. I want you to call me on my cell so the number shows up. I know what to do. I agree with you about those gold shields."

Jack grimaced. "Now I know how you ladies feel about getting revenge. It's all I can think about. No one should have that kind of power and have no one to answer to. That's the part I can't deal with. Good burger, huh?"

Nikki wiped at a smear of ketchup on her chin. She laughed. "The best, Jack, the very best. Charles is making pecan-crusted salmon and shoestring sweet potatoes for dinner. I'll take a burger any day."

Nikki finished her coffee and motioned to the waitress for a refill. "I called Jenny while I was waiting for you. She's really miserable and can't wait to deliver. Did you know her mother changed her mind about retiring?"

Jack shook his head. "No, the last I heard was that Judge Easter was looking forward to stepping down. I always liked her. She's never been appealed and that's a plus in my book. Says a lot for the judge, too. Wonder why."

"No clue. That's all Jenny said. She's going to call the baby Barbara Caroline if it's a girl and, if it's a boy, Brad is going to name him Joshua Adam. Strong names. You up for a slice of that peach pie on the counter?"

Jack laughed. "Only if it has two scoops of

vanilla ice cream." He wiggled his hand in the waitress' direction. She walked over, poured more coffee and took their dessert order.

The couple talked about Jenny, Allison Banks, and some of the court cases that were under way and in the newspapers throughout their dessert. When they were finished, Nikki looked Jack in the eye and said, "I don't want to have to worry about you, Jack. Do you know what you're doing?"

"I hope so. I can't see those gold shields scaring off the newspaper. If anything, it will just whet their appetite. Am I going to get beat up again? My guess would be they'll take a shot at it. I just have to be prepared. Have a little faith in me, OK?"

"OK, Jack. I'm still going to worry. Be careful."

"I will. Guess you have to get back, huh?"

"I should. I'd like to stay but I don't want to arouse suspicion among the girls. Myra . . . I'm not sure Myra bought my story of going shopping. I bought a ton of stuff I don't even need. Just so you know, Jack, I'm walking a tightrope."

Jack nodded as he peeled bills off his money clip. "I do know, and I worry about you as much as you worry about me. What's wrong with this picture? Are we ever going to get married?"

"God, I hope so. I still have my wedding dress. And I still have this," Nikki said, pulling out her engagement ring from under her sweatshirt. "When this is all over—and it will be over at some point, Jack—then we can talk about it."

"OK, that's good enough for me. Be careful, OK?"

"You got it. Same goes for you."

They held hands as they walked out of the café.

Jack kissed Nikki when they reached her car. It was a long, sweet kiss that spoke of many things. "I'll call you in five minutes. I love you," he called over his shoulder as he sprinted toward his car.

"Me too. I mean, I love you, too," Nikki said, laughing.

Neither one of them saw the three men in the black Chevy Suburban.

Eleven

The women looked at one another across the kitchen table, their expressions blank. Nikki knew their thoughts were on her and what they considered her odd behavior. Well, they'd just have to get over it.

Nikki got up and pushed her chair back under the table. Her eyes on the clock, her voice cool, she said, "Time to go!"

Like robots, the others got up and followed her out of the room.

Kathryn, directly behind Nikki, touched her arm lightly and said, "You sound like you're in a hurry, Nikki."

Nikki didn't break her stride. "I *am* in a hurry, Kathryn. I have something to tell all of you but I didn't want to say anything in the kitchen." Kathryn was rapidly becoming a real itch that needed to be scratched. Nikki didn't like the feeling at all.

Myra's smile was huge and welcoming when the women took their assigned seats around the table in the war room. They sat back to wait for the meeting to be called to order. The moment the formalities were over, Myra said, "Is there anything that needs to be discussed before we get down to work?"

Nikki reached in her pocket for her cell phone and held it up. She turned her head slightly and said, "Charles, you should step down here so you can hear this conversation."

Charles set aside what he was working on to descend the steps to the round table. Nikki clicked the Play Message button. Jack Emery's voice circled round the room, crystal clear.

"Nikki, it's Jack. I'm calling to tell you something. I'm probably a little late in reporting it, and I'm sure you already know, but on the off chance you don't, my friend Ted Robinson, who works for the *Post*, was beaten up by those goons of Charles Martin's. You know the ones, the guys with those special gold shields. The same guys who beat the living shit out of me. Well, this time, they went too far. Ted just got out of surgery. The surgeons had to remove his spleen. You know what, Nik; Ted could have died on the operating table. That would have made you and all those women, Myra included—and let's not forget Charles—accessories to murder. But you're not sorry. None of you are sorry. Don't give it another thought. The paper is behind Ted on this. Before it was just me. I packed it in but I turned it over to Ted. You know those newshound guys. Well, Ted leads the pack. He's pissed now. He liked his spleen. He didn't want to have to give it up. The paper agrees. Consider this a shot over the bow. But anyway, listen, I gave it up. You win. You win, OK? I'm going back to the DA's office. But know this, Nik. When—and I say when, not if—Ted breaks your story, I'm the one you'll be looking at in the courtroom. That's all I have to say."

Nikki clicked the Save Message button before she turned off her cell phone. She didn't say a word. She leaned back and waited. It was a sobering moment for them all.

Isabelle was the first to speak. "People have their spleens removed all the time and live long lives. What did he mean, he could have died on the operating table? Was there something else wrong with him? I think we need more details before we push the panic button."

Myra looked from one to the other. She wouldn't admit it, but she was shaken at what she'd just heard. "I think what Mr. Emery meant was that any operation has risks. I think what he meant was that Mr. Robinson could have had an adverse reaction to the anesthetic, his heart could have given out, that sort of thing."

Alexis's voice was edgy, almost angry. "If that had happened, Jack's right, we'd be accessories to murder even though we didn't hold the scalpel. I don't like the sound of this."

Yoko sat up straighter in her chair. Her small hands were flat on the table. "He said—Mr. Emery, I mean—he said he wasn't going to bother us anymore, or words to that effect. He said we win. That means we outsmarted him. He isn't going to bother us anymore. I thought he sounded angry but truthful. So why did those men have to hurt the reporter? We would have outwitted him, too. We would have, wouldn't we?"

"Will you get real, Yoko! Robinson is a reporter," Kathryn said. "They live for the scoop, the byline, the story above the fold. The man probably has sources Jack Emery can only dream about. The reporter is more of a threat than Jack ever was. If Robinson's paper is behind him on this, then that means they believe the story Jack managed to spin to the reporter. All he did was pass the torch to someone more powerful with the means to come after us. The man isn't dead; he survived. Sticking your nose into other people's business is always dangerous. Wait a minute. I do have one other thing to say. The Cold War is over. How is it, Charles, that you still, after all these years, carry so much weight in the circles you used to travel? Who could possibly be interested in your activities all these years later?"

"I'm sorry, Kathryn, I am not at liberty to discuss my past or my present personal affairs. When we formed the Sisterhood, you were all told that there would be things you wouldn't like, that things would be done that might interfere with your personal beliefs, and you all agreed. You wanted vengeance and vengeance comes at a price. You all said you were willing to pay that price. Are you telling me now that you're changing your minds?"

The women all shook their heads, even Nikki.

"Then what is it you want me to do, ladies?"

"Nothing," Alexis muttered. "We need you and your resources. We just don't like hearing this kind of thing. I know that sounds foolish considering what we're doing. My bottom line is I don't want to go back to prison, so whatever you have to do, you do. You won't hear another word from me."

The others nodded and mumbled words that echoed Alexis's sentiments.

Kathryn turned to Nikki and tapped her arm. "Do you believe Jack? Do you believe he caved in and is no longer a threat?"

"Yes. Jack never says anything he doesn't mean. He *will* prosecute us if we get caught. And he'll love every minute of it."

"Then we'll just have to make sure we don't get caught," Kathryn said coldly.

Nikki looked across the table at Myra. They locked gazes and Nikki knew in that one breathless moment that Myra knew she'd sold out to Jack. She knew but was keeping her own counsel. Mothers did that. Nikki didn't relax until a small smile tugged at the corners of Myra's mouth. Her thoughts switched from Myra to Jack as she wondered what he was doing.

What Jack was doing would have surprised Nikki Quinn. With a handful of quarters and two prepaid phone cards, he was at the hospital's one pay phone that actually took change and the prepaid cards in place of the automated credit gibberish he hated. No sense in giving the gold shields an edge if they were monitoring his cell-phone calls or his credit card usage.

Jack knew he was safe from the shields here on the sixth floor, which was reserved for family members. Somehow, he'd managed to convince the nurses he was Ted's half-brother. In the scheme of things, it was a small lie and one he could live with.

The hospital was like any other: antiseptic-smelling, mind-numbing white walls and shiny tiled floors that showed your reflection. Right now it was hushed and quiet with most of the patients either sleeping or getting ready to sleep. The perfect time for his allotted five-minute visit on the hour. If Ted was sleeping, he'd leave and make his phone calls. He opened the door and poked his head in. The small fixture over the bed cast Ted in an artificial light. Jack stumbled as he remembered a scene just like this not too long ago at his mother's bedside. He'd been so angry that night, angry with the doctors, angry with God and everyone in the universe for taking his mother from him. Tonight, he was just plain old angry.

"Hey, buddy, you awake?" Jack whispered.

"No, I'm sound asleep. Jesus, can't I get away from you even here in this hospital?"

"No. No, you can't. I'm going to get those bastards and you get first crack at them. But only if there's anything left after I get done with them. You in pain?"

"Hell yes, I'm in pain. This is a morphine drip in my arm. Go home, Jack. Let me die in misery."

"You aren't going to die. You have to be old and

sick to die, like my mother. And you're meaner than cat shit, Ted, so God doesn't want someone like you. Think about grassy meadows and wild-flowers and that woman you've been seeing who you think no one knows about. By the way, where is she?"

"Shut up, Jack. I want to hate you for this pain. Stop being nice to me. The first thing I'm gonna do when I recover is to kick your ass all the way to the Canadian border."

"That'll be the day. Listen, I only have a few more minutes. That old dragon out there watches the clock. So, do you want to hear my plan or not? By the way, I fed your cats and cleaned out the litter box. I will continue to do that until you get out of here."

"No, Jack, I do not want to hear your plan. What is it? You really cleaned out the litter box and fed my cats?"

"Before I tell you, you have to agree to let me use you as bait. Yeah, yeah, I did that. It was the least I could do. They hiss and snarl a lot."

Ted made a funny sound. Alarmed, Jack stood up and shouted, "What? What's wrong?" Then he realized Ted was laughing, or rather trying not to laugh. "Stop! Lie still, you'll do damage to your stitches."

Ted made the sound again. "Crazy glue and clamps. You're a dipshit, Emery."

"Guess that means you don't want to be the bait, huh?"

The dragon nurse opened the door. "Out!" she said adamantly. Her finger pointed to the door and Jack scurried through it.

"OK," he said. "I'll be the bait!"

Jack looked at his watch as he made his way to the telephone in the waiting room. He fished around in his pocket for his stash of quarters and prepaid phone cards. He was still up, so that meant everyone else should still be up answering their phones.

Voices on the other end of the phone variously threatened to kill him, maim him, strangle him and slit his throat when they answered.

"Yeah, yeah, I know, it's eight minutes past midnight. Now, let me tell you why I'm calling."

Ninety minutes later, Jack hung up the phone, his pile of coins seriously depleted, his phone cards minus half their minutes.

At one forty-five in the morning, Jack Emery exited the hospital lobby and sprinted down the walkway to the parking lot. He unlocked his car, climbed in and started the engine. Even though the night was cool and damp, he drove with the window down. He was two blocks away when he knew he had a tail. He leaned his arm on the open door as his middle finger shot upward. He drove that way all the way to Nikki's house.

Jack parked his car on the quiet street, five spaces up from the house. He looked around to see if a car followed him down the dark street. It would be just like those cowardly shields to ambush him.

Some of the houses had their stoop lights on. Across the street there was a dim yellow light in the front part of the house. Somewhere off to his left, he heard a trash can bounce on the sidewalk. Probably a stray cat looking for food. There were no night sounds tonight, probably because it was too blustery. The birds were socked away in the trees, knowing it would rain before morning.

Jack loped up the steps that led to the front door. He fumbled with the key and finally made contact. The voice, when he heard it, sounded like it was at the foot of the brick steps.

"Good night, Mr. Emery."

Jack whirled around but didn't see anyone in the blackness. He made a mental note to leave the stoop light on, day and night, and to buy a whole bag full of light bulbs.

"The same to you, you son of a bitch!" Jack slammed the door, bolted it and then shot home the two vertical locks, top and bottom. But he was realistic enough to know no amount of bolts could keep the shields out if they wanted in.

Twelve

It started out as one of those dreary, lazy days when the sisters met in the kitchen for breakfast. Then the rain came in torrents. From that point on, the day turned into what the women later referred to as the day from hell.

Charles stepped aside as the women carried their breakfast plates to the dishwasher. He was so quiet, they all knew something was on his mind. When he spoke, they stopped what they were doing to stare at him, their expressions tense and tight.

"I have some . . . bad news. It seems the Barringtons, as we know them, disappeared sometime yesterday. When I say disappeared, I mean just that. They walked out of their apartment at the Watergate with the clothes on their backs. At some point during the night, the horses that remained at the farm were taken away. The house is burn-ing to the ground as we speak. I just saw it on our local news station. We're upwind, so to speak, so didn't hear the sirens. The smoke is traveling in another direction because of the storm we're presently experiencing."

No one said anything. Yoko leaned over to place her plate in the dishwasher. It clinked against another plate, the only sound to be heard in the kitchen.

Charles looked pointedly at Nikki, waiting for her to say something.

"Is that your way of telling me my mission is off for the moment? What about Allison and the judge? If we can get to them, they might lead us to the Barringtons. Isn't it worth a shot?"

Charles shrugged. He'd worked so many long hours setting up the plan to deal with the Barring-tons. He didn't like to work piecemeal projects. When you deviated from a given plan, something always went awry. He said so.

Nikki's voice was cold and bitter. "So does that mean I go on hold for the moment and we pick someone else? Is that what it means, Charles?"

Charles didn't respond to the question. "We'll reconvene in the war room in forty-five minutes. We can discuss matters and vote at that time." Without another word, he turned and walked out of the room. Again, no one said anything as they returned to what they had been doing.

When the phone rang again, no one made a move to answer it. Finally, on the eighth ring, Myra picked up the portable phone and said,

"Hello." The others continued to tidy up the kitchen.

The sound they all heard was somewhere between a whimper and a moan as Myra dropped the phone and slid to the floor. Alarmed, the women rushed forward.

"Go get Charles!" Nikki barked as she cradled Myra in her arms.

No one thought to pick up the phone until strange noises could be heard coming from across the room where it had slid. Isabelle picked it up and spoke softly. She listened, her eyes growing wide. Somehow she managed to say, "Thank you," before she clicked the off button.

"That was . . . that was a man named Brad Kelly. He said . . . what he said . . . was that Jennifer and . . . and the baby are gone."

"What does that mean? Gone where?" Alexis shrilled, not liking the look she was seeing on Isabelle's face.

Isabelle swallowed hard just as Kathryn and Charles raced into the room. The women scattered to make room for them.

Isabelle struggled to clear her throat. "It means Jennifer and the baby are dead. This man Brad said he was taking Jennifer to the hospital when he skidded on an oil slick in the rain. One of those big delivery trucks hit him head-on. He's in the hospital himself but said he was all right."

Nikki rocked back on her heels, her face as white as the refrigerator she stood next to. Jenny and her baby were gone. Just like Barbara and her baby. It couldn't be. It just couldn't be. But it was, and she knew it. Dazed with what she'd just heard and at what she was feeling, Nikki walked to the door, opened it, and walked outside into the rain that was sluicing against the house. Kathryn followed her.

Myra struggled to sit up, Charles's arms around her. "It's just like it was with Barbara. Oh, Charles, how could this have happened? My godchild is gone. Nellie . . . We have to go to Nellie. She's going to need us."

"Yes, dear, Nellie is going to need us. I'll get the car ready. Here, let me help you."

Charles looked around, dazed. Alexis handed him the keys to the Mercedes that was sitting outside. Isabelle rushed to the coat rack for two slickers. Yoko searched till she found Myra's purse. Charles reached for it and tucked it under his arm.

The women huddled. "I don't think either one of them is in any condition to drive," Alexis whispered. The others agreed.

"I'll drive them," Isabelle said as she reached for a slicker, knowing it was probably Nikki's. She was gone a second later, following her hosts to the black Mercedes.

Outside in the pouring rain, Kathryn did her best to herd Nikki under a tree to get out of the driving rain. There wasn't any thunder or lightning so she felt reasonably safe. It was a cold rain and she shivered. Nikki was crying, her shoulders shaking uncontrollably. All Kathryn could do was murmur soothing words that were whipped away on the wind.

Inside the cozy warm kitchen, the phone rang

yet again. Yoko answered it and listened, her face impassive. She blinked once before she handed the phone to Alexis, who in turn listened and, without saying a word, burst into tears. Yoko set the portable phone back in the cradle before she ran to the kitchen door to shout for Kathryn and Nikki to come in. She had no way of knowing if either woman heard her. She kept calling until she was hoarse. Exhausted, soaking wet from the rain that was driving across the porch, she stepped back inside the kitchen.

Alexis looked up at Yoko. In a strangled voice she said, "You should take off those wet clothes or you'll get pneumonia." Her gaze swept over to the portable phone. "I can't believe it. Don't you think we should have felt something? Sensed something?"

Yoko licked at her lips. "I do not know. I felt nothing, sensed nothing. Kathryn will be devastated."

Alexis wiped her eyes on the sleeve of her shirt. "I bet that doctor who was treating Julia was a quack. Old people die in their sleep. Not people like Julia. She can't be dead. She was supposed to come here soon. She was recovering. I know he's a quack. I just know it." Sobs rocked her shoulders.

Yoko placed a tiny hand on Alexis's shoulder. "No, he was not a quack, Alexis. He was a fine man. Charles showed us his credentials. He is well known, sought after by people all over the world. The treatments were all experimental. Julia knew that from the beginning. We all knew it could go either way, including Charles. Julia made the final decision. Passing away in one's sleep is . . ." She didn't finish her sentence because Kathryn and Nikki suddenly swept through the door to stand puddling in the middle of the floor.

Yoko ran to the laundry room and returned with a pile of thick yellow towels. She handed them out before she ran back to the laundry room to strip off her own wet clothes.

Alexis wiped her eyes again. "Julia passed away in her sleep," she blurted out. "Her doctor just called. He said . . . he said Julia made all her final arrangements when she signed into the hospital for her initial visit. She's to be cremated this very afternoon and her ashes will be spread somewhere near the Alps. Maybe he said over the Alps. I can't remember. He said it was what she wanted." She burst into tears and ran from the room, leaving Kathryn and Nikki to stare at one another.

The only sounds to be heard were the dryer clicking on in the laundry room, and Alexis's choked sobs.

Kathryn was the first to act. Her face grim, she stomped her way to the little stand under the skylight where Julia's plant sat. Purposely, she counted the new shiny leaves, checked the soil for dampness and then stepped back. Nikki watched, her eyes full of tears. Kathryn picked up the plant, looked at it again and stomped her way to the door. She opened it and, with a baseball player's arm, pitched the plant as far as it would go. The rain continued to pour down, driving inward to the kitchen, flooding the floor. Before Yoko could stop it the door slammed and a long stemmed leaf with the root still attached and full of tiny white pellets blew into the kitchen and settled on the floor at Kathryn's feet. Kathryn howled an ungodly sound and ran from the room. Nikki followed her, tears running down her cheeks as she fled.

Left alone, wrapped in her two yellow towels, Yoko picked up the leaf and stuck it in a glass of water. Some things, she thought sadly, were not meant to die.

As Yoko made her way upstairs she thought about Julia's empty chair in the war room and what it would mean to her and the others. They were minus a sister now. Would things start to unravel and fall apart? She looked down at the watch on her slim wrist. It wasn't even nine o'clock and already there had been enough bad news to last a lifetime.

Yoko walked past Nikki's room. She could hear her crying inside. She raised her hand to knock on the door but changed her mind. Everyone needed to grieve in their own way.

Inside her room, Nikki sat cross-legged in the middle of the bed, Willie clutched to her breast, tears gushing down her face. Jenny *and* Julia gone. Within hours of one another. How could that be? Did the universe tilt, did God get angry, what? More to the point, why?

Nikki brought her knees up to her chest, squeezing the worn, fragile teddy bear so tightly against her that she let out a yelp of pain. Jenny with the pug nose, freckles and laughing eyes. Jenny who could make a joke about anything, more often than not at her own expense. Best friend Jenny. A hell of a lawyer. How she'd been looking forward to motherhood, just the way Barbara had looked forward to it. Now, like Barbara, she was gone.

Nikki's gaze went to the pile of rainbow-colored presents she'd accumulated for Jenny's baby shower. Most of them had been purchased before she went to the islands. Others had been ordered from catalogs while on the islands. For some strange reason, her host on the island had allowed catalog and Internet shopping. Now what was she going to do with the mountain of presents? Like that was really important. She'd donate them to someone. End of story.

Nikki hiccuped. She always hiccuped when she was angry and she was so angry right now she thought she was capable of chewing iron and spitting out rust. Willie hit the floor as Nikki went on a rampage, ripping and gouging, tossing and kicking every single thing she could see in the bedroom she'd shared with Barbara. She even upturned the rocker and then kicked it, knowing she probably broke all her toes doing so. The pain ricocheted up her leg but she ignored it. She started to curse and when she ran through her list of dirty words, she made up some that shocked even her.

Her wet hair flying in all directions and still wearing the same wet clothes, Nikki looked up when her bedroom door opened. The four women took in the scene at a glance. As one, they moved into the room, tidying up as they went along.

Isabelle nudged a trembling Nikki toward the

bathroom where she turned on the shower. "Get in! Your lips are blue. We can't afford to lose you, too." Her tone was firm and stern but not unkind. Nikki's shoulders slumped but she did as she was told.

Ten minutes later, Nikki emerged from the bathroom to see the four women sitting on her now made-up bed. They all started to jabber at once. Nikki just shook her head. "You don't understand; Jenny, Barb and me, we were inseparable. We were best friends. Don't you think it a little strange that they both died while they were pregnant and both died in car accidents?"

Kathryn shrugged. "I admit it's freaky, but freaky things happen all the time. We didn't know your friend Jenny, Nikki. We're sorry for your loss, we really are. Right now, all the four of us can think of is Julia, and I know you're as upset as we are over that. You'll be able to lay your friend to rest. We can't do that for Julia. I'm never going to get over the fact that she planned her own . . . you know . . . funeral. Scattered over the Alps. Why do people do that? It's like they were never here."

Their heads jerked upright at Murphy's and Grady's furious barking. A second later, both dogs bounded into the room. Isabelle ran to the window. "We have company!" she shouted. "Did anyone lock the kitchen door? Whoever it is knows the code to the gate. It's not Myra and Charles!"

Kathryn grabbed the poker from the stand beside Nikki's fireplace and then led the charge downstairs, the dogs running ahead. The women huddled together as they watched what appeared to be a woman holding an umbrella in front of her advancing to the back door. The dogs continued to bark and howl. The women did nothing to stop them.

A violent gust of wind sent the visitor's umbrella straight up in the air, affording the women a clear view of the unwelcome intruder.

"It's Maddie, my office manager," Nikki said. "Quick, open the door and quiet the dogs down, then you all need to retire to the second floor. I'll make the explanations to Maddie."

Maddie stood in the middle of the floor, rain dripping from her clothes. "I hope I'm not interrupting anything. Nikki, I didn't know what else to do. I suppose I could have called you but . . . but I decided you might need to see for yourself. It took me almost three hours to get here. This storm is terrible. If you have company," Maddie said, motioning to the kitchen staircase, "I can come back later."

Three hours on the road has to mean she doesn't know about Jenny. She's here for something else, Nikki thought. *Jack? Oh, God, maybe something happened to Jack.* Finally, Nikki managed to get her tongue to work. "What is it you want me to see?"

"Nikki, what's wrong? Has something happened? Where's Myra?"

Nikki's shoulders slumped. "It's Jenny. Brad was taking her to the hospital earlier and they were hit head-on by one of those big delivery trucks. Jenny is . . . she's dead, Maddie, and so is the baby. Myra and Charles went to town to be with Aunt Cornelia. Brad's OK," she added, almost as an afterthought.

Shocked at the news, Maddie sat down on one of the kitchen chairs, rainwater puddling at her feet. Her eyes were glazed as she tried to come to terms with what she'd just heard. Finally she raised her head and said, "Brad walked away from a head-on collision with a delivery truck? They weigh tons. I am so very sorry, Nikki. I loved that spitfire. The three of you—Barbara, Jenny and you—made it a joy to come to the office in the morning. You three were the best of the best."

Nikki ran her hands through her wet hair. "And now there's just me. Kind of spooky, eh? I want you to close the office, Maddie. Put up a sign that says we're closed due to a death in the family. But you aren't leaving here until this storm lets up. Do you hear me?"

Maddie wiped her tear-stained cheeks. "Yes, boss, I hear you."

"Now, why did you drive all the way out here? Don't tell me Allison Banks had us served at the office."

Maddie shook her head. "No, nothing like that. I brought someone out here to see you. Nikki, I didn't know what else to do or where else to go. Can I bring her inside?"

"Of course you can bring her inside. Is it anyone I know?"

"I'm not sure if you know her or not. I'm going to . . . to need some help, Nikki. Put your slicker on."

Nikki obliged and both women ran to the car. Maddie jerked the door open. Nikki craned her neck to see into the corner of the car where a strangely familiar face stared back at her. A sound of pain escaped Nikki's lips. "Oh, my God!"

"She can barely walk, Nikki. I don't know if we'll hurt her more by carrying her or not, but we have to get her inside. I didn't know where else to take her. Before you can ask, she refused to go to the hospital."

The woman in the back seat whimpered as Nikki and Maddie did their best to extricate her from the car. She cried openly as they made a seat with their hands and carried her into Myra's house and on into the sunroom and to the sofa.

Her grief temporarily shelved, Nikki whispered, "She needs a doctor, Maddie."

"I know. I thought Myra might know a doctor who wouldn't have a loose lip. I didn't know what to do, Nikki. I keep saying that, don't I?"

"Well, I sure as hell know what to do. Please tell me she isn't going to go back to where this happened."

"No, she isn't going back. I want you to help her the way you helped those other women who had insurmountable problems and who came through our offices. Will you do it, Nikki?"

Nikki didn't have to think twice. "Yes."

Thirteen

Nikki motioned Maddie to follow her out of earshot of the woman sitting on the sofa.

"Maddie, I'm no doctor. I don't know if I can even reach Charles to ask for his help. Why didn't you insist on going to the hospital? What if she's bleeding internally? She's the wife of the President's national security advisor, isn't she? I've seen her pictures in the paper. What's her name?"

"Paula Woodley. We have to do something. I'm not sure about this but I think she's been to every hospital in the area. How many accidents can one person have? You know all about spousal abuse. I wouldn't be surprised to find out she used other names, too, for hospital visits. We have to do something. Nikki, I don't know the lady personally, but I know her sister Nancy. Nancy is the one who called me to ask if I would check on her sister. She lives in Pennsylvania. She said she'd been trying to call Paula but there was no answer and she was worried. I guess no one knows about . . . all of this. Like most battered wives, Paula hasn't told anyone. It's hard for her to talk; the bastard broke her front teeth. She did allow me to bring her here and she did tell me her husband is the one who beat her. I really didn't want to ask too many questions. To tell you the truth, I was scared out of my wits that someone would try to stop me when I went to get her."

Nikki seethed. The anger raging through her was almost a welcome relief, driving her grief to the back of her mind and heart. "I'll take it from here, Maddie. I don't want you involved in any of this. I want you to go back to the office. Don't answer any questions if you get caught up in this. In other words, you've had a memory lapse. You know the drill."

"OK. She's going to be all right, isn't she, Nikki?"

Nikki massaged her temples. "I don't know, Maddie. Call me to let me know you got back all right."

"I will. I think the rain is letting up."

The minute Maddie swept through the security gates, Nikki ran upstairs. "Quick!" she shouted. "Come with me. I need your help."

The women dropped what they were doing to follow Nikki down the stairs, through the kitchen and into the sunroom where Paula Woodley was lying on the sofa.

"Get her some brandy. I'm going to call

Charles. See if there's anything we can do for her other than the brandy, and I'm not even sure we should be giving her that."

In the kitchen, Nikki dialed Charles's private cell phone number. The minute she heard his strained voice, with her own high-pitched in response she updated him on Julia and Paula Woodley.

"Charles, are you there? Tell me what to do! Charles! Look, there's nothing we can do about Julia. We're all as devastated as you are. I need some help here. The woman could be bleeding internally. She's the wife of the president's national security advisor. Do you want me to call EMS?"

Finally Charles's voice came through, strong and assured-sounding. "I'll send someone immediately. I'm not going to say anything to Myra about Julia just yet. She's coping right now, reliving Barbara's death, and trying to be strong for Cornelia. I'll check back with you in a little while."

Nikki didn't respond; she simply clicked off the phone and then clicked it back on to call Jack. She relaxed the moment she heard his sleepy voice. Oh, how she wished she were there to kiss him fully awake. The fact that she'd woken him had to mean he didn't know about Jenny. She didn't waste any time in blurting out the facts as she knew them.

"Oh, God, Nik, I am so sorry. I'll go right over there. Where are you? Are you OK?"

"I'm at the farm. No, I'm not all right. How could I be? On top of that, Julia, Dr. Webster, passed away in her sleep last night. I know I shouldn't be telling you that, but I don't want to keep anything from you. I have to hang up because I have a crisis here at the farm I have to deal with. Stay in touch, Jack."

"I love you," was all he said in reply.

Nikki was about to respond when Alexis entered the kitchen. "OK. Me too. Gotta go now."

"The lady wants a drink. We decided to veto the brandy. Any luck with Charles?" Alexis asked as she poured iced water from a pitcher in the refrigerator.

"Yes. He's sending someone. I had to tell him about Julia. I think he's as devastated as we all are. He's not going to tell Myra until later. She's doing her best to be strong for Judge Easter. Hey, we're women, we can handle this."

Alexis set the pitcher of water back in the refrigerator. "Who is she, Nikki? She looks familiar."

Nikki didn't even consider lying. "Her name is Paula Woodley. Her husband is the President's national security advisor. You might have seen her picture in the paper at some White House function."

Alexis's jaw dropped. Nikki reached out to take the glass of water from her hands. "Did he do that to her? What a stupid question, of course he did. I bet you this isn't the first time he's done it, either. God, how I hate wife-beaters."

"Me, too," Nikki muttered as she looked down at the numbers on her watch. How long, she wondered, would it take the help Charles promised to arrive?

Kathryn, Isabelle and Yoko were kneeling on the floor in front of the sofa. They took turns talking to the almost comatose woman.

Nikki handed the glass of water to Kathryn, who looked at it, then at the woman. "I think she needs a straw." Alexis ran back to the kitchen and returned with one.

Paula Woodley tried to suck on the straw, her eyes filling with tears when she couldn't quite manage it. Alexis ran back to the kitchen and returned with a wad of paper napkins. "Soak them and rub it over her lips. Some will ooze into her mouth."

Nikki tried not to look at the battered woman but her eyes were drawn to the bruises, the open cuts, her black and blue face, her swollen eyes and split lips. What kind of monster was allowed to do things like this? Someone like Karl Woodley, that's who, she answered herself.

The hair on the back of Murphy's neck went straight up as he raced to the kitchen door. Nikki ran to the door and opened it. Two white-jacketed men and two nurses entered carrying a portable stretcher. No one said a word as Nikki led the foursome into the sunroom. She motioned the others to follow her back to the kitchen.

Just to have something to do, Isabelle started to make coffee. Then they started to babble quietly to one another. Alexis told them the woman's identity. The others simply gaped.

"The bastard!" Kathryn said.

"And he advises the President of our country!" Isabelle hissed.

"I saw his picture in the paper a few days ago. He looks like a fat little bully. He probably suffers from a Napoleon complex," Alexis said.

"He needs to be taught a lesson," Yoko said.

Nikki reached up into the cabinet to get the coffee cups. She turned around, her eyes narrowed. "Yoko, you are absolutely right. And do you know what else? We're just the little group who could do that. Think about it," she whispered. "My mission is more or less postponed for the moment. It's hardly worth our concentrated efforts to go after Allison Banks and Judge Krackhoff. We can go after them later on when Charles finds out where the Barringtons are. Of course, we'd have to agree among ourselves because, in essence, that would give me two missions. Or, if we agree, we can call this one a united mission. I'm sure Myra will vote along with us. What do you think?"

"I'd personally like to be alone with that guy for fifteen minutes. There wouldn't be anything left for the rest of you. I'm in. That means you have my vote," Kathryn said.

The others agreed with Kathryn just as one of the white-jacketed men appeared in the doorway. In stilted English, the man said, "We will take the lady now to our clinic."

"Will . . . will she be all right?"

The man looked at her with piercing dark eyes. He said nothing. He made a motion with his right hand. The two nurses were carrying the portable stretcher while the second white-jacketed figure held on to a metal pole with an IV drip. Nikki thought it strange that the women were carrying the stretcher and the men were doing nothing but holding a pole and opening the door. No one said goodbye.

Yoko poured coffee. "Will we ever know what happens to the lady?" she asked.

Nikki added cream to her coffee. "I'm sure Charles will tell us at some point. Let's just be grateful for the moment that we probably helped to save her life."

"Why do women stay in such abusive situations?" Isabelle queried. "Why don't they just leave? There's all kinds of help out there. I just don't get it. And another thing, do they even try to fight back?"

"Fear," Nikki said succinctly. "If there are children, the women are even more fearful. They suffer the beating hoping the batterer won't go after the children. Shame. Low self-esteem. It does sound rather lofty to say, why don't they just leave. Where will they go? How will they live? The batterer always promises not to do it again, and he doesn't, for a little while, then he starts up again. It's a vicious circle. I represented too many women in my practice not to know that very few women ever press charges. Mostly out of shame. Most end up going back to their husband or significant other. Anger-management classes are usually mandatory but I haven't seen them work yet."

"But this guy . . . He's such a high-profile public figure. How does he get away with it?" Kathryn snarled. "Fifteen minutes with him, that's all I want."

"That high profile, the stress, is probably the

reason he gives for using his wife as a punching bag. Batterers threaten the person they're abusing. Then they play with the abused heads. I can almost guarantee the first words out of his mouth if the wife threatens are, 'who's going to believe you?' That kind of thing. She buys into it. That Paula Woodley finally got the guts to do something is amazing. Maybe this beating was the worst one. Too bad she didn't do it sooner," Nikki said.

"She didn't say a word to any of us. But her eyes were grateful. I hope there are no children involved in this," Alexis said.

"Let's adjourn to the war room so we can kick this around and come up with a plan," Nikki said as she picked up her coffee cup to lead the way.

Inside the war room, all the women slumped in their seats except Nikki, who remained standing. She set her cup down and then walked around the table to push Julia's chair to the other end of the room. "Move your chairs closer, ladies. The chair will stay there until we find someone to fill it. That may happen, it may not happen."

Nikki took her seat and looked from one to the other. "We have voting power. There are five of us. Just because Myra isn't here doesn't mean we can't make decisions and carry through on them. I can access most of Charles's programs. That means I can find out where Paula and her husband, Karl, live. I don't know this for a fact but I tend to think the government provides a driver for Karl. That means it's going to be pretty hard to get to him. I said hard, I didn't say impossible. We just have to find a way so we don't get caught."

"Won't that unleash those guys with the special gold shields?" Kathryn asked.

"Without a doubt. We have to outwit them. Hey, I keep telling you, we're *women*. Now, who would you put your money on if you were a betting lady, us or them?" Nikki asked.

The women chuckled on cue, but they were worried, Nikki could tell. She herself was beyond worried. She hoped the others weren't sensing her fear.

Nikki got up and took two steps at a time. She turned on Charles's computer, the one-of-a-kind computer with so many bells and whistles it looked like it had come out of the White House war room. She turned it on and waited. Then she poked her head over the top of the computer and spoke to the girls.

"I'm sure there's a profile of Karl Woodley and his family somewhere. It will be the public profile, not the one they don't want the public to see. Charles knows how to get that information but I don't. This will have to do for now. OK, look up at the middle screen."

The women leaned forward, trying to envision how the little man they were looking at could do what he'd done to Paula Woodley— until Nikki brought up a head shot that showed Karl Woodley's eyes. All four women at the round table reared back into their chairs. Their comments were crude, brutal and derogatory.

"Here's his stats. Karl Woodley is 52 years old. He went to West Point with the President. He did his stint in the army and then went to the CIA. He's five feet seven and weighs one hundred and sixty-five pounds. He was on the wrestling team. He likes to sail and the family has a cabin cruiser moored somewhere up the Chesapeake. He married Paula Oxford when he graduated from West Point. The President was his best man. The Woodleys have no children. This is just a guess on my part, but I'd wager old Karl doesn't have any swimmers.

"Paula Oxford was an Olympic gymnast but she won only the silver. She's quite tiny, as we know. She is also the heiress to a shoe-polish fortune. Karl didn't bring anything to the table. This next picture is a shot of their house but there is no address for security reasons. It's a Tudor. Looks expensive and lush. It has an Olympic-size pool and tennis court. They have matching Mercedes.

"Mrs. Woodley is supposedly shy and doesn't like being in the public eye. Of course, we know why. She likes to garden. Supposedly she has some prize-winning roses. She paints a little. She was quite outgoing and popular before she married Karl. She has a sister who lives in Pennsylvania. No other family is listed for Paula. Karl has two brothers. One lives in England, the other one lives in Washington State. That's all the information there is for public viewing."

Nikki shut down the computer and hopped down the steps to plop onto her chair. "OK, girls, let's kick it around. No matter how stupid, how inane, spit it out. We might be able to make it work. Kathryn, you first."

Kathryn's face was grim. "He's going to be impossible to get to. Federal security is tough. Personally speaking, I'd like to get my hands around that fat neck of his and give it a good twist."

"If we can't get to him, maybe we can get him to come to us," Alexis said.

"With or without his backup?" Isabelle queried.

"If the man was worried his sordid activities might get out, he just might be motivated to elude his people to try and shut us up," Alexis said.

Nikki stared off into space. "People like Karl Woodley aren't afraid of innocuous threats, and that's what he would consider us. Alexis is right, we have to find a way to get him to come to us, minus his security."

"Are we sure Mrs. Woodley will not go back to her husband once she recovers?" Yoko asked.

Nikki shook her head. "There's no way to know. I guess it depends on how afraid she is. The fact that she allowed Maddie to bring her here must mean something. Abused women almost always have a breaking point. Still, we can't go by that fact. If Paula's sister, who is a friend of Maddie's, hadn't called her, Mrs. Woodley wouldn't be here. At this point, we don't even know how extensive her injuries are. In the end, it doesn't matter as far as we're concerned. We'll take on the mission if we all agree. We'll be doing her a favor. At least, that's how I see it."

The women's expressions were glum.

Nikki looked at them and said, "Listen, I know we're all sitting here with Julia in the back of our minds. I don't know this for sure, but I rather think Julia would want us to go on. I, for one, will miss her. She was a bright light to all of us for a little while. If it would do any of us any good, I would be the first one to suggest we go to Switzerland. Julia took care of that by being cremated and having her ashes scattered. She left us with our memories and we have to accept that."

Yoko pushed her chair closer to the table. "Let's get to work."

"Let's give some thought to the sister in Pennsylvania. Maybe there's a way we can work through her to get to Karl Woodley. Or, maybe we could pretend to be her, call him and simply announce a visit. What could he do? It would get one of us in the house," Isabelle said.

"And then what?" Alexis asked.

"It isn't as crazy as it sounds. Let's consider it a jumping-off place," Nikki said as she reached for a yellow legal pad and pen. "Let's go first with the worst case scenario and then the best case scenario to see if we can come up with something doable."

Fourteen

Nikki tried to juggle the oversize umbrella that the funeral home had provided. Numb with grief, she did her best not to look at the shiny bronze casket laden with flowers that sat under the green awning. She turned to stare at Judge Easter, Myra and Charles. They looked the way she felt: shocked and numb. She felt her heart flutter in her chest when Myra turned to stare at her. She was hollow-eyed, gaunt, the same way she'd looked when she'd stood at her daughter's grave years ago. Now she was standing here at her goddaughter's grave.

The minister spoke softly, his voice barely audible. Nikki found that strange. Shouldn't he be shouting his words so the mourners could carry away some comfort?

If there was anything to be grateful for, it was

the private cemetery with no more than a dozen people in attendance. Across from her was Jack, holding a green and white striped umbrella. He was dressed in a dark suit with a pristine white shirt and dark tie. Brad, Jenny's husband, didn't have an umbrella. He stood, stone faced, soaking wet. Jack would take care of Brad.

And then it was over, the small group lining up to walk past the bronze casket. Nikki looked down at the limp yellow rose in her hand. Jenny had loved yellow roses. When it was her turn, Nikki crooked the handle of the umbrella under her arm, the umbrella tilting backward. Her right hand touched Jenny's last resting place. "Goodbye, old friend." She laid the limp rose next to the others.

Disgusted with the umbrella, Nikki closed it and walked toward her car. She stopped at the lead car to embrace Judge Easter, Myra, and then Charles. She knew that Myra and Charles were going back to the farm later in the day. Judge Easter was going to stay with Brad for a day or so and then join Myra at the farm for a while.

"I'm going to stay in town and will go to the farm tomorrow if that's all right with you," Nikki whispered to Charles. "Is there any news on Mrs. Woodley?"

"Do what you have to do, Nikki. She'll survive, but she'll never be the same. We can talk about it when you return to the farm. Myra . . . Myra is devastated."

Like she didn't already know that. "I know," was all she said. She saw Jack approaching out of the corner of her eye. She said, just loud enough for him to hear, "I'll see you back at the farm to-morrow then." She knew Jack wanted to offer his condolences to Judge Easter so she moved quickly to her car.

Nikki settled herself in the car, turned the key in the ignition and then burst into tears. Good-byes were so hard. Final goodbyes were beyond hard. The windshield wipers swiped across but did nothing to clear her vision. *Get a grip*, she told herself. She did her best to blink away the tears as she inched her car forward to follow the pro-cession out of the cemetery.

Shivering in her lightweight suit, Nikki turned on the heater, hoping it would warm her cold, wet feet. She craved a long, hot shower. When, she wondered, had she slept last? She couldn't re-member. The cars ahead of her turned right; she turned left and sped down the road.

"Whoa! Slow down, Nik. I don't want to have to show up here for a long time. Keep your eyes on the road. I want you to get home safe and sound."

"I don't want to talk to you now, Barbara. I'm too vulnerable. Why couldn't the sun shine to-day? Jenny loved the sun. Remember that year we planted all those sunflowers and gave them names? It's not fair. You're both gone. Go away, Barb, I have to deal with this on my own."

"I'll stay with you till you get home. You haven't slept in two days and you haven't eaten, either. That's not a good combination."

A sob caught in Nikki's throat. "Is she there with you, Barb? Is she OK?"

"Yes, and yes. Keep your eyes on the road, Nik. The weather is terrible. Do you hear me, Nik?"

A horn blared, warning Nikki that she was straddling the middle line in the road. She moved her foot off the gas pedal and clenched the wheel. One more block to go.

"OK, kiddo, park this boat and get in the house."

Nikki sat perfectly still once she turned off the engine. She was so tired she could barely hold her head upright. Did she just talk to Barbara? Of course she did. What was it Barbara told her to do? Oh, yes, get out of the car and go in the house. She stepped out of the car into an ankle-high puddle. She slogged her way to the curb and up the stairs to her house. She looked up to see that the outside light was on. Jack must have forgotten to turn it off. Maybe he didn't like the dark any more than she did. She locked her door, kicked off her sodden shoes and padded her way to the steps. She grasped the banister to pull herself forward. In the end she was too tired to climb the stairs so she sat down and leaned her head against the newel post. A second later she was sound asleep.

An hour later, Jack entered the house. His heart beat faster when he saw Nikki sleeping on the stairs. He shrugged out of his drenched Burberry and hung it up. His eyes felt moist when he stared down at the slim young woman in her rain-soaked clothing. In the blink of an eye, he scooped her up into his arms and carried her upstairs. She stirred once, opened her eyes and smiled.

"Jack." A second later she was asleep again.

Jack felt like a doting mother as he stripped off Nikki's damp suit and then covered her with a flowered quilt. He sat on the side of the bed watching the woman he loved. Satisfied that her breathing was deep and even, he shed his own clothing and then dressed in jeans and a tee shirt.

He'd wanted to stay with Brad, but Brad had said he needed to be alone. All he could do was respect his friend's wishes. He shuddered when he tried to imagine how he would feel if it had been Nikki carrying his child. In time, Brad would be able to deal with his loss, because life was for the living and Jenny would want Brad to get on with his life.

Jack looked around the kitchen. He was like a homing pigeon, always returning to the kitchen. He'd read somewhere that a kitchen was the heart of a home. He thought it was true. He walked around aimlessly, trying to decide what he should be doing. When he was a boy, his mother used to tell him to put on his happy face and do whatever he'd been balking at.

He hadn't eaten this morning, hadn't even had coffee. Sustenance. That's what he needed. He made coffee, toast and scrambled two eggs, which he wolfed down. He cleaned up and then sat down, twiddling his thumbs. Now, what should he do? Maybe he should go into the office. This was, after all, supposed to be his first day back at work, but he'd delayed his arrival because of the funeral. Well, hell, he'd just changed out of his suit and he wasn't about to change again.

On his way to the second floor, Jack gathered up Nikki's shoes, carried them to the laundry room and placed them on top of the dryer. He retraced his steps to the second floor, his thoughts going in all directions.

He settled himself in a comfortable stuffed chair and watched Nikki as she slept. The rain continued to pour down, lulling Jack into a deep, sound sleep. The morning crawled into afternoon and then into early evening. He stirred when he felt a light touch on his arm. He cracked open one eye and then smiled as he held out his arms. Nikki sat down on his lap and snuggled next to him.

"How long have you been sitting here?" she asked in a sleep-filled voice.

Jack looked at his watch. He laughed. "All day. Like you, I guess I needed the sleep. Are you OK?"

"Personally, I'm fine. I just feel sad that I've lost my two best friends. I'm sad for Judge Easter. She lost her only daughter just the way Myra lost Barbara. I know they must be thinking that I'm not blood to either of them, and yet here I am alive and well. I almost feel like I shouldn't be here. Then again, maybe they aren't thinking about that at all. And there's Julia, passing away in her sleep. Two very special people are gone from my life on the same day, so, yes, I'm sad. How is Brad?"

"He's a basket case. The judge is with him. I know he didn't want that but he didn't know how to tell her he didn't want anyone around. Time will help. He and Jenny have a lot of friends and they'll be there for him. I'm kind of hungry, how about you?" Jack asked, hoping to change the subject.

"I'm starved. How about you fixing something or ordering in? I want to take a shower. And a fire would be nice. We can eat by the fire, nothing fancy, a sandwich will do and some nice wine. I need to talk to you about something, Jack," Nikki called over her shoulder.

Jack blinked. Food, fire, talk. "Sure."

Jack couldn't remember the last time he'd built a fire this early in the year. His mother, before she became ill, liked to sit and knit in front of a fire. Once, in the middle of summer, he'd gone to visit her and she'd had the air-conditioning set at fifty-five degrees with a fire going. She'd knitted him a bright-blue watch cap that summer. He felt so choked up at the memory he had to bite down on his lower lip. Then he thought about Brad and how many memories he'd have to contend with.

Jack stood back when the dry wood and the artificial log caught and sparked upward. Done. Now he had to rummage for something to eat. He knew his choices were limited, but he was game. In the end he fried up bacon and two eggs and made sandwiches. He was carrying the tray along with a bottle of wine into the living room just as Nikki plopped down on the sofa.

"Fried bacon and egg sandwiches, mmmm. They look good," she said. Jack preened at the compliment.

They sat together, egg yolk and ketchup dribbling down their chins. "These really are good. The last time I had one of these was—"

"When we were together and happy and planning a future together," Jack said without missing a beat. "So, what do you want to talk to me about? Brad will be all right in time. He has to go through the grieving process. The judge . . . I don't know, Nik. I want to believe she's a tough old bird and will get through it. Myra did."

Nikki wiped her chin. "Myra almost didn't; you know that."

"Yeah," Jack said softly as he poured more wine. "Life is for the living. Some doctor told me that. I wanted to smash his face in. Come on, what do you want to talk about?"

Nikki cleared her throat. "This is all hypothetical, Jack. What would you do as a friend, an outsider, if you found out that Brad was a wife-beater? Let's say a year ago, before Jenny got pregnant but it was going on for years. And Jenny wouldn't press charges. Let's say you found all this out in a circuitous way."

Jack bolted upright. His face was a mixture of anger, disbelief and then red-hot rage. "Are you saying . . . No, I know Brad. He would never . . . I'd beat the living shit out of him and then haul his ass to jail."

"No, no, not Brad. That was just an example. I'm sorry, I guess I didn't phrase that very well. We're still in our hypothetical mode here. How about a high-profile man, someone high up in the present administration? Someone you'd never think would do something like that. Same scenario, just a different man. A powerful man."

Jack sat down with a plop. The relief on his face was almost comical. "Those bastards are clever. I prosecuted quite a few. The kicker is, the woman usually goes back, eight times out of ten. It's all up to the woman."

Nikki played with the stem of her wineglass. "What if she's afraid of this high-profile guy? I said he's high up in the administration. What if she's afraid he'll kill her because his career in that high-powered job would be over and he'd face jail time?"

Jack squirmed on the couch until he was facing Nikki. "This isn't hypothetical at all, is it?"

Nikki shook her head. "No, it isn't. I don't know what to do."

Jack chewed on his lower lip, never taking his eyes away from Nikki. "You personally, Nik, or your little . . . organization out there at ye olde farm? Why don't you tell me everything and then we can talk it to death?"

She did. Jack listened, his jaw dropping. "Holy fucking shit!"

"Well, yes, that pretty much sums it up," Nikki said as she poured more wine into both their glasses. "We both know the court system won't work for Mrs. Woodley. Even if it ever got close to an actual courthouse. Let's not bullshit each other, Jack."

"Nikki, listen to me. Knowing what you and your buddies are doing is one thing. Helping you is something else. Do you have any idea what you're asking me to do here? You *are* asking me, aren't you?"

Nikki looked Jack straight in the eye. "Yes, I'm asking for your help. You know how the Feds work, you know people who can help you."

"Not those kinds of people. They're real high up there on the food chain. Remember those guys with the presidential gold shields? I'm dead meat if I poke my nose into shit like that."

Nikki's shoulders slumped. "Is that a no? You didn't see her, Jack. She was almost dead."

Jack threw another log on the fire just to have something to do. "No, it's not a no. I need to think about this. The guy is best friends with the President of the United States."

"I know. It's asking a lot, Jack. I think we can take him on and pull it off, but we're going to need some backup. You're the backup."

"That's just another way of saying we're all dead. The guy has three more years in office, so that means Woodley will be at his side for those three years. He's going to want to cover his ass all the way. If his wife didn't turn him in by now, she's never going to do it."

"I know that too, Jack. That's why we're going to do it for her. We aren't even going to tell her. She's got a long road of recovery ahead of her. For now she's safe and sound and hopefully on the mend, but Charles said she's never going to be the same. I don't know what that means exactly."

"You better find out damn quick before you start anything. For God's sake, give some thought to the possibility she'll recant. Then where will you be?"

"We'll keep her safe and away from him. We know how to do that. You know, those guys you had spying on us are pretty good. Do you think . . . ?"

"No, don't even go there. This is a whole other

ball game. You're going to be messing with some over-the-top powerful people."

"What about your friend from the *Post*? A dropped word here or there. You know, to start the ball rolling."

Jack poked at the fire. A shower of sparks shot upward. It was getting warm in here. Still, he added another birch log. When he was satisfied with his fire, he returned to the sofa. "Don't go there either, Nik. Are you thinking of a smash and grab? What? You do know people like Woodley have special security, right?"

"I'm aware of that. Don't sell us short, Jack."

"God forbid. OK, let's formulate a plan that you can take back to your . . . vigilante group."

"You're in then?"

"I'm in."

Fifteen

September gave way to a dismal gray October and a briskness in the air that hinted at snow in the not-too-distant future. The days simply cried for a cozy fire and a mug of hot apple cider. The brilliant fall foliage was almost gone, replaced with bare, arthritic branches that looked like skeletons. The lawn this morning was covered in frost, and it was just a little past nine o'clock.

Nikki climbed out of her BMW and walked around to the front porch to see the Halloween display the girls had created for Julia's homecoming. Her eyes started to burn at the memory of Julia. Halloween was just two days away.

Nikki lifted the top off one of the carved pumpkins. No one had bothered to light the candles at night. She shrugged. Having Judge Easter as a month-long guest wouldn't have allowed for such frivolous things. She was here now to drive the judge back to the city. She shrugged again at the thought that Nellie had put a time limit on her mourning period. A month was all she'd allowed herself to grieve, and now that month was up. Maybe putting a time limit on her grief was the only way she could go on without her daughter and the grandchild she was never going to see.

Judge Easter was sitting in the kitchen, her packed bag by the back door. She was dressed in a dull gray pantsuit that matched her pallor. She sipped coffee. The moment Nikki entered the kitchen, she was on her feet. She carried her cup to the sink before she hugged Myra and Charles, her eyes brimming with tears.

"I'm ready, Nikki. I must say, you folks do provide service. I was prepared to take a car service but Myra wouldn't hear of it." She turned to Myra. "Thank you, my friend, for allowing me to stay here and for putting up with me. Charles, thank you for all the wonderful dinners."

Nikki picked up the judge's bag. She turned and mouthed the words, "I'll be back by noon. Call the girls."

Myra nodded.

The women all wore somber expressions as they took their seats in the war room. Charles took his position on the raised dais, his fingers poised over his computer keyboard. He looked down at the little group, noting the absence of any paperwork on the table. The shoe box sat in the middle of the table. He waited as Myra brought the little meeting to order. Once, his gaze strayed to the far end of the room where Julia's chair nestled in the corner. He quickly averted his eyes.

"Ladies, I personally want to thank you for your condolences and your patience. It's been a horrific month, but life and time go on, as we all know. We're all women so we will persevere and prevail. Now, I yield the floor to Nikki," Myra said.

Nikki nodded before she turned to look up at Charles. "Has anything changed in regard to the Barringtons?"

"No, I'm sorry to say. If you'll allow me, I'd like to make a suggestion." He looked down to see all the women nod for him to continue. "I suggest then that we hold the Barringtons in abeyance and continue with Nikki's suggestion that her mission becomes what you all discussed among yourselves during our tragic misfortune. Nikki, tell us what you want done."

"I would like to see that little weasel, Karl Woodley, the President's national security advisor, put to the test. I'd like to see how he holds up under a battering. The kind he gave his wife, Paula. The problem is, how do we get to him?

"I know for a fact that the Woodleys live in the Kalorama section of Washington. No one sells houses or rents them there. I don't think people die there. It's very exclusive and I doubt Woodley could afford to live there if it weren't for his wife's money. Considering his position, I would imagine he has top-notch security. How do we penetrate that?

"We need to know, Charles, where Mrs. Woodley is and how she's doing. One of us has to talk to her. My office manager, Maddie, told me that when she picked up Mrs. Woodley, at Mrs. Woodley's sister's request, she wrote a note for the husband and Mrs. Woodley signed it. It said simply that she'd had enough and was leaving. Period. I've been scouring all the papers every day and there has not been one word about either one of the Woodleys in regard to their personal lives. The NSA is all over the place with his government duties but I have to think he's worried that word of his ugly deeds might be forthcoming.

"Paula Woodley gave my law firm her power of attorney and as such we closed down all her bank and brokerage accounts. Right now, Karl Woodley doesn't have a dime except for his salary as national security advisor. I have to believe the upkeep is tremendous on the Kalorama house. Maddie is working on the sister to see what, if anything, she knows that can help us without alerting the sister to the extent of Mrs. Woodley's precarious life."

Alexis leaned forward. "Where is Mrs. Woodley? Don't you think her husband, considering his position in the administration, can find out? Are you prepared to have your office subpoenaed and your files taken?"

"We have it covered," Nikki said. "I personally do not want to know where Mrs. Woodley is located. If we don't know, we can't tell. However, I do want to talk to her. As to the NSA, I doubt he would raise any red flags in regard to his wife. Wife-beaters go to great lengths to keep their habit secret. And make no mistake, it is a habit."

"I can arrange a phone conversation," Charles said.

Kathryn spoke. "I suppose it's possible the NSA is just going to suck it up. Maybe he's afraid if he makes waves, it will get out. But," she said and held up her hand, "creeps like him only feel good when they have some woman to use as a punching bag. Who is he going to vent on if she's gone? I think he's got private people looking for her. Is she safe, Charles? I mean *really* safe?"

Charles looked especially smug. "She is *really* safe, Kathryn. I also think you're right. There are people searching for Mrs. Woodley, but probably from the private sector. Rest assured, Paula Woodley will never be found unless she wants to be found."

Nikki's sigh was long and loud. She took the floor again. "Should we assume that someone is watching the sister in Pennsylvania? If so, and if her phone is tapped, I don't want Maddie anywhere near her."

"I think we must assume Mrs. Woodley's sister is under surveillance of some sort. I'll run a profile on both the NSA and Mrs. Woodley. I'll also get the blueprints of their house. While I'm doing that, the rest of you decide how you want to handle this particular punishment. Almost a month has gone by since Maddie spirited Mrs. Woodley away. The NSA could either be resigned that she isn't coming back or he could be livid. Keep that in mind as you plot your course."

The women huddled around the table throwing out idea after idea. Finally, when everyone was turning testy, Kathryn said, "Why don't we just get a bead on the guy's habits. Like what time he gets home from work, what times he does whatever he does. We boldly go up to the door, knock, and say we're there to talk about his wife. Maybe we could pretend to be reporters doing an article for the Sunday lifestyle section of the paper. There's a lot to be said for boldness."

Alexis had a sour expression on her face. Her time in prison and her dealings with the police were all too fresh in her mind. "While we're doing that, what will his private security be doing? They'll be hauling our asses off to jail, that's what they'll be doing."

"You'll be altering our appearance, for one thing. How about if we show up, calling ahead and leaving a message, that we're in the area and will stop by for a hen party, for want of a better explanation? We could pretend to be old friends interested in renewing old friendships, that kind of thing. We can pretend we're old college friends or high school friends, or some of her Olympic friends, something like that. If we call from the District and use one of those prepaid phone cards, there's no way it can be traced. We can call during the day when the NSA is at work. He won't get the message till he gets home. We won't be leaving a number for a call back. I'll bet you a hundred bucks he'll be waiting for us when we arrive. That's how we get into his house. Why are you all looking at me like that?" Isabelle demanded.

"Because it's a good idea," Nikki said. "Let's kick it around a little. We have to remember who we're dealing with and how powerful the man is. And if we *do* manage to get inside the Kalorama house, we have to decide what we're going to do to Mr. Woodley."

The women laughed. Up on his dais, Charles thought he'd never heard a more evil sound in his life. He looked down to see his lady love smacking her hands together in anticipation. He was glad that he was on the good side of these talented, dedicated women who were trying to right serious wrongs in the judicial system.

Back at the table, Nikki was speaking. "I'll go on the Web to see if I can find an alumni list from Mrs. Woodley's college and her friends from the Olympic team. We need legitimate names in case the NSA decides to check out the message we leave him."

Yoko spoke softly. "Do you think it might be a good idea to pick one of the neighbors to talk to? I could deliver a flower arrangement with some made-up sender, or maybe we could pretend it was for Mrs. Woodley. We might be able to get access to the inside of the neighbor's house and maybe they'll talk."

"Another great idea," Nikki said. "We can get Charles to check the property listings and run checks on the neighbors. I think we're on a roll, girls. Any more ideas?"

The women batted ideas back and forth and finally decided that Yoko would say, if anyone asked, that a woman came into her flower shop saying she was from a real estate office and wanted flower arrangements sent to all the residents on Benton Street in Kalorama in the hopes of securing a house listing.

"All any of Yoko's people will be able to remember is that the request came via a Century 21 realtor, in case anyone asks. And the customer paid in cash. But we can't do that until Charles comes up with a list of homeowners on Benton Street. Yoko can use her business van and deliver to one side of the street and one of us will deliver to the other side. We're sure to get at least one person who will invite us in," Nikki said.

"Brilliant, dear. Just brilliant," said Myra. "Perhaps I should be one of the delivery people. People are comfortable talking to an older person. I would like to do it."

"OK, you and Yoko will be the delivery people. Now, we're going to need someone to go to Yoko's shop with a wad of money. Who wants to volunteer?" Nikki grinned.

"I'll do it," Kathryn said.

"It's coming together. Keep talking, girls. I'm going into the house. I want to call Maddie. On second thought, I think I'll drive to the drugstore and pick up some prepaid phone cards and call Maddie from there. No sense giving anyone an edge. If you come up with any more ideas, write them down. Do you want me to take Murphy and Grady?" Alexis and Kathryn nodded. "Good, I'll be back in an hour. Anyone want anything from town?" The women declined the offer. "Then I'm outta here."

* * *

With Murphy and Grady on leashes, Nikki walked along aimlessly until she came to a phone booth off the beaten path. She used her brand new phone card to call Maddie.

"Just checking in. Anything going on? I'm in town walking the dogs. I think I'll head over to the park for an hour or so."

Quick on the uptake, Maddie responded by saying, "I feel like taking a walk in this nice brisk air myself. I had to turn the heat on. By the way, we have two new clients. Nothing big, but kind of intense. I should be going now, Nikki, I have a slew of paperwork that needs to get filed."

"Do you have a purse? You know how you always forget yours."

Nikki could hear the sigh on the other end of the phone. "I know, I know. The office is in good hands, Nikki."

With time on her hands, Nikki huddled inside her warm jacket and headed for the park. She unhooked the dogs' leashes before she sat down on a dark green bench to wait for Maddie. The dogs looked at her and then sat down, making it obvious they weren't interested in chasing squirrels or stray cats. Nikki smiled as she dialed Jack's number. Her smile widened when she heard his voice. "How's it going, District Attorney Emery?"

"Oh, it's going. I just got back from court. This place is a zoo. What's going on with you?"

"I came into town to buy . . . a few things. I brought Murphy and Grady with me. Do you believe how cold it is for this early in the season? Anything going on?"

"Same old, same old. I'm meeting Ted for a drink after work. He's back at work and pissed to the teeth. I'll get details this evening. I miss you."

"I miss you, too. Judge Easter left the farm today. I think she plans on going back to work tomorrow. I drove her into town. Send some flowers to her office, Jack. I think she'd like that. She won't think of it as brownnosing. The woman has shifted her mental gears and . . . I think she's shelved Jenny's death and will only think about it in private. She reminded me of a robot on the ride in. What about Brad, how's he doing?"

"Brad headed up to the Big Apple last week. He has family upstate. This is just a guess on my part, but I don't think he's coming back. I helped him pack up the nursery last week and that was real bad. We donated everything to the Salvation Army. He left Jenny's things for the judge to . . . you know."

"Yes, I do know. Maddie took care of the firm's insurance and Jenny's partnership shares. Do you have an address for Brad? If you do, call it in to Maddie."

"Will do. When am I going to see you, Nikki?"

"Not till we complete our . . . Soon, Jack."

Jack laughed, an intimate sound. Nikki smiled. "In the meantime, I'll dream about you."

"Me, too. Bye, Jack."

"Bye, Nik."

Nikki slid her cell phone into her jacket pocket. She leaned back to wait for Maddie. The dogs lay at her feet, their eyes alert.

Thirty minutes later, the dogs were up on their feet, the hair on the backs of their necks standing on end. Maddie approached and waited for Nikki to admonish the dogs when Murphy's ears went flat against his head, a signal he wasn't happy with someone coming so close to Nikki.

Nikki's voice was soothing. "It's OK, boys. Sit down, Maddie, and just talk normally. They need to get your scent and decide for themselves that you're a friend."

It only took five minutes before the dogs lay down, their heads on their paws.

"Listen to me, Maddie. I need you to tell me everything you know about Paula Woodley. Any little thing that the sister, your friend, may have told you. I also need you to tell me anything Paula might have said to you when you picked her up after the sister's call. Do they have security at the house in Kalorama? I don't mean just an alarm system. Does the NSA have any kind of security? Like bodyguards. I don't want you to ask me any questions. You know the rules."

"Nikki, Nancy doesn't really talk about her sister. I do know she hates the little squirt. That's what she calls the NSA. When Nancy and her family moved to Pennsylvania, we were reduced to a phone call once a month, exchanging Christmas cards, that kind of thing. As far as I know, Nancy doesn't know about the abuse. She may suspect, but she sure didn't let on to me that she knew anything. She was just concerned that Paula wasn't answering the phone. I do know that Nancy is the one who always does the calling. The two of them haven't seen each other in six

years. Because every time Nancy would suggest
a meeting, Paula would tell her they were going
either out of state or out of the country."

"Six years!" Nikki gasped. "How can that be?"

"That's what I asked, and Nancy said Paula
was a big girl and moved in the circles of the
pretty people. Movers and shakers. Nancy is just a
down-home girl with a family who comes first.
She's involved with things that concern her kids.
She teaches part-time. She has her own life."

"What exactly did you tell Nancy after you res-
cued Paula?"

"Just what Mr. Martin told me to tell her. That
Paula was rushing around getting ready to go
on a trip abroad. Nancy was satisfied and hasn't
called back. She cares about her sister and once
I reassured her she was OK, she went back to
her own life."

Nikki fixed her gaze on two squirrels racing
up and down one of the maple trees across from
the bench. Murphy was eyeing both squirrels
with interest, but he didn't move. "How did you
get into the house?"

"Actually, it's kind of funny. The house was
locked up tight. I rang every doorbell at least
ten times with no response. Nancy said Paula
used to keep a key in one of the birdhouses in
the backyard. I found five keys. I let myself in.
This may surprise you, and then again, maybe it
won't. The Woodleys do not have household
help. Paula does . . . *did* everything. Anyway, she
was in the living room on the sofa. She looked
scared out of her wits when I told her who I was
and why I was there. She begged me to take her

someplace. The phone rang the entire time I was there. Several hundred times at least. I'll never forget the number on the caller ID. I repeated it to Paula and asked if it was her husband and she nodded. I got her out of there as quick as I could. She could hardly talk but she managed to tell me I had to take her book bag that was hanging on her dressing-room door. It looked at first glance like it just had reading books in it, but on the bottom, under the other books, were her bank records and her important papers. I just grabbed it and her purse and away we went. That's all I can tell you, Nikki."

Nikki kept watching the squirrels. Now there was a third one who could run faster than the other two. Grady raised his head to watch, but, like Murphy, he didn't move. A sudden gust of wind swept through the small park. A little boy tugging on his mother's skirt howled his displeasure when the wind buffeted him forward. The mother bent down to pick him up. He buried his little face in her shoulder.

"Think, Maddie. Did Paula say anything else? No matter how inane it might have seemed. Did she say *anything* about that bastard?"

"She was in so much pain. I think she was just lying on that couch hoping she would die. He shattered her teeth, hit her with a candlestick. It was metal. It was still on the floor. All she said was, 'no more.' She came willingly, even gratefully. She's OK, isn't she, Nikki?"

Nikki diverted her gaze from the squirrels in the tree. "She's mending. Has anyone been calling or asking questions?"

Maddie shook her head. "No. I had my story all ready if they did, which was that Jenny handled everything even though she was on maternity leave. The fact that Jenny died the same day I brought Paula to the farm made it work perfectly. The story, I mean. I know in my heart, Jenny would have approved of what I did. God won't punish me, will He, Nikki?"

Nikki hugged her friend. "No, Maddie, God isn't going to punish you, and you're right, Jenny would approve."

"So, what now?"

"It's better that you don't know. Did you bring the key? Where is the rest of Paula's stuff?"

"At first it was in the firm's safe. I made copies of everything. I sent everything to Mr. Martin by messenger. I cleaned out the safe after we did all our filing and sent Mr. Martin those files too, by messenger. There's nothing in the safe now to tie us to Paula. For all intents and purposes, Jenny had everything. I brought all five keys," Maddie said, handing over a small white envelope. "The NSA's cell phone number is on the envelope in case you need it."

Nikki pocketed the envelope and stood up. The women hugged before they started toward the parking lot, the dogs walking alongside them.

An hour later, Nikki walked into the kitchen of Pinewood. She held out the small white envelope. "Ladies, here is our entrance to the Kalorama house. And the NSA's private cell phone number."

Sixteen

Dressed in his pajamas and ready to retire for the evening, Ted Robinson was about to slide the last dead bolt home on his front door when he heard a loud knock. Unwilling to open the door at this hour—past ten o'clock—he looked through the peephole to see Jack Emery standing on the other side. He undid the other five locks that Jack had installed while he was in the hospital. The two cats, Mickey and Minnie, hissed their disapproval at these goings-on until they saw Jack, at which point they brushed up against him and started to purr.

"Kind of late for a social visit, isn't it, Jack?"

Jack moved into the living room, the cats following him. "I tried to get here earlier in the week but the office is such a zoo, I haven't been getting home till after midnight. Now *that's* late.

I just wanted to see how you were doing and if you needed anything."

"I'm OK. I work a few hours a day, hang out and catch up on the soap operas." Ted guffawed. "I mostly order in so I don't have to go shopping. I'm OK, Jack, and I don't blame you. Can we please get past that?"

"If it works for you, go for it. OK, we're past it. Anything going on in the world of journalism? Anyone exciting kill anyone less exciting? I only ask so I can put said killer on my schedule. Personally, I wish all those whack jobs out there would kill each other. Would make my job a lot easier."

"Nah, it's kind of quiet, crimewise. Lots of gossip if you're into gossip."

Jack yawned. He wanted a beer but he noticed Ted's pajamas and decided it was time to go home. The cats were still purring at his feet. "Gossip doesn't cut it for me, Ted. Look, if you're OK and don't need anything, I'm going to head on home. I've been dragging my ass for the last three days and I'm bushed."

Ted held up his hand. "Hold on, Jack. Sit down. Wanna beer? I think you might be interested in this particular gossip." He padded across to the small kitchen for two beers and returned to the living room. Jack noticed how slowly Ted was walking, and felt bad for his friend. The friend who wasn't blaming him for his condition. He accepted the beer and sat down.

Ted took a huge swig from the bottle before he set it down on the coffee table. Minnie, or maybe it was Mickey, hopped on his lap. He stroked her black silky head as he spoke. "When I was in the office today I heard Maggie Spritzer on the phone. She covers the political gossip, in case you didn't know. Anyway, what made me sit up and pay attention was the mention of your girlfriend's name. Now follow me here. The national security advisor is married to a shoe polish heiress. Years ago she won a silver in gymnastics at the Olympics. Her name is Paula and she refuses to be part of the Washington fishbowl. The press refers to her as reclusive. They live in Kalorama in a house that has been in the wife's family for years and years and more years. You know no one ever sells in Kalorama and, if you believe the rumors, no one dies in Kalorama. Anyway, your old girlfriend's law firm represents the wife, Paula Woodley. Rumor has it the wife split and hired the law firm to cut off the NSA from all her personal accounts and cleaned out the joint accounts. It's a rumor and can't be nailed down, Jack. You need two sources and all Maggie has is rumor. I thought you might be interested."

Jack pretended to be puzzled. "So the woman hired Nikki's firm. It's a good firm, even though it took a serious hit with the Barrington case. I've gone up against just about every lawyer in that firm and let me tell you, they gave me a run for my money. I lost more cases than I won. Maybe Mrs. Woodley wants a divorce. It happens, Ted. What are you seeing that I'm not seeing?"

Ted shrugged, his eyes narrowing as he

watched Jack. He continued to stroke the cat in his lap. "Do you know which lawyer handled Mrs. Woodley's affairs?"

"Nikki? If she hired Nik, she's in good hands."

"Nice try, Jack. Not Nikki. Jenny. Jenny's gone now and so are the records. This is just rumor, OK?" Ted stood up. "Now you can go."

Jack's head buzzed. "And you think I needed to know this . . . Why?"

"I'm just passing it on. I thought maybe you could make some sense out of it."

"I think I'll pass on it. Marital problems don't do anything for me. Just because the guy is the NSA doesn't mean he's a saint. He probably had an affair and his wife caught him. Happens all the time. Don't go spooking yourself or try to tie that in to what's been going on at Pinewood. Thanks for the beer."

Ted closed the door and then closed all six locks. He leaned against the door, the cats pawing at his bare feet. "You're about as transparent as cellophane, Jack, and I think Maggie Spritzer is going to be my new best friend," he muttered to the cats at his feet.

Outside in the dark, Jack walked to his car, his thoughts going in all directions. He wished now that he hadn't stopped at Ted's apartment. He looked up at the star-filled night. In a day or so there would be a full moon, at which point all the crazies in town would pop out of their hiding places and raise all kinds of hell. It never failed. He had to call Nikki and alert her because he knew in his gut that Ted was going to pursue Maggie Spritzer's gossip even though he said he wasn't interested.

On the drive back to Georgetown, Jack let his mind veer off in two different directions. If the presidential gold shields were called upon to help the NSA, what would they do to the women of Pinewood? After all, the presidential gold shields had an allegiance to Charles Martin. He definitely had to call Nikki, but eyebrows might shoot up if he called Pinewood at such a late hour. Better to wait for morning to make the call.

A smile tugged at the corners of his mouth when he thought about Nikki. It was two weeks since she'd called him from the shopping center to alert him to her meeting with Maddie. He'd begged her not to tell him her plan but she hadn't listened and told him anyway. Fucking with the NSA was not a good thing. He'd told her so but she'd paid him no attention.

Two weeks. Fourteen days. God alone knew what that little group of women had come up with in all those hours. Whatever it was, the NSA wasn't going to like it. Jack knew that he personally was going to *hate* it.

Jack couldn't believe his good luck when he found a parking spot right in front of Nikki's house. Normally, every spot was already taken at this late hour. He parked his car, then gathered up his briefcase and cell phone. Before he got out of the car, he looked out the window at Nikki's front stoop to see if the light was still on. It was. Still, he looked both ways before he got out of the car. His foot was on the first step when the hairs on the back of his neck moved. He whirled around to see a man standing in the shadows near the parked car in front of his.

"Good evening, Mr. Emery. Welcome home. Keeping late hours, I see."

"Fuck you, you creep. Why are you tailing me? I'm going to write to my congressman and protest my taxpayer dollars going to pay your salary. Then I'm going to call the *New York Times* and tell them about you guys. You can't interfere with the Old Gray Lady and we both know it. Now, get your ass outta here and leave me alone."

The man standing in the shadows clucked his tongue. "I'm standing on a public sidewalk. I can make you eat your words, you crud. Don't ever make the mistake of threatening me again."

Jack's mind raced. If he went in the house and didn't respond, the shield would think he was afraid. If he opened his mouth with a smart-ass retort, the shield would probably break every bone in his body. Since he was only half-turned toward the man in the shadows, he moved slightly, stuck his hand inside his jacket, and whipped out his gun just as he swiveled around to confront the man. "I'm a dead-aim shot, you asshole. You're lurking outside my residence and you're harassing me. I'm protecting my castle. You want to bring this to a head, let's go for it."

"Another time, another place, Mr. Emery. Just for the record, I had the drop on you five minutes ago."

Jack snorted. "Yeah, right. That's what I would say if I were in your position, too," he said as he backed up the steps to the front door. Inside, he let out his breath in a loud *swoosh*. He hated it that his hand shook when he jammed his gun back into his shoulder holster. Most DAs didn't pack their guns on their persons but carried them in their briefcases. He wasn't one of those DAs. More than once his gun had come in handy and he wasn't about to give up his habit. Not for some asshole carrying a gold shield. "Your day is coming, you bastard, and I'm going to be there to see it."

Jack walked back to the kitchen to make himself a cup of hot chocolate. He made some toast and spread butter and jam on it. He ate five slices before he made his way to Nikki's bedroom. He looked around, missing her so much he wanted to cry. He bit down on his lip and picked up the picture of the two of them from the nightstand. He didn't feel silly at all when he kissed Nikki's photograph. Now, he could go to bed.

Myra called the meeting of the Sisterhood to order. "It's been two weeks since we last met. Now, let's bring out all our ideas so we can arrange a plan to take care of Mr. Karl Woodley."

Kathryn spoke first. "I'm not comfortable snatching the guy. I'm even less comfortable going after him inside his own house. I don't see any way to foolproof this gig. I'll go along with the majority, but I want you all to know I think this is incredibly risky."

"I like the idea of delivering the flowers to all the residents on the street," Isabelle said. "We've been up and down the Woodleys' street a hundred times and there is no outside security that we could detect. My guess is the guy has a driver who picks him up and drops him off. Once he's inside, he puts on his alarm system. He's safe till the next day. The surveillance we conducted proved to us that once he's home for the night, he stays put. We have the floor plans of his house. Nikki now has a key to the house. We can get in and out during the day if we have to, as long as someone covers the neighborhood. We can do it at night, too, if Charles shows us how to disarm his alarm system. I read this spy novel not too long ago where the main character was worried about getting kidnapped. The CIA gave him this gadget he wore twenty-four-seven. All he had to do was press a button and everyone came on the run to save him. Is there such a gadget? I don't know. The book was, after all, fiction."

Nikki leaned forward. "If we went in at night, we could get to him while he's sleeping. If there is such a personal alarm, he'd probably wear it around his neck or on his wrist. Maybe it's something built into his watch. If that's the case, we sneak up and grab his arms. The guy's a little squirt. I think we can take him with one hand tied behind our backs. Lights out is between twelve and one o'clock. The guy leaves at six thirty in the morning. That would give us five hours. Or, we can have him call his driver to say he's sick if we need more time. I think we can do it."

"I think so, too," Myra said. "Charles, is it possible the NSA has a gadget like Isabelle described?"

"Absolutely, and probably more high-tech than you can imagine. If we knew for certain, I could jam the frequency, but I'd need to know exactly what it is."

Nikki grimaced. "We need to get real here. There's no way we can possibly find out what kind of security the NSA wears, much less the specific type. We'll have to wing it. We could, of course, call him up and ask for the model number." This last was said tongue in cheek.

"There are no animals that we know of to alert Mr. Woodley if we decide to go in at night. If we take Mr. Woodley away from the premises, that is kidnapping a federal employee," Yoko said.

Kathryn made an ugly sound. "What do you think we did to Senator Webster, who was also going to run for the second highest office in the land? That little caper was about as federal as you can get."

Alexis toyed with the pencil she was holding. "Then I vote we go in at night, do what we have to do and then leave. Before it gets light outside. Five hours is a pretty long time. If we synchronize our movements we shouldn't have any problem. That's my vote."

"Girls, do you agree or disagree?" Myra asked.

Five hands, including Myra's, shot in the air.

"All right, we're in agreement. Now let's plot out the night. Until we pick a specific evening, I think it would be wise if we continue our surveillance of Mr. Woodley and his residence," Myra said quietly. "Charles, do you have anything you'd like to add?"

"Only that you all study the floor plans of the house so that you can find your way around in the dark. In addition, you're going to need a secure parameter outside as well as at the entrance road to Kalorama. I'd like to make a suggestion. When you do your surveillance, pay close attention to the other houses on Benton and see what time the lights go out. Make a note of which houses leave their outside lights on. See if any of the houses have sensor lights. That might prove a little hard to do, as motion lights click on only if someone or something passes across the beam. If you all think it wise, I can place a call to Mrs. Woodley and ask her some of these questions, but by doing that I will be alerting her that something might be going on. She's mending nicely and might be having second thoughts. It's indicative of battered women once they start to heal."

Nikki's head bobbed up and down. "Charles is right; battered women, once they start to feel better, often backpedal. I vote no on calling Mrs. Woodley." The others agreed. "That's a no, Charles."

Kathryn stood up. She looked down at her wrist. "It's nine thirty. We might as well get ready and head for the District. I'll have to take your car, Myra, if that's all right with you. I'm going to take Murphy with me. After we do our drive-by I can park on a side street and walk him. A loose dog will give me a reason to go up over the lawn and around the back, especially if I toss a piece of meat in that direction."

"That's a great idea," Isabelle said.

"I can do the same thing with Grady. Pick a time, Kathryn, so we don't overlap our walk. We can meet back here at, let's say one thirty, to be on the safe side."

"It's a plan," Nikki said. "Let's do it! But, I'm going to go home this evening after the surveillance. I need some clean clothes. We can meet up at that all-night burger stand on Pennington Street. Is that OK with everyone?"

The women agreed.

"Good luck, girls," Myra said.

They all waved as they filed into a straggly line to exit the war room.

"You don't look happy, dear. Is something bothering you?" Myra asked Charles.

"I am concerned about Mrs. Woodley. In the aftermath, the authorities will want to talk to her. I'm going to have to make plans to move her somewhere so that she can have an airtight alibi. I need to do that ASAP. She may balk. I'm going to have to come up with some plausible reason for moving her without giving anything away. As Kathryn would say, it's not going to be an easy gig."

"I'm sure you'll come up with something, dear; you always do, and then we all marvel at how brilliant you are. Let's go upstairs and have a nice glass of wine and watch some television for a little while. I can fix us a sandwich if you like."

Charles smiled. "Why is it you always say exactly the right thing at exactly the right time? Give me thirty minutes. I want to send off a few e-mails. A ham and cheese sandwich will be nice and a few of those fat sugar cookies. I'll leave the wine up to you. Now scoot and let me get to work."

Myra winked at Charles. He burst out laughing. She giggled all the way to the kitchen.

Seventeen

Ted Robinson let his gaze sweep the news-room not once but twice. He blinked, unable to comprehend that Maggie Spritzer wasn't at her computer. She was always the first one in, box of Krispy Kremes and a tray of decadent-flavored coffees for all of them. He knew she put it on her expense account, but it wasn't about the money, it was that she cared enough to go out of her way for her colleagues. "Everyone," she would say, "needs a sugar high to start the day at this zoo." And she was right. He, for one, always looked forward to his hazelnut coffee and jelly doughnut. Today there was no coffee, no doughnuts and no Maggie Spritzer.

At thirty-five, she said, her biological clock was ticking but she was healthy as a horse, or so she claimed. Maggie never got sick. At least, he couldn't ever remember her being sick or absent. Hell, she never even got a cold or the flu. She never took a vacation, either.

Ted shuffled over to Maggie's desk as though the very act would make the freckle-faced redhead appear. He sniffed like a hound dog, hoping to pick up the scent of flavored coffee and fresh doughnuts. He looked around. "Anyone seen Maggie this morning?" A chorus of "no"s caused him to narrow his eyes. "Did anyone call to see if she's all right?" For this question he received a block of blank stares. Ted shrugged and walked back to his own desk. His antenna went up as he continued to peruse the newsroom. There was still no sign of Maggie.

Ted flopped down in his ergonomic chair and swiveled it around so that he was facing the door to the newsroom as he struggled to remember what he knew about Maggie Spritzer. None of the staff were what you would call personal friends. Oh, they might meet up at the local watering hole for a beer at the end of the day, but they didn't socialize beyond the doors of the *Post*. Maggie was a dynamo; everything they said about reporters fit Maggie to a T. She was relentless, tireless, and she had the nose of a bloodhound, something the staff also said about Ted himself. The bottom line was that Maggie was damn good at what she did. Almost as good as he was. The space between his shoulder blades started to itch as he rummaged in his bottom desk drawer to find the staff list with all their addresses and home phone numbers. He didn't stop to think; he simply dialed the number and listened to it ring on the other end. Seven rings later a curt message came on.

"We're not here right now. Leave your name and number and one of us will return your call as soon as possible." The "we" referred to Maggie and her Jack Russell, Daisy Mae. If you lived alone, it paid to pretend you shared an apartment with someone else because of all the nut cases walking around out there who had it in for reporters.

Ted left a message. "Maggie, it's Ted. I'm just calling to see if you're OK. I missed you this morning. If you're there, give me a call at the paper." He looked down at the sheet of paper in his hand. Maggie lived in a high-rise in Crystal City. He could go there if he wanted to. He looked up at the clock. He'd give her another hour and then he'd call again. If there was still no answer, he'd drive to Crystal City.

The newsroom took on a life of its own as reporters straggled in. The chatter was deafening as computers were turned on, the clicking of keys like a symphony. With nothing really pressing on his personal agenda today, Ted flipped his Rolodex till he found Jack Emery's number at the DA's office.

"Emery," Jack said.

"It's Ted, Jack. Listen, Maggie Spritzer didn't come to work this morning."

"And I need to know this . . . why? I sure as hell hope you aren't calling me to ask the cops to put out an APB on your friend. Listen, I have to be in court in fifteen minutes."

"Don't you remember what I told you last

night?" Talking as fast as he could, Ted outlined Maggie Spritzer's work ethic, her attendance, her stamina and her bulldog tendencies where a story was concerned.

On the other end of the phone, Jack Emery's own antenna shot upward. He knew exactly where Ted was going with all this. He needed to chop him off at the knees and he needed to do it right this minute. "Stop whining because you didn't get your doughnut and coffee hand-delivered. Get some exercise and go buy your own. I gotta run, Ted. I'll call you later in the day. Forget all that shit, OK, and keep remembering what happened last time you stuck your nose where it didn't belong." Like that was really going to happen.

Ted gave the ergonomic chair a shove to the right. He swiveled around twice, disoriented when he finally stood up. Screw the hour's wait. His gut told him something was wrong where Maggie Spritzer was concerned. He looked down at the staff roster again to memorize Maggie's address. Since he was pretty much top dog at the paper, he didn't have to report his comings and goings. He reached for his backpack and his jacket.

Ted tried calling Maggie twice during the forty-minute ride to Crystal City, but there was no answer. He now knew her greeting to callers by heart.

The high-rise boasted an underground parking lot. For some reason he was surprised at Maggie's digs. He'd more or less expected her to live in a little cottage-style house with lots of flowers, trees and a backyard for her dog, Daisy Mae. He parked and took the elevator to the seventeenth floor. It was a nice building, he decided. Mirrored elevators and carpeted hallways with green plants in the corner. Everything smelled like it had just been painted.

Ted looked at the numbers on the apartment doors. Maggie's was 1706, three doors down from the elevator. He rang the bell. When there was no response, he rang it again and kept his finger on it. He could hear nothing from inside the apartment. He took his finger off the bell and yelled that he wasn't going to go away until she opened the door. When there was no response, he tried again.

"Open the goddamn door, Maggie, or I'm going to tell all your neighbors what you did at the last Christmas party." To make his point, Ted jabbed the button and held it down again. That's when he heard steps inside the apartment. The door opened with such force that Ted was thrown off balance.

"What the hell do you think you're doing, Robinson? What are you doing here?"

For the first time in his life, Ted felt stupid. Shit, what if she had some guy in her bed? Maybe she *was* sick. She sure as hell looked sick. Where was the damn dog?

"You didn't come to work," he said stupidly. "You always come to work. You bring doughnuts and coffee. I wanted some this morning. I called you three times. I don't care if you do have some guy in here, I'm coming in. Where's the dog?"

Maggie burst into tears as Ted brushed past her. He quickly made the rounds of the two-bedroom, two-bathroom apartment. Satisfied there was no one else there, he joined Maggie in the living room. To his reporter's eye it looked to him like she was wearing the same clothes he'd seen her in yesterday.

"Talk."

"About what?" Maggie said as she wiped her eyes on the sleeve of her yellow shirt.

"Well, let's start with your dog. Where is she?"

"Daisy's at the vet's."

"Is she going to be all right?"

"I don't know. What are you doing here, Ted?"

"I want to know what happened. You're a real hard-ass and I say that as a compliment. Why didn't you come in today? I was worried about you. Things happen to people who live alone."

"I didn't feel like it, OK? Where is it written that I have to explain myself to you? You live alone and I don't worry about you. Why should you be worried about me?"

"You're a woman," Ted said flatly. "Don't make me beat it out of you. All this," Ted said, waving his hand about, "has something to do with the NSA, right? You asked the wrong questions of the wrong people and some guys paid you a visit to warn you off. They probably kicked your dog to make a point. How am I doing so far?"

"You're crazy, Robinson."

"Yeah, crazy like a fox. Ask yourself why I'm walking around without a spleen these days. I can describe those guys right down to their socks. There's also the little matter of those presidential gold shields. They scared the crap out of you, didn't they? To make their point, they did something to your dog. Now, talk to me, Maggie. Between the two of us, we might be able to come up with a plan to get them off our backs. If it's any consolation to you, those guys still have me in their sights."

Maggie heaved herself to her feet and walked to the kitchen. She started to make coffee. Ted followed her and watched while she rummaged in one of the drawers for a pack of cigarettes. She fired one up.

"I didn't know you smoked."

"I don't. Not really. Well, I do, usually one in the morning with coffee, sometimes one after dinner. Never in the car or the office. Some days I don't smoke at all. I don't consider myself a smoker. Why do you care anyway?"

"I don't care, they're your lungs. I was making conversation because you're nervous and jittery. Maybe if you took a shower and changed your clothes you'd feel better. I'm a reporter so I notice things like that."

"You need to mind your own business, Robinson. Do you want some coffee?"

"Well, sure. I don't suppose you have any doughnuts, do you?"

Maggie rolled her eyes. "No, I do not have doughnuts." She poured coffee, the cigarette hanging out of the corner of her mouth. She sat down and blew a perfect smoke ring. "You were right. It happened just like you said. They scared me, Ted. I didn't think anything could scare me.

I'm supposed to be this tough reporter. I *am* a tough reporter, but when they kicked my dog, that was something else. That's when I got scared."

Ted leaned across the table. "What did you do? Who did you talk to?"

Maggie crushed out her cigarette and lit another one. She blew another perfect smoke ring. "After you left the office yesterday, I went to ask some questions at the law firm Mrs. Woodley used. They showed me the door in quick order. I went out to Kalorama to nose around. No one answered the Woodleys' door. The neighbors are a closed-mouth bunch. It might have something to do with Woodley being the NSA. One lady said she hadn't seen Mrs. Woodley in quite some time but said that wasn't unusual because Mrs. Woodley keeps to herself. It's not the kind of neighborhood where the ladies meet to gossip and drink coffee. All in all, it got me zip."

"There has to be more to warrant a visit from the gold shields. What else did you do?"

"I called the NSA himself. I had to leave three messages but he finally called me back. In a very nice, cold, deadly voice, he told me to mind my own business. He said his personal life was no one's business. By that time I started to realize there was more to it all than a man and a woman separating and possibly divorcing. None of my sources in the food chain claimed to know anything about the Woodleys' private life. I came away knowing the Woodleys do not socialize with the powerful elite in Washington. No one ever remembered them entertaining. Do you know something I don't know?"

Ted decided to play it close to his vest. "Not really. I was working on something else and those guys paid me a visit. I ended up in the hospital. I guess I wanted to warn you to drop whatever it is that involves the NSA."

"Consider it dropped. Look, I'm no wimp. I just needed to get myself together this morning. If it weren't for Daisy, I would have spit in that guy's eye. I love that dog, Ted."

Ted thought about Mickey and Minnie and how devastated he'd be if anything happened to either one of them. "So you're dropping the whole thing?"

"It was just a thread. Gossip. Another player getting divorced. Washington is not the place for enduring marriages. I am no longer interested in Karl Woodley's private life. The son of a bitch can drop dead and I won't blink an eye. If that's all, Ted, I'm going to take a shower and go to work . . . Wait, there was one other thing. I drove out to Kalorama and parked down the street from the Woodleys' house last night. Don't ask me why, I just did. There was a hell of a lot of traffic on that street last night. Some woman had a big German shepherd and he ran up and around the Woodleys' house. She chased after him. I can't be sure, but I thought she threw something and the dog ran after it. It was dark so I can't be really sure. Then about forty minutes later, another woman was walking her dog. She had to chase her dog up over the lawn, too. Just for the hell of it, I copied down two license plates. Like I said, there was lots of traffic."

"Can I see those plate numbers?"

Maggie set her coffee cup down and walked over to the kitchen counter where her purse was. She pulled out a small notebook and then ripped off the page. "I don't want to know who those cars belong to, so don't tell me. You can leave now, Ted."

"What time did the NSA get home last night?"

"No idea. I left at nine thirty. My company showed up at ten thirty, just ten minutes after I finished walking Daisy. Go, Ted!" At the door, Maggie managed a tiny smile. "Thanks for . . . for worrying about me, Ted. I'll try to return the favor sometime."

Ted took a really good look at his colleague. He decided he liked what he was seeing. He shuffled his feet as he jammed his hands into his pockets. "You wanna take in a movie, maybe go to dinner first?"

Maggie's bright-green eyes blinked rapidly. "You mean like a date? You show up at the door, ring my bell, bring me flowers, that kind of thing?" Her tone suggested it was the next thing to picking up the Holy Grail.

Shit. When was he going to learn to keep his mouth shut? "Yeah," was all he could say.

"OK. When?"

When? That must be a yes. Confirmation. She wanted a specific time, a date. "Well, how about tomorrow night?"

"OK. You aren't going to blab this around the office, are you?"

"Who, me? Nah."

The door closed behind him. Ted finally picked up his feet and headed for the elevator.

He had a date with Maggie Spritzer. He started to whistle. He was still whistling when he made his way across the lobby and out to his car.

He actually, honest to God, had a date with Maggie Spritzer.

His next stop: the police station.

Every building in the world has its own distinctive smell. The *Post* building smelled like paper and ink. A pleasant if not overpowering scent. The police station smelled of stale sweat, burned coffee, mold and more sweat. The smell matched the baby-poop-yellow walls, the dirty wood floors, the cigarette-scarred desks, the weary-eyed detectives, and the incessant sound of ringing phones.

He'd been here a thousand times, maybe more, during his career at the *Post*, so Ted knew where he was going—the detective's unit and his old friend Bobby Sanchez. He rapped sharply on the glass door before he opened it. Detective Sanchez groaned and pretended to fall off his chair.

"The answer is no, no, and no."

"How do you know I want you to do something? Maybe I just stopped by to see if you got divorced yet. I worry about you. Did you? Get a divorce?"

"No, I didn't get a divorce. My wife loves me. It's my job she hates."

Ted looked at his friend. He was an ugly man with a head of black, unruly, curly hair that refused to be tamed. But you forgot the ugliness the minute you looked into his big dark eyes that were so full of compassion you had to do a double take. His grin was infectious. Ted found himself grinning in return.

"I will never understand how you got that beautiful wife of yours to marry you. You look like you fell out of the ugly tree and hit every branch on the way down." They both laughed.

"OK, whaddaya want, Ted?"

There was no use pretending he was here for a social visit. "I need you to run two license plate numbers for me. I'll send your wife some flowers and sign your name on them."

"Christ, Robinson, don't do that. She'll think I did something and am sending her flowers out of guilt. Don't you have any other friends in the department you can ask to do your dirty work?"

"Well, yeah, but I like you best. C'mon, it will take you five minutes and you'll make me a happy man."

"Gimme the numbers. You do know I could get my ass in a sling if the captain finds out I'm doing favors for you? Reporters are the enemy around here."

"I always give you guys good press."

"And that's the only reason I'm doing this. OK, here it is. The first one is registered to Alexis Thorne. The second one is registered to Myra Rutledge. Now are you happy?"

Damn. I knew it. I knew it! "Bobby, my cup runneth over. Thanks, buddy. I owe you one."

"You owe me a hundred and one. So, how are you feeling? I tried and wanted to see you after my initial visit in the hospital. Crazy damn hours, my wife, the kids. Shit, there's not a free five minutes anywhere in my day. You really OK, Ted?"

"I have my moments. A twinge here, a twinge there. There are some things I still can't do. Maybe I'll never be able to do them again. I have to live with it. I'm back at work part-time. Life goes on."

Sanchez pointed to the paper in Ted's hand. "Do those numbers have anything to do with what happened to you?"

"Always the detective, huh? The short answer is, yes." Ted looked at his watch. "Bobby, you want to go to an early lunch?"

"Can't. Got desk duty." He motioned to a brown bag on the corner of his desk. "Thanks for asking, though. Ah, listen, Ted, if there's anything I can do for you in regard to . . ." He pointed to the paper in Ted's hand. "Just ask. I can get some of the guys to watch out for you."

"Thanks. You'll be the first guy I call if I need help. I mean that, Bobby. Call me if you find some free time and we can pound a few beers. See ya."

"You got it. Remember now, do not—I repeat, do not—send my wife flowers."

Ted laughed as he closed the door behind him.

Eighteen

Jack Emery's assistant took one look at her boss and quickly scurried away to avoid what she called "one of Jack's moods," which were cranky, really cranky, and then pissed-to-the-teeth cranky. From her cubicle she could see him throw his briefcase across the room. Things must have gotten hateful in court today. She then opted to make herself scarce when she heard his phone ring at the same moment she saw a tall, lanky man make his way toward Jack's desk. Friend or foe? From the look on her boss's face it looked like foe. Better to get herself out of the line of fire.

"That ugly look on your face tells me you'd like to kill someone," Ted Robinson said cheerfully. "I hope it isn't me," he added as an afterthought.

Jack jerked at his tie to loosen it before he removed his suit jacket. He tossed it on to another chair. "I lost in court today. Police screw-up. What are you doing here, Ted?"

"I got good news and bad news. The good news is I have a date with Maggie Spritzer tomorrow night. The bad news is those fucking gold shields paid her a visit and sent her dog to the vet. They scared the living hell out of her. They didn't harm her though. Sometimes intimidation is worse than a physical beating."

"Well, Ted, I'm happy for you and your date. I warned you about those guys. You have to back off and warn Maggie to do the same thing. Anyone who hurts an animal is a crud in my book . . . There's more, isn't there?" Jack said, working at the still-too-tight tie that he seemed to think was strangling him.

"Yeah. See this," Ted said, holding out the slip of notebook paper with the two numbers Maggie had given him. "These license plate numbers belong to two of the ladies at Pinewood. Alexis Thorne and Myra Rutledge. Maggie was staking out the NSA's house in Kalorama last night. The ladies of Pinewood did some drive-bys. I have to believe they were doing what Maggie was doing, but on the move as opposed to parking and watching. Then two women with dogs managed to check out the Woodley yard, front and back. Maggie couldn't make out the features of either woman."

Jack's insides started to churn. "You here for advice or to confide?" That sounded good to his ears. He had to call Nikki and warn her.

"Heavy on confiding and light on the advice."

"Is this about the fact that the NSA is possibly separating or maybe worse, going for the big D word? In this town people get divorced every five minutes. What's the big deal? Is this a scoop thing, a byline, a picture of the NSA above the fold, what? I'm not getting it." Jack realized his words sounded like a crock of the dark-brown stuff. Even he couldn't believe they'd just spewed from his mouth.

"If this were a perfect world, I'd probably think like you're thinking. But what were the ladies of Pinewood doing out there at night, driving around, letting their dogs pee on the Woodleys' shrubs? I notice you didn't say anything about our mutual buddies with their impressive, I-can-do-whatever-I-want-to-you-and-you-can't-do-a-damn-thing-about-it shields."

Jack snorted as he stretched his neck muscles. "You know what it means, Ted. It means you tell Maggie to mind her own business, that the NSA's private life is his own and doesn't concern her. Now, you're sticking your nose into it. Let it lie, for Christ's sake, before your new best friend gets hurt. The world really doesn't give a shit if the NSA gets a divorce or not. A bunch of bull-shit gossip isn't worth getting thrown into the hospital for. Tell Maggie Spritzer I said that, too."

Ted sucked on his bottom lip for a full minute before he replied. "What about the ladies of Pinewood?"

"The gold shields will tell you it's a free coun-try and they can drive all around Kalorama twenty-four-seven and unless they commit a crime there's nothing anyone can do. The road is a public road. As for the dogs, we all know dogs are unpredictable. If they have to go, they go. If they see a squirrel or a bird, it's fair game."

Ted looked so disgusted that Jack knew he wasn't going to get past square one with the hard-nosed reporter. He waited, knowing exactly how Ted was going to respond.

"You're so full of bullshit, Jack, your eyes are turning brown. Those gals are setting up the NSA and we both know it. I'm thinking it has something to do with the NSA's wife. It's called Reporting 101. I'm going to stake out Kalorama tonight myself."

"Well that's a dumb-ass move if I ever heard one. I suppose that's in Reporting 101, too?"

"Did I mention that Maggie actually spoke to the NSA himself? It took a few calls before he actually called her back. He was not warm and fuzzy about it either."

Jack slapped his hands on the desktop. Papers scattered in all directions. "What does that tell you, Ted? Back off, forget it. He's the one who sent the shields after Maggie. Do you want to see her get hurt? The next time they might *really* hurt the dog and rough up Maggie. Do you want that on your conscience?"

The look of disgust was still on Ted's face. "Man, you have changed. What happened to fearless Jack Emery, rising star in the District Attorney's office?"

Jack wished he could wipe the smug, disgusted look off his friend's face. "He got smart is what happened. I like my life just the way it is, thank you very much. I'm all healed up and I want to stay that way. You go ahead and do whatever it is you feel you have to do so you can get your name in the paper. The day after it appears, it's old news and dogs and cats are peeing all over it. Get the hell out of here, Ted, I have a ton of paperwork to do and I'd like to get out of here before midnight. All I had to eat today was a stale bagel and I'm starved, but I don't have time to fucking eat. Say hello to Maggie for me."

Ted was dismissed and he knew it. Something stank where Jack was concerned. Maybe he should be staking out Jack instead of the house on Kalorama. Yeah, yeah, that's exactly what he should be doing.

Jack raced over to the door and closed it the moment Ted left the office. He looked around to see where everyone was. Gone. Great. He yanked out his cell phone and dialed Nikki's number. Her greeting was cautious but he closed his eyes at the sound of her voice.

"It's me. Here's the short version. Just listen. Maggie Spritzer of the *Post* was staking out the NSA's house in Kalorama last night. She copied down two license plates belonging to Alexis Thorne and Myra Rutledge. She also spotted two women with dogs. Said dogs were racing around the NSA's front and back yard. In addition to all of that, those guys that Martin sicced on me paid her a visit and put her dog in the dog hospital and scared the living crap out of her. You're on a real slippery slope, Nik. It's all I know. Call me the first chance you get, OK?"

"Will do. Thanks, Maddie. I appreciate you calling."

Maddie? Nikki must be surrounded by people and didn't want them to know who she was talking to.

Jack felt the beginnings of a headache. Now what the hell was he supposed to do? He'd warned Nikki. He'd tried his best to bluff it through with Ted Robinson. He yanked at his cell phone and called Mark Lane. He didn't bother with pleasantries but got right to the point.

"I want you to put a tail on Ted Robinson at the *Post*. He just left here. He's probably on his way home but I figure he's going to head out to Kalorama after he takes care of his cats and has some dinner. His home address is in the Rolodex. Try to pick him up at home. Use Moody, he hates reporters. Tell him to call me on my cell on the hour. Just for tonight. I'll let you know if I want to continue tomorrow night. Thanks, buddy."

Jack looked down at his cluttered desk. Well, shit, all this crap would still be here tomorrow if he wanted to cut out now. He was still bristling at his defeat in court. What the hell was that dumb-ass cop thinking when he entered the guy's apartment without a search warrant? Probable cause, my ass. He looked in the corner where he'd tossed his briefcase. It would still be there tomorrow. He decided to go home to wait for Nikki's call. Tomorrow would damn well take care of itself.

* * *

Nikki slapped the cell phone shut. The others were looking at her expectantly. She would have to tell them something, improvise as she went along.

"That was Maddie, our . . . silent spy. She took it upon herself to go out to Kalorama to see if . . ." Nikki shrugged. "If there was anything to see. She said there was a parked car down at the end of Benton Street and she copied down the license plate and then cajoled a cop whom the office had represented at one time to run the plate. It belonged to a *Post* reporter named Maggie Spritzer. Before you can ask, I don't know if she saw us or not. If she did, she didn't let on to me. Maddie is the epitome of discretion. With all the drive-bys we did last night and with Kathryn and Alexis walking the dogs, I think it's safe to say she's got our license plate numbers and she might have seen Alexis and Kathryn clearly. Right now there is no way to know if she did or not." There was no way she could let the others know the rest of what Jack had told her.

Kathryn jammed her hands in her pockets. "So, what exactly does all this mean, Nikki? Are we on or are we off?"

Nikki looked to Myra and Charles. "I say we go for it and stop futzing around with drive-bys and stakeouts. Let's hit the place around eleven tomorrow night. We have all day tomorrow to firm up what we'll do. I still think we should do the flower thing. Myra and Yoko can do that in the morning. If they come up with any good intel, we can use it at night when we go in, but I think we should vote on it. The reason I think we should do it tomorrow is that if Spritzer is simply on a stakeout mode, she's not ready to go public."

Every hand in the war room shot upward, including Charles's.

"Then it's settled. All right, let's get busy and make our plans. We've got—" Nikki looked at her watch—"less than thirty hours to bring it all together. Get started. I'll be back in five minutes. I left my briefcase in the kitchen."

Jack answered his cell phone, his mouth full of chow mein. He gulped and swallowed. "I hope you took my message seriously. Are you going to call it off?"

"I took your message very seriously. We put it to a vote. But to answer your question, no, we are not going to call it off. Listen, Jack, I have to get back to the others. I'll try to call you later."

Jack looked at the cell phone in his hand and then down at the white box of shrimp chow mein. Damn, he hadn't even gotten to the hard noodles yet, or the sweet and sour soup. He closed up everything and stuck it in the refrigerator. Then he changed his clothes, hanging his suit up and pulling on fleece-lined sweatpants and a hooded sweatshirt. At the last minute he switched his black socks for heavy wool ones and put on his Nike running shoes. He jammed his keys and wallet into the zippered pocket of his sweatpants. His gun went into a second zippered pocket. It felt uncomfortable and yet comforting at the same time. If he stuck it in the back of his waistband he just might shoot off his ass. Better to be uncomfortable.

In the kitchen he looked down at his bottle of Tsingtao. He loved Chinese beer. Well, he wasn't about to give *that* up. Besides, he needed to think and not go off half-cocked. What was Nikki going to do? Maybe he could outthink her and head her off at the pass. Maybe he should consider what he would do if he were Nikki. For starters, he'd jump the gun. Knowing reporters were on the scene, he'd create a diversion of some kind to get rid of them. Then he'd storm the house on Kalorama and choke the life out of the fat little NSA. But that was him. Nikki and her merry band of cutthroats probably had a very well-thought-out plan of action. Since the shields were tailing everyone, the outcome could turn into a free-for-all with the girls going down for the count. Unless . . .

Jack drained the bottle of Tsingtao and longed for a second. Ah, well, he'd have something to look forward to when he got home.

Outside in the crisp October air, Jack sniffed. Somewhere, someplace, someone had burned leaves. It was against the law but nobody obeyed the law these days, he thought bitterly. It was blustery, the wind ripping through the naked branches of the trees. It was a scary, mournful sound to Jack's ears.

Jack looked up and down the street. He smiled at the lit pumpkins, knowing there were battery-operated flashlights inside the pumpkins instead of the little votive candles. The candles could never survive the wild wind that was kicking up. He hoped to hell it didn't rain.

On the short drive to Kalorama from Georgetown, Jack wondered why he was doing what he was doing. What a stupid thought. He was doing it for Nikki.

As Jack drove up and down the quiet streets he wondered how much money a person needed to live in one of these fine big old houses. The only way he'd ever be able to live in a place like this was if he won a lottery of some kind. As long as he stayed in law enforcement, that would never happen. The thought didn't make him unhappy. All he wanted was a house with a yard for kids and a dog, maybe a cat. A guest bedroom, a fireplace and a nice bathroom and kitchen would do the trick for him. Maybe a front porch so he and Nikki could sit out there on warm summer nights listening to the crickets and watching the fireflies. Holding hands, getting up every so often to check on the kids sleeping upstairs. The dog would be between them. It was all he wanted. He hoped he wasn't asking for too much. Well, if he was, he'd have to downsize, that's all.

Jack parked down at the end of 39th Street and Benton Street to wait. For what, he didn't know. When he started to get cold, he climbed out of the car, locked it, and jogged in place before he took off slowly so he could scan the neighborhood. The gun slapped against his leg but he ignored it. He knew in the morning his thigh was going to be black and blue. He would live with it. Some houses had lights on; others didn't. There were no lit pumpkins that he could see. The houses that were dark on the outside told him the occupants were probably in for the evening. Why waste electricity?

Jack continued to jog around the block and did a second jog past the Woodley house that was lit up like a Christmas tree. Did that mean the NSA was home or did it mean his lights came on with timers? When he started to sweat, he turned around and headed back down 39th Street and got in his car. A 1997 Jaguar passed him and then sailed up a driveway six car lengths from where he parked. With his window half down he could hear a garage door open and then close. He craned his neck to see if the outside light went out. It did. The people must be frugal. Maybe that's how you got rich, by being frugal. He hunkered down to wait.

Two more front lights went out, then a post light at the end of a driveway went out. The night turned to pitch black; the air was damp. The outside light on the Woodley house was still on. If he stayed here much longer he was going to freeze his ass off. He started the car's engine and drove to the nearest convenience store where he pulled out one of his prepaid phone cards and called the NSA's house. Sometimes he felt superior because he had the private number of every politician in Washington.

The phone rang seven times before Jack hung up. Either the NSA wasn't answering the phone or he simply wasn't home. Jack decided the guy used timers and wasn't home. A man in his position would have to answer his phone even if he carried one of the government's specially en-crypted phones.

Jack mulled over his situation as he sat quietly in his car. Everything appeared normal as far as he could see. He might as well go home to his Chinese food and Tsingtao. He didn't feel right leaving, but he didn't seem to have any other options at the moment.

He checked his cell phone to make sure it was still on. He hoped he would remember to charge it when he got back to the house. If there was one thing he wanted, it was not to miss Nikki's call.

Jack drove around the streets of Kalorama one last time but saw nothing out of the ordinary. It appeared the residents were socked in for the night just the way he should be—and would be in less than fifteen minutes.

He knew before he got out of the car that someone was waiting for him. He unzipped the pocket of his sweatpants. The cold steel of the gun felt good in his hand. He climbed out, waved the gun and yelled, "Good night, all!" He didn't feel half as brave as his voice sounded.

A voice came out of the darkness. "You had a regular parade tonight, Mr. Emery. Guess you're kind of tired. I'd like it if you'd tell me why you felt the need to go to Kalorama to jog when you have all these beautiful tree-lined streets here in Georgetown."

"You know what I would like? I'd like you to kiss my ass, you asshole. Make a move on me and I'll shoot you right in the gut. They say a man is never the same once he's shot in the gut;

can't poop or do any of those things we all take for granted. Hell, you might as well forget you ever knew the word 'sex'."

The man in the shadows ignored Jack's threat. "You had two tails tonight, *Mister* Emery. A Mr. Theodore Robinson was on your tail and a man named Moody was on his. I thought that was very curious. I wonder if you have an explanation."

Ted was tailing him. Well, shit, that really screwed things up. "Why don't you ask him? I'm tired from my jog. I'm going to bed. You should do the same thing unless you want to be carted out of here in an ambulance."

The soft chuckle in the shadows made the hair on Jack's neck stand straight up. He fumbled with his key, got the door opened and then he was inside. He bolted the door and set the alarm.

So, he hadn't fooled Ted after all. And Moody hadn't called him on the hour the way he was supposed to. Why in the damn hell didn't people do what they were supposed to do?

Nineteen

The ladies of Pinewood were dressed for the start of a very busy day.

Kathryn wagged her finger as she cast a critical eye over her hostess's attire. "The pearls have to go, Myra."

"Oh, dear, are you saying I'm overdressed? This is what I wore when we did our truck run."

"Yep, but minus the pearls. You're going to deliver flowers, so that means working duds like what you have on. No pearls."

"This is so exciting," Myra gushed. "I've been rehearsing ever since I got up. I'm driving to Yoko's nursery. She is going to drive the van. I'll ride shotgun like I did on our . . . our road trip. I'll deliver on one side of the street and Yoko will deliver on the other side. The magnetic decal for Yoko's van is in my car. All I have to do is . . .

ah . . . slap it on the side and Flowers For You is born. Kathryn, you went to the nursery and paid cash to one of the workers?" Kathryn nodded. "It's a good thing none of Yoko's employees speak or read English in case anyone . . . What's that phrase? Oh yes, *sniffs around.* I can do this. I'm not going to make notes about any conversations I have with our flower recipients. I will trust my memory. When I get back, I feel sure I will have something of merit to report. Charles, take care of my pearls. Goodbye, everyone!"

No one laughed until the door closed behind Myra.

"She's getting off on this," Isabelle said and giggled. "And she looks damn good in those jeans, too."

"I hope this works and they come back with some kind of information," Nikki muttered under her breath. "Charles, where is Mrs. Woodley?"

"She's where you spent the summer, in the islands. I have all her medical reports—even the ones where she went to hospitals using assumed names. I told her only what I wanted her to know. She asked very few questions but she will know how to respond should the authorities want to question her at some point in the future. My people will swear she's been there for months. Mrs. Woodley gave me, albeit reluctantly, her husband's private office number, his pager, his cell phone number, as well as their private unlisted number at home. She's very afraid of government people because of the power they hold."

Nikki reached for the accordion-pleated envelope, stunned at how heavy it was. She looked at Charles, who nodded solemnly. "Just about every bone in that woman's body has been either fractured, broken or traumatized. I took the liberty of marking all the breaks and fractures on the X-rays. The portable panel only needs to be plugged into an ordinary light socket to highlight the X-rays. You should put it in the car now to be sure you don't forget it. Never mind, it's heavy, I'll do it. Alexis, do you have everything you need?" he asked.

Alexis pointed to her red bag of tricks. "And then some, Charles."

"Good. I'll leave you all to your plans. I have things to do in the war room. If you need me, call."

"Let's take this upstairs so we can go over our plans again," Kathryn said. "I hate that bastard and I don't even know him. I just don't understand how a woman can let herself be battered like that, over and over again. I heard everything you said, Nikki, and part of me understands it, but another part of me refuses to comprehend allowing someone to beat you to a pulp. The lady was rich; all she had to do was walk out of the house after the son of a bitch left for work. She could have gone anywhere in the world."

"Fear and shame can be terrible, Kathryn. Maybe we'll never *really* know why Mrs. Woodley stayed. My guess is the NSA threatened to kill her and she wasn't ready to die. Maybe she knew no matter where she went, her husband would find her since he has all the resources at his disposal to do just that. The doctors told Charles yesterday that Mrs. Woodley is going to need years of intense therapy. The *why* of it can't concern us. We're going to make sure it never happens again. Now, let's get to it," Nikki said.

"First question," Alexis said as she dropped the red bag on the floor. "Are we or are we not going to call the NSA and say we're bringing Mrs. Woodley home and he should meet us?"

"It would certainly be to our advantage to have him *in* the house when we get there," Kathryn said. "The man is such a pig I'm thinking he'll want to be there to welcome his wife home so he can beat the crap out of her again once he shows us the door. Don't forget, he hasn't had anyone to punch out since Maddie whisked Mrs. Woodley away. Do we give it a shot or not?"

"I'm all for that," Nikki said. "However, give this some thought. None of us sound like Mrs. Woodley. If we call and say we're bringing her home, isn't he going to be suspicious? Won't he wonder why his wife isn't calling him herself? In addition to that, I'm sure Mrs. Woodley has instructions to never give out the NSA's numbers. Maybe we can have Charles intervene and actually have Mrs. Woodley call him at a specific time, even if it's just to leave a message. That will work if she agrees to do it."

The others concurred.

"Good. Let me call Charles in the war room and arrange it. What time do we want to make the call?" Nikki said.

"Sixish for the call. We go to the house at nine," Kathryn said. "If we get there and he isn't home, we go to Plan B, which is to park at a gas station so Alexis can fix up Isabelle to look like

Paula Woodley. Then we go back and are inside waiting for him."

"That works for me," Nikki said. The others nodded.

Their heads together, they watched as Alexis started to inventory the contents of her red bag. A wide grin spread across her face. "We got it covered, girls!"

Myra hopped out of the van with the agility of a thirty-year-old. She walked around to the back where Yoko was opening the panel doors. "Oh, my dear, these arrangements are lovely. All these people are going to be so surprised to get these beautiful flowers. I can hardly wait to deliver them."

"I am so glad you approve, Myra. I stayed up all night making them. I didn't skimp on the flowers. I wanted to feel proud when we deliver them. Take your clipboard. All they have to do is initial the space next to their address. When they ask who sent them, point to the Century 21 card and say it is a promotion the office is conducting."

Myra nodded as she picked up an arrangement and tucked the clipboard under her arm. She walked up the driveway and on to the front porch where she rang the bell. "A delivery for you, ma'am," she said when the woman opened the door. "Just initial here." She thrust out the clipboard.

The gray-haired lady smiled. "Oh, I do so hope these are from my son."

Myra smiled weakly. "No, ma'am, they're from

Century 21. They're doing a promotion. We're delivering to everyone on the street. You could help me a little, if you don't mind. I'm delivering on this side of the street. It's rather cold and I'm a little nervous about leaving flowers on the porch. The wind, the rain, that kind of thing."

"Yes, yes, I see your dilemma. Just about everyone is home or their housekeepers are inside. Except for the Woodleys. He's the National Security Advisor, you know."

"No, no, I didn't know that. Are you saying I should leave their flowers with a neighbor?" Myra asked.

"I suppose so. I did so want these flowers to be from my son. Wait just a minute."

The minute turned into five. Myra used the time to scan the neighborhood. She had five houses to go before she could see the Woodleys' place. She turned when the woman opened the door again to hand her two dollars. Myra looked at the money in the woman's hand. "It's a tip. Even though the flowers aren't from my son."

"A tip! Ah, yes. Thank you. I'm sorry the flowers weren't from your son."

"Oh, well, maybe he'll send some for Thanksgiving."

"What's your son's name, ma'am?"

"Anthony," the woman said before she closed the door.

Myra made a note on her clipboard. She'd send the woman some flowers from Anthony.

The next four deliveries went like clockwork. Myra gleaned no information, but she did make twelve dollars in tips, to her amazement. She could hardly wait to tell Charles.

The house next to the Woodleys' was almost an exact replica, at least on the outside. A giant of a man opened the door. When he saw the flowers in Myra's hands, he bellowed over his shoulder, "Mother, there's someone here with flowers."

A pretty little lady with clicking dentures, rosy cheeks and flour on her hands appeared. "Goodness gracious, come in, come in. It's so windy out there. Now, aren't these pretty! Who in the world would be sending John and me flowers?"

Myra gave her practiced speech, then said, "You must be baking bread."

"I am. John insists. He won't eat store-bought anything. I can't believe he left you standing outside like that. Men!" she huffed. "If you like homemade bread, I can give you a loaf. In lieu of the tip for delivering the flowers."

"I'll take it," Myra said smartly.

"Come along then and watch me wrap it up. Would you care for a cup of coffee?"

"No, thank you. I have a lot of deliveries to make. Do you happen to know if your neighbors are home?"

The woman clicked her dentures. "You mean the Woodleys? He is the National Security Advisor to the President of the United States. He and his wife don't bother with us common folk. Honey, I can't tell you if anyone is home or not. He leaves in the dark and comes home in the dark. The last time I saw Mrs. Woodley was a year ago. She must have some crippling arthritis, because she could hardly walk. She was a gymnast when she was young. I imagine she abused her body and now is paying the price. And she wears a hearing aid. One never knows if they're home or not. They never have company."

"That's a shame. Oh, this bread smells heavenly. Thank you so much. Do you think I should leave their flowers on the porch or possibly around back?" Before the woman could answer, Myra leaned forward and whispered, "What's it like to live next door to someone so important? Does the President ever visit, or some of those other important people? Mr. Woodley must have all kinds of security, Secret Service, that kind of thing."

The chubby little woman laughed. "No and no," she said. "John thought for sure there would be all kinds of security around them but there isn't. A car does pick up the NSA at five thirty every morning. Usually seven days a week. The drapes and shades are always closed on the first floor, so I guess that's their security. Like everyone else on the street, they have an alarm system. I've never heard it go off."

Sensing the woman had little more to offer, Myra made her way to the front door, the loaf of bread in her hand.

"John, say goodbye to our guest."

"Goodbye!" the bear bellowed. Mama bear rolled her eyes as she closed the door behind Myra.

Back at the van for her next delivery, Myra held up her loaf of bread. "It's a tip! Doesn't it smell marvelous? I found out a little information but not much. Let's finish this up so we can call Charles."

"I finished my side of the street, so I will help you," Yoko said. "You do the Woodley house and I will do the three beyond it and then we can leave. It's really getting cold. I think it feels like snow. Maybe just a cold rain."

"More likely snow. As Nikki would say, that sounds like a plan. How much did you make in tips?"

Yoko laughed. "Twenty dollars! But you got a loaf of bread!"

Myra walked up the Woodleys' driveway. She looked all around as she tripped her way to the front porch and rang the bell. She stayed there just long enough, in case anyone was watching, to show she was simply a delivery person. She walked down the steps and around to the back, making a careful note of everything she saw. A coiled-up hose was nestled against the side of the house. No one would trip over that in the dark. The backyard had a picnic table that was in need of paint sitting under a maple tree. It looked lopsided to Myra. The patio was bare except for a rusty outdoor grill that was pushed up against the house. There was a storm door that was locked, the blind on the inside door closed. All the windows were shuttered. Myra rang the bell several times. When there was no answer, she walked around to the front and back up to the front porch where she left the flowers by the door.

Five minutes later the white van left Benton Street.

"I found this whole experience enlightening, Yoko. People really do love to get flowers. We should do this again sometime. There's a whole world out here I never got to experience. Instead of saying 'let them eat cake,' we should say 'send them flowers.'"

Yoko had no idea what Myra was talking about. She just smiled.

Jack stuffed half a hot dog in his mouth, mustard and sauerkraut dribbling down his chin. He chewed carefully, his narrowed eyes on Moody.

"If I had known this hot dog stand was what you meant by lunch, I would have declined. Those things will kill you. Do you have any idea what's *in* a hot dog?" asked Moody.

"No, and I don't want to know either. When I leave an order for you to call me on the hour, I mean on the hour. I don't want to have to chase you down."

Moody grimaced. When he spoke it was as though he were talking to a backward child. "Jack, Robinson was tailing you and I was tailing Robinson, so in actuality, I was tailing you, too. Think about it. Did you really want me calling you and have Robinson see you talking on your cell when you were somewhere you probably weren't supposed to be to begin with? And for your information, Jack, I had a tail on me, too. We were a regular fucking parade out there in Kalorama. Under the circumstances, I used my best judgment. Fire me. See if I care, but pay me first."

"Where and when did you pick up Robinson,

and when did you notice your own tail?" Jack shoved the rest of the hot dog in his mouth and motioned for the vendor to make him another one. Moody opted for a salted pretzel.

"I picked up the news hound at his apartment and followed him to where you're staying in Georgetown. We followed you when you left. I didn't pick up the tail until we were almost at Kalorama. Whoever they are, they're good."

Jack chomped down on his second hot dog. It was every bit as good as the first one. Now he was going to have heartburn all afternoon.

"I might need you tonight, Moody. Stay available and keep your cell phone on. It will be a last-minute thing, if at all. You got that?"

"I'm not stupid, Jack, I got it. Stay available and keep my cell phone on. You're a pain in the ass, you know that?"

"I've been called worse." Jack eyed the hot dog vendor and couldn't make up his mind if he should go for a third dog or call it quits. "Gimme one of those hot pretzels."

As he walked back to the courthouse, Jack wondered if there was a way for him to track the NSA's movements. It was a stupid thought. He needed to call Nikki but the last four times he'd called, she hadn't answered her cell phone. He didn't have to be a rocket scientist to know what that meant. They were going to do their thing tonight.

And where did that goddamn nosy reporter get off tailing *him?*

Twenty

The ladies of Pinewood scurried to their chairs when the time appeared on the Fox Network screen in front of them. Charles had pressed the mute button, so no sound emerged. The time was one minute to six. As one, the women sucked in their breath. When the time rolled over to precisely six o'clock, they exhaled. The minutes ticked by. The silence in the room roared in their ears. At seven minutes past six, Charles's phone rang. He listened, his expression blank. All he said was "thank you," before he ended the call.

"Mrs. Woodley had to leave a message. Before you can ask, let me explain about the call to the NSA. Because he has the ability to trace the call, my people bounced the call off a satellite. There is no way he can find out where the call came from. Maybe a year from now, if his people worked on it twenty-four-seven, he might come up with it, but I doubt it." Charles chuckled. "Mrs. Woodley is safe. What we don't know is what time the NSA will check his messages. With nothing going on in the news, I take it to be a slow day, security-wise. I rather imagine he will check them shortly. I have one of my people watching both entrances to his office. I'll know within minutes if he leaves. He left the White House a little after two this afternoon and has been in his office since.

"Mrs. Woodley volunteered a few tidbits. I think you'll find them interesting. There is a yellow light over the walk-through garage door. It was Mrs. Woodley's job to turn it on at twilight. If the light is on, as it always is, the security drive-bys during the evening know everything is all right. Be sure to check to see if it's on. The second thing is that the NSA *does* wear a security bracelet but it's on his ankle, under his sock. It has a spring lock, quite easy to remove, according to Mrs. Woodley. The panic button, for want of a better word, is under the spring clasp. You'll want to remove that posthaste. This," Charles said, withdrawing a hypodermic syringe, "will literally freeze him in a nanosecond. It lasts two minutes. That's all the time you have to remove the bracelet. You can jab him anywhere. Do not ask what this is or where I got it," he said.

Nikki felt her heart give a little jump when Charles handed the syringe to her. She pocketed it without changing her facial expression. "What if that reporter, or maybe those high-security people, are prowling around out there? Our license plates can be checked."

Charles sighed. "There are two cars sitting outside our gates right now, right this minute. One is a Mustang with a Minnesota license plate. The identical plate that is on Carolyn Movani's car back in Minnesota. Miss Movani was one of Mrs. Woodley's fellow Olympic gymnasts from years ago. The other car is a Chevy Suburban with an Ohio license plate. Identical to Betty Ann Openhimer, Mrs. Woodley's best friend in college. I'm sure the NSA will recognize both ladies' married names. If not, their first names will register. The important thing is that if the plates are run, they match to the names."

"How do you do that?" Isabelle demanded.

Charles smiled but he didn't answer.

"I think it's time for dinner," Myra said. "We're eating light this evening. Sandwiches on fresh homemade bread. My tip." She gurgled with laughter. "I can hardly wait to taste that bread."

The others laughed as Myra led the way out of the war room and into the kitchen. They all pitched in, with Kathryn slicing ham, Alexis cutting the fresh bread, Isabelle setting the table, Nikki making coffee and Myra spreading the bread with assorted condiments. Charles, his cell phone to his ear, walked around as he listened to someone on the other end.

Finally, Charles took his place at the table and reached for a sandwich. "I will be joining you this evening. More or less. I will be stopping by to thank the lovely lady for the tasty loaf of bread Myra brought home. At least, that's my plan at the moment. As you know, things change rapidly when we're down to the wire. The lady does make good bread," Charles said as he reached for a second sandwich.

After they'd eaten, the women worked together to tidy the kitchen. From time to time, one or another of them would let her gaze go to the digital clock on the stove. Charles's cell phone remained silent. Myra poured coffee into clean cups, not so much because anyone wanted coffee, but because they could toy with the cup, twirl it around on the saucer to give them something to do. Time was moving too slowly. There didn't seem to be a need for conversation. The time was ten minutes past eight.

"The fact that my phone isn't ringing doesn't mean anything, ladies. The NSA could very well have gotten his wife's message. Perhaps he can't get away as quickly as he would like. I will call you if I receive a call once you're on your way. Remember, from here on in, anything can go wrong, so be prepared. Pay attention to your instincts and remember the kind of person we're dealing with. Now, it's time to make the necessary changes to your appearance. Alexis, you have exactly thirty minutes," Charles said, looking at his watch.

Alexis went to work. It took her exactly five minutes to turn Myra into a buck-toothed harridan with corkscrew gray hair, thanks to two mini wiglets. Tinted glasses that she perched on her nose jiggled when she moved. Isabelle was transformed into a street girl with a skimpy spandex dress that she could have stuffed in her ear if she needed to hide it. Her makeup was theatrical, as was the jewelry that she wore by the pound. She clinked and clanked as she moved around. The black fishnet stockings had a hole in the right knee.

Kathryn's cheeks were filled with cotton balls, a small adjustment that changed her appearance completely. She now wore a blonde wig that swirled and twirled when she moved her head.

With a little spirit gum and a black kohl pencil, Nikki's eyes took on an Asian cast. Her wig was long and shiny black with a severe row of bangs down to her eyebrows. She looked nothing like Nikki Quinn.

Yoko stepped forward to slip into a sack dress the color of putty. A skullcap made of shimmering silver slipped down over her head and matched her new huge silver glasses that covered almost her entire face.

With eight minutes to spare, Alexis raced into the bathroom off the laundry room to alter her own appearance. When she returned, everyone gasped. Her chin was longer, her eyebrows more pronounced, her bosom larger. She now sported inch-long fingernails that looked like talons. Her dark hair was now a mysterious shade of orange-brown to match her orange-brown eyes. Hollywood had missed a bet when they cast Halle Berry as Catwoman.

Charles looked them over carefully. He nodded with approval as he held the door for them, careful to lock it behind him. Murphy barked sharply, angry at being left behind.

Charles's cell phone was still silent. He sat in

his car and waited for the gate to open. He could see the two cars with the out-of-state license plates go down the mile-long driveway.

The ladies of Pinewood were on the move.

Jack Emery ran around, turning on all the lights in Nikki's house. He looked at his watch just as the doorbell rang. He raced to open it. Mark Lane entered, carrying a bag of food and a six pack of Heineken beer. The next guest to arrive was Moody, also carrying a six pack of beer: Budweiser. Five minutes later, Carmody showed up carrying a shopping bag of food and a six pack of Coors Light. Boys' night in. Well, almost. *This* boy was leaving as soon as he could get himself together.

"You know the drill. Make a fire in the living room. Those guys will see and smell the smoke. An indication we're in for the evening. The drapes are closed in the living room. Will it work? I don't know, but I gotta get out of here with no one seeing me. I'm going out the laundry-room window. I turned off the lights in the kitchen and the laundry room. Be sure to answer the phone in case I call. On the first ring. You got that?" Three heads bobbed up and down in unison. "Where'd you park that pickup truck, Moody?"

"On Dunbarton. Here's the key."

Jack pocketed the key. A minute later he was out the window, closing it softly. He dropped to the ground, barely making a sound. He was dressed all in black, so he knew he blended with the dark night. He yanked at the black watch cap, pulling it down over his ears. He waited till his eyes grew accustomed to the darkness before he took off, running through the neighbors' yards. He was almost to Dunbarton when he stopped dead in his tracks. Why the hell was he doing this? Ted had a date with Maggie Spritzer tonight. Christ, how could he have forgotten that? Overload, that's how. Good old Ted wasn't going to be out in Kalorama freezing his ass off. Right now the only thing on Ted's mind was how to get Maggie back to his apartment and into his bed. That left only the shields to worry about. They were out there somewhere; he knew it as surely as he knew what his destination was. Well, there were only three of them.

Jack eyed the battered pickup with the lawn-mower and six bags of peat moss in the back. He climbed in, turned the key and listened to the engine grind and protest. It took him five tries before the truck sputtered to life. Even with the windows closed he could smell the junk spewing from the tailpipe. It would be just his luck to get a ticket for polluting the air. He peeled away from the curb at a rousing five miles an hour. He knew in his gut that if he tried goosing the truck past fifteen miles an hour it would stall out on him, never to be started again. As he chugged along he tried calling Nikki again and again. A generic voice finally came on and said the customer he was trying to reach was out of the area.

"Out of the area, my ass." He knew that Nik must have turned her phone off.

It was five minutes to nine when Jack hit Kalorama. The first thing he saw was Ted Robinson and Maggie Spritzer sitting in a champagne-colored Honda Civic. He chugged past them, turning his face to the right so they wouldn't see him. *Shit.* If Ted was here that meant the shields were here, too. So much for trying to elude every-one. He felt like a jerk. He chugged to the cor-ner of Calvert and Unlaw and parked. He climbed out and headed for Benton, careful to stay in the shadows. He was three doors away from the NSA's house, hiding under a thick evergreen tree, when he saw a Crown Victoria turn into the Woodleys' driveway. Must be the NSA, he thought. He held his breath, waiting to see if it was Woodleys' dri-ver or Woodley himself. In the still night he heard a door close and then the headlights of the Crown Victoria swept across the yard as it backed up and went down the street. It looked like the NSA was home for the night. Now what the hell was he supposed to do?

Was he here on a wild goose chase? Jack poked his head out of the spreading yew to see if he could spot anything. The street was dark and silent. He decided to wait a few more min-utes before melting into the backyards that would take him back to the ancient pickup truck. That's when he saw the two cars almost bumper to bumper on the street behind him. The moment both cars turned on 39th, he knew who it was. Sure-ly they'd do a drive-by. Surely that's what they would do. He was counting on Nikki's honed in-stincts. He clenched his teeth in frustration as he waited.

The cell phone was in Jack's hand a second

later. He dialed the local police and said, "This is Harry Davis at 3244 Benton Street. There's a suspicious car parked on the street and it's been there since it got dark. There are two people in it. I'd like you to check it out. Like *now*, officer." He was told a patrol car would be on the street within minutes. From his position under the spreading yew, Jack could see the red and blue flashing lights on the street behind within minutes. Then he heard the siren. He saw the two cars that he was sure held the ladies of Pinewood pull to the side of the road to allow the cruiser to take the corner.

"C'mon, c'mon, drive by, Nik." He almost fainted in relief when he saw the two cars continue down Unlaw Road. He turned back in time to see the police cruiser swerve in front of the champagne-colored Honda Civic. A moment later he saw Ted and Maggie exit the car. He almost laughed. Some date this was.

Now, if he could just figure out where the shields were, he could go home happy. Maybe he lucked out and they didn't know he was out here. Oh, yeah, and pigs fly. He watched as Ted and Maggie got back in the car and drove away. He knew Ted was cursing up a storm. Maggie probably was, too. They'd get over it.

Jack sat back on his haunches. The women would be back because they had a plan. He just wasn't privy to that exact plan. He yanked out his cell phone, squeezed his eyes shut as he tried to remember the number he'd called the night he'd visited Ted in the hospital. "My house, forty-five minutes." He dropped down lower into the spreading yew and continued to whisper. "Are you sure you got all this? OK, I'll be waiting. Here's the address. I left the laundry-room window unlocked. Try not to be late."

Nikki wiped at the sweat beading on her forehead. "Damn, that was close." She pulled into the Mobil station, parked and waited for the car with the Ohio license plates to park alongside her.

Isabelle poked her head out the window and said, "Charles called and said the NSA is home. The yellow light is on over the door. The cops won't be back for a while if they're on patrol. Let's just go for it! He's waiting for his wife so he's going to open the door. Remember, Myra said the storm door at the back was locked so we can't sneak in and he probably has his alarm system turned on. The front door is our best bet. Bold as brass. Just have that needle in your hand."

Nikki thought about it for a full minute. "OK, let's do it." She backed up and waited for a break in traffic before she pulled out on to 37th Street, Alexis right behind her.

"Thith ith tho exthiting," Myra gurgled as she tried to get her tongue to work around the chipmunk false teeth. Nikki burst out laughing and couldn't stop. Kathryn pounded her on the back but she was laughing herself.

"For God's sake, Myra, don't talk or we'll blow this gig by laughing our heads off," Kathryn said.

Myra offered a thumbs up as she nodded.

"Here we go. Everyone out on the count of three. The porch light is on. He's expecting his wife." Nikki cut the engine at the same time Alexis did. "One, two, three, and we're out of here." The syringe in her hand, the cap off, Nikki led the parade up the walkway and on to the small front porch. She drew in her breath as she pushed the doorbell. She could hear it chime inside. She counted the seconds. One, two, three, four, five, six, seven, eight. The door opened. Her first crazy thought was that he was a pissant and probably the ugliest man she'd ever seen.

"Mr. Woodley, I'm Betty Ann Openhimer, Paula's friend. We brought her home."

Woodley's voice was a deep baritone. "Well, where is she?"

Nikki looked over her shoulder. "Paula, honey, your husband can't see you." Quicker than lightning she moved forward, the needle going into the NSA's neck, just under his ear. He tilted forward but Kathryn caught him and dragged him backward into the house. The others piled in. It took two seconds to shove him on to the foyer settee, another three seconds to remove the ankle bracelet and another three to lock and bolt the front door.

"Damn, we're good. We have time to spare," Alexis said. "OK, let's get him over to the couch. Who has the flexi cuffs?"

Nikki yanked the flexi cuffs out of her pocket and tossed them to Alexis. The NSA was cuffed and dumped on the couch within seconds. "OK, scatter, ladies, and let's check out this place. Ten minutes. Alexis, give me that panel and the X-rays. I'll set it up on the mantel. There's an electrical outlet just above it. I can do it myself; do what you have to do. He's coming around. Quick, cuff one of his legs to that pine table." Nikki tossed a second set of flexi cuffs to Alexis. She finished just as the NSA started to shake his big head like a wet bear.

"What the hell . . . ! Is this a home invasion?"

Alexis, all six foot three of her, stood at attention. "I prefer to call it a par-tee. A sort of come-to-Jesus meeting. Shut up and speak only when we address you." To make her point, she whacked him across the face so hard his big head rolled backward.

"Stop!" came the commanding voice. "Do you have any idea who I am?"

"Oh, yeah," Nikki drawled. "We know *exactly* who you are. You're the son of a bitch who beats up his wife. Well, Mr. National Security Advisor, we're here to even up that score."

Isabelle strolled into the room. The NSA blinked and then blinked again at her slutty appearance. "The guy has twelve, count 'em, twelve Hugo Boss suits. The gray one will look real nice to get laid out in. They have gray caskets now. Bronze used to be the in color but I read that the silvery-gray is a good seller. Yeah, the gray suit. Red tie. Red's a power tie. Befitting this little shit. Maybe a gray shirt."

"Gray it is!" Alexis said cheerfully. "How you doing over there?" she shouted to Nikki.

"I demand you stop this instantly. I'll . . . I'll . . . You can't get away with this."

"Helloooo there, Mr. National Security Advisor. You need to get with the program. We're here, and you're sitting there begging us to let you go. That means we *are* getting away with it," Isabelle said. "You ready?" she shouted to Nikki.

"Got it all ready," Nikki responded. She waited for the others to join her.

"The place is clean," Yoko said. She handed out latex gloves to everyone. The women made a production of pulling them on and snapping them into place.

"Who wants to tell this son of a bitch why we're here?" Nikki said.

"Me!" Kathryn said. "We're here, Mr. National Security Advisor, to give you a real taste of your own medicine. What that means, you sick bastard, is this: we're going to do everything to you that you've done to your wife, Paula. Hit it, girl!"

Nikki could have been a doctor or a technician the way she slapped the first X-ray on to the lighted panel. "This little work of art is from 1987. Fractured collarbone. I have another one almost just like this where the collarbone is *shattered*. But we'll get to that later." The women all watched in silence as Nikki continued with X-ray after X-ray. "And this particular masterpiece is when you ruptured your wife's eardrum. I think you get the picture, Mr. National Security Advisor."

The NSA tried to lean forward. Yoko grabbed his hair but it came off in her hands. She tried not to laugh as the man tried to reach for it with his cuffed hands. She clipped him on the side of the head before she grabbed for both ears and held them tight in her tiny hands.

"Stop this instant. Do you know who I am? I'll

have you locked in prison for the rest of your life. The President of the United States is my best friend."

"Name-dropper," Kathryn said. "Just out of curiosity, how are you going to do anything? Look around you. There's five of us. There's one of you. We have weapons and you're handcuffed. In my book, that means we got you! You ain't going nowhere, you little piece of shit! When we're done with you, you aren't even going to know your own name. Now, shut up."

The women used up five minutes as they arranged a grouping of Queen Anne chairs so that they could all face the NSA. Nikki pointed to the huge red bag. Alexis opened it and withdrew a long serrated carving knife and a thick, heavy book. She handed the knife to Kathryn as she took her seat and opened the book. The NSA's face was bone white, his eyes frantic as he struggled on the sofa.

"All right," Alexis said as she opened the book and pretended to read. "This is how you cut up a whole chicken. Same principle as cutting up a body. First you spread the legs wide and cut downward on the joint. Then you do the other leg. That leaves you with the torso and the wings, which you then cut at the joint in the same manner."

"How long will it take for him to bleed out?" Isabelle asked as she picked at the hole in her fishnets.

"Thath methie," Myra said.

"Oh, well, what's a little mess? We'll be leaving and won't have to clean it up. But to answer your question, maybe five minutes. Ten at the most. What's it say in the book?" Nikki asked.

"Well, the chicken is dead so it can't bleed out. Let's go with eight minutes," Alexis said.

The NSA tried to twist his head but Yoko leaped up and chopped at his neck. He ceased struggling but only for a moment.

"Where's my wife? Did she put you up to this? You're all wrong about this. What do you want?"

"Now, if we tell you that, we'll have to kill you," Isabelle singsonged. The hole in the fishnets was getting bigger by the minute as she kept picking at it.

"Continue," Nikki said to Alexis.

Happiness rang in Alexis's voice. "OK. We did the wings, right? OK, now we have the rest of the carcass. You flip it over and cut down the sides. Then you flatten the breast and slice down the middle. Oh, shoot, I forgot. You have to cut off the part that goes over the fence last." She made a slicing motion with her hand. "You know, the private parts. That's it. Anyone have any questions?"

It appeared no one had any questions.

Nikki stood up. "Take off the flexi cuffs. Do his leg first. If he behaves, we'll take off the wrist cuffs."

Kathryn bent down to undo the flexi cuff on the NSA's ankle. His foot shot upward, narrowly missing Kathryn's head.

"Try something like that again, you piece of crap, and they'll be carrying you out of here in a body bag." She balled up her fist and socked him in the middle of his fat stomach. He cursed as he doubled forward. "Not so tough, are you?" Kathryn reached out for the man's ankle, gave it a twist sideways and didn't release her grip until she heard the bone snap. The NSA squealed like a stuck pig. "Is that how your wife sounded when you beat her?"

Kathryn bounded to her feet. "Look how brave he is! I'm impressed. Are you all impressed? That's bone number one."

Yoko hopped off her chair and ran behind the couch to grab the NSA's neck in both her little hands. "Answer the question or I'll do to your neck what she just did to your foot. Now, are you impressed with my colleagues' expertise?"

His teeth clenched, his face white, the NSA said, "Fuck you!"

"What a guy! No guts, no glory, Mr. National Security Advisor. I wonder if the Prez would still consider you his best friend if he could see you right now. Show him we mean business," Kathryn said to Yoko.

Yoko's hands slipped down under Woodley's arms. She pulled and lifted him backward, giving Isabelle a perfect shot at his rib cage with the billy club. She took it, and then tossed it to Nikki. The pig in Woodley squealed so loudly that Myra clapped her hands over her ears.

"Isn't it time for a coffee break?" Alexis asked.

"Why, yes, it is." Nikki pulled the small .22 caliber gun out of her backpack. She stood back, took careful aim, but didn't fire. Instead, in the blink of an eye she brought down the billy club on Woodley's kneecap. She waved the gun again and fired off a shot, missing Woodley's ear by a hair. "That should take care of his eardrum. He ruptured his wife's eardrum. She wears a hearing aid. How many bones does a crushed kneecap count? Oh, I must have nicked his ear. That's a lot of blood."

"Not enough. Yeah, it is a lot of blood. And here we sit with no Band-Aids," Kathryn snapped. "I'll make the coffee."

Everyone called out their sugar and cream orders as Nikki watched the blood soak through the NSA's trousers.

"Oh, look, he's got a bone sticking out of his knee. Looks like it's in slivers."

"Ith methie," Myra said.

"Do we care?" Nikki asked.

Myra pushed the chipmunk teeth higher on her upper gum. "No!" she said clearly and distinctly.

Twenty-One

The women sipped at coffee they didn't want. "I couldn't find any cookies," Kathryn said. "Guess this guy eats out since his slave isn't here to cater to him.

"Hey, you, Mr. National Security Advisor, look alive here. We want to talk to you and we don't want to hear any cussing. We're going to ask each question once. If you don't respond instantly, we'll break another bone. Whatever you do, don't confuse us with someone who might care about how much pain you're in." Kathryn jerked her head in Isabelle's direction and made clicking noises. Isabelle got up to get a disposable camera out of Alexis's red bag. "Be sure you get all the blood."

"Tell us why you beat your wife, Mr. Woodley."

"Anger," came the response, right on cue. "You

have to call a doctor. I could bleed to death. Please," he begged.

Nikki pretended to consider the request. "No. You don't deserve a doctor. How long have you been abusing your wife?"

"Since we got married. Please. I'll never do it again."

"That's a lie and we both know it. Don't lie to me again. I hate liars." Nikki looked at Kathryn. "Take off his cuffs. He isn't going anywhere."

"Did your wife beg you to stop when you were beating her?"

"Yes."

"Did you stop?"

"No."

"I'm not going to stop either." In the blink of an eye, Nikki whipped out the billy club and whacked him in the elbow. The breaking bone made a loud popping sound. All the women looked on with clinical interest as the NSA's body catapulted upward then bounced down on the sofa.

"Get his head! Get his face!" Alexis shouted to Isabelle who was busy snapping pictures. The NSA was crying, his hairpiece clutched in his good hand. She walked over to the whimpering man, took the hairpiece, plopped it on his head. Crooked, of course.

Isabelle giggled as she clicked and clicked. "Tell me this isn't a Kodak moment!"

"It's a Kodak moment," Nikki agreed. "You almost killed your wife the last time and you walked out and left her. Why did you do that?"

"I was angry," the NSA gasped.

"Guess what? I'm angry, too." Nikki walked over to the mantel to pick up the tall metal candlestick the NSA had beaten his wife with. She tossed it to Kathryn who caught it in midair. Woodley held up his good arm to ward off the blow he knew was coming.

"Big mistake." Kathryn brought down the candlestick on his shoulder. She winced at the sound of crushing bones.

"He blacked out," Yoko said.

"Well, we'll just have to fix that right now." Kathryn stomped her way to the kitchen to return with the leftover coffee. It was still hot when she poured it over the man's head. Coffee dripped from the crooked hairpiece. Yoko clapped her hands in approval.

Woodley opened his eyes. "Please. Stop. I can't stand the pain. Call a doctor. I won't tell anyone what you look like."

"Is that what your wife said? Only in your dreams will you get a doctor. I don't like your nose, Mr. Woodley, or your teeth."

"Oh, Jesus, please don't do this. Why are you doing this to me?"

"You can't be that stupid. You beat your wife to within an inch of her life. You terrorized her. She lived in fear of you. For whatever reason, she felt powerless to stop you. As you can see, we are not powerless. We are *women*. Women are doing this to you." Nikki jerked her head at Kathryn.

Kathryn did a pirouette and swung the metal candlestick. Teeth and cartilage flew in all directions.

"He blacked out again," Alexis said. "He still has his hips, one good knee and his fingers. How many pictures you got left, girl? Ooh, and the ribs on his other side."

"Seven," Isabelle responded.

"Allow me," Yoko said, stepping forward. The others watched as her tiny hands reached for the NSA's right hand. One by one she broke every finger.

"Wake him up," Nikki ordered. Alexis ran to her bag for smelling salts. She waved them under the NSA's nose.

"Look alive, Mr. Woodley. Tell me what I want to hear. I want to hear you tell me you're sorry for what you did to your wife. I'm waiting."

"I'm . . ."

"You're what?"

"He blacked out again," Alexis said.

"Wake him up," Nikki said. Alexis waved the smelling salts.

"Go to fucking hell!" the revived NSA screamed.

"Did you hear that? Did you *hear* that?" Isabelle squealed as she snapped the last picture with the throwaway camera.

"We're outta here. Clean up, ladies. We weren't wearing the latex when we arrived. Clean everything. Quick."

The ladies of Pinewood worked in unison as they gathered up everything they'd brought with them. They were at the door when Nikki asked, "Where's the security bracelet?" Isabelle pointed to the table in the foyer.

"Yoko, give us time to dump this stuff in the car and back out to the road. Isabelle, you go one way, I'll go the other way. Yoko, take the bracelet to the bathroom, activate the panic button and then drop it in the toilet. We should have five minutes to get away before his security arrives. Run like hell. All right, let's go."

The car with the Ohio license plates was already moving when Yoko leaped into the front seat.

The ladies of Pinewood were on the move. Again.

Jack didn't know when he'd last been this cold. He felt like he was rooted to the ground under the spreading yew. One hour and ten minutes was all it had taken the ladies of Pinewood to do whatever the hell they'd done. They were gone now, on their way back to Pinewood, he figured. Time for him to leave, too. He struggled to stand upright, his cell phone an open line.

"OK, I'm ready." He heard the cars before he actually saw them. The screech of tires told him he was a minute too late. He stepped back into the shadows and waited, hardly daring to breathe. Car doors swung open; men emerged, guns drawn as they ran at full throttle up the walkway, up the steps to the porch. In the dim whitish glow of the porch light, Jack was able to make out the faces of the men with the drawn guns. Like he really didn't know who they were.

He heard the motorcycle at the end of the street. Well, it was now or never. He hunched down and ran like the hounds of hell were on his heels. The cycle barely stopped as he leaped on the back. The three men on the porch turned. Two went inside and the third one ran to his car.

Jack clamped the extra helmet on his head with his free hand, the other securely around the waist of the driver of the Harley. "Make these wheels fly, mister. That's a Fed on our tail."

The Harley ate up the road, going through stop signs and red lights. They made it back to the alley behind Nikki's house in Georgetown in eleven minutes. The driver parked the cycle and both men ran to the house and crawled through the laundry-room window.

Jack cringed when he saw the mess in Nikki's living room. He barked orders as he stripped down. Minutes later he was dressed in a pair of plaid flannel pants and a Georgetown sweatshirt.

"I've been here all night," he said, reaching for a beer. He looked around at the expectant faces of his friends and his new friends. He issued orders like a general. The men scattered, leaving Mark and himself in front of the fire. Jack eyed his shoulder holster that he'd dumped on the chair in the living room.

The doorbell rang. Mark flinched. Jack took his time finishing the rest of his beer. He popped another one, took a swig as he sauntered to the door. "Showtime, guys!" he called over his shoulder. He looked out the side panel before he opened the door.

"You're a little late. The party's over, but then I bet you already know that. What the hell do you want now?"

The tall man shouldered his way inside.

"Just a goddamn minute. Do you have a warrant?"

"I don't need a warrant, Emery."

"Yeah, you do, you asshole."

Before he knew what was happening, the intruder was surrounded by dark figures clad in Ninja attire. His gun, his special shield, his keys, his cell phone, and everything in his pockets were tossed onto the coffee table.

"First rule of law enforcement, you asshole, is you never give up your gun. What's the Prez going to think when he hears we took you?" Jack said.

"Don't do this, Emery; you're in enough hot water."

The agent's phone rang, saving Jack from a reply. "I'm going to let you answer the call, but I want to hear what you say. If you utter so much as one word I don't approve of, this big guy behind me is going to crush your larynx. Tell me you understand."

"I understand."

"No matter what your buddy says, this is what you say: 'I'm at Emery's. He was the guy on the cycle. Get over here.' Got it? OK, click it on and make sure I can hear."

The agent, his eyes twitching, brought the cell phone to his ear. "Yeah, what?"

"Never mind *what*. Where the hell are you?"

"Emery was the guy on the cycle. I went after him. You need to get over here."

"Yeah, well, our hands are a little full right now. Somebody busted into the NSA's house and damn near killed him. He's pretty busted up. I think every bone in his body is broken. He's out of it, but he keeps saying a bunch of women invaded his home."

Jack pinched the agent's neck and nodded. The agent repeated, "I told you, you need to get over here."

Jack reached over to take the phone. He cut off the call.

"What do you think you're doing, Emery? You can't possibly think you're going to get away with this. The President himself will throw the switch on you."

"Yeah, yeah, yeah. Somebody shut this guy up."

One of the dark-clad figures raised his hand and chopped down on the agent's neck. He crumpled and dropped to the ground with a thump.

"And to think we don't even know this guy's name," Jack muttered.

Fifteen minutes and two beers later, the doorbell rang again. The agent was sitting up on the floor, massaging his neck.

"I think you should answer the door, Special Agent whatever the hell your name is. I'll plug you right in the spine if you even blink your eyes when you open that door. Say 'Thank you, Mr. Emery.' "

"Fuck you," the agent said as he shambled to the door. He stopped when he heard the hammer slide back on Jack's gun. "Thank you, Mr. Emery."

Jack felt the draft from the open door as the three agents made their way into the living room, where he was sitting on the edge of the coffee table, his legs crossed, his gun pointed at all three of them.

They were cranky; Jack could tell that by their surly expressions. They also didn't like guns being pointed at them. Like he cared. This was pay-back time.

"Look, tough guy, put away the gun or you'll wish you had," one of the three said.

"This gun?" Jack said, placing it on the coffee table next to the first agent's gun. "Are we gonna dance now? I wish you'd given me a signal. My social skills are sadly lacking." He whistled. A second later a blur of black invaded the living room.

"This is not pretty," Mark said.

"Noooo, it isn't," Jack drawled as he popped another beer. "They don't need their spleens," he shouted to be heard over the Ninjas' *eeyow* and *aieeee* cries. "Let me know when you get tired."

"You're really pushing it, Jack. Who the hell are those guys?" Mark asked. Moody and Carmody stood in the kitchen doorway, their jaws slack, their eyes glazed.

"They teach that crap to the cops three times a week. It's mandatory. They're all black belts. Kneecaps, boys, kneecaps!" Jack shouted again. "I hate that bastard in the middle. He's the one who cracked my ribs on the President's orders. Smash his shoulder. Don't be gentle, either. How are those spleens coming? I thought you guys were the best of the best. *Sheeittt*," Jack chortled. "You're pussies!"

"Well, that's one down," Mark said in awe.

"Two down!" Jack said, clapping his hands.

"Three!" Mark said, getting carried away. He was jumping up and down with excitement. Moody and Carmody were still standing in a trance.

"You get those spleens?"

"Hell yes, and a few other things. You owe us, Emery. Big-time."

"Yeah. All we have to do now is get them back to Kalorama and dump them in the NSA's back yard. They won't die, will they?"

"Do we care?" one of the Ninjas asked.

"Well, I certainly don't. You brought the van, right?"

"Yep, it's parked in the alley. Can we go out the door this time instead of the window? I wish I didn't know you, Emery," the leader of the black-clad figures said.

"Wait a minute. I have to clean out their junk." When he was done, Jack had enough hardware to open his own store. "OK, you're good to go."

"Aren't you going to help?"

"Hell no! If I'm ever asked about this little caper, I don't want to have to lie. Thanks, Harry."

"For you, Jack, any time."

Twenty minutes later, Jack Emery was singing in the shower.

All's well that ends well.

Epilogue

"You smell like wildflowers," Jack said, nuzzling his face in Nikki's neck.

"Hmmm, and you smell earthy. This is nice, isn't it?"

"The best," Jack said, nibbling on her ear.

Nikki giggled. "I have to get up, Jack. They're expecting me at Pinewood. Loose ends and all of that."

"It's been a week and not a word has filtered out," Jack said, swinging his legs over the side of the bed. Nikki did the same thing. "My ear has been to the ground but nothing is coming through. I don't know if that's bad or good."

"I think it's good. Somebody would be banging on our doors if they had even half a clue we were responsible for what happened. Wanna take a shower together? I'll wash your back if you wash mine. No fooling around, though."

Jack groaned. "You go first. I have to be in court and can't afford to be late. I'm appearing before Judge Easter this morning. She loves me. Well, sometimes she loves me. No, that's a lie; she hates me most of the time."

Nikki turned around. "No, Jack, she doesn't hate you. She's going through a bad time. She hasn't had enough time to grieve over Jenny. She put too many limits on herself. She needs time, that's all. Myra is her confidante these days. Make some coffee, OK? Maybe some toasted muffins."

"You got it." Jack looked down at the messy bed. It smelled like Nikki. He liked the little blue flowers on the sheets that were crisp and ironed when they'd gone to bed last night. A sigh escaped his lips as he pulled on the bottoms of his pajamas and walked out to the kitchen where he turned on the small TV to catch the early-morning news. As he spooned coffee into the wire basket he half-watched and listened to the anchor going on about private jets and the people who could afford to fly in them.

Jack, his eyes on the TV now, watched as a woman wrapped in some kind of shawl, wearing a huge straw hat and sunglasses, walked carefully down the steps to the tarmac. To the right he could see a small limousine. A reporter, one of many, rushed forward.

"Mrs. Woodley, do you care to comment?"

"Nik!" Jack bellowed at the top of his lungs.

Nikki came running through, wrapped in a cotton-candy-pink towel. She looked at the TV. "It's the wife!"

"I came as soon as I heard about the home invasion. I was vacationing in the islands when I heard about . . . *it,*" the woman on the television said.

"They say it's touch and go with the National Security Advisor. Has the government told you anything different, Mrs. Woodley?"

Paula Woodley tilted the huge sun hat farther back on her head and removed her sunglasses. She smiled from ear to ear. "Only that what my husband needs now is my loving care, which I intend to give him twenty-four hours a day. My husband's doctors tell me his recovery will be long and painful. The President has assured me that Karl's position as National Security Advisor will be there for him when and if he's able to return to work."

Another reporter stepped forward. "How do you feel about the lack of arrest in regard to the home invasion?"

"I don't think I understand the question. I thought when there was a home invasion the people doing the invading robbed you. It's my understanding that nothing was taken from the house; none of my mother's antiques, none of my jewelry and none of the electronics. I think someone had a vendetta against my husband. Possibly terrorists. Nothing else makes sense."

A third reporter shoved a microphone in Paula's face. "It's been said that a group of women broke almost every bone in your husband's body. They say he's going to be crippled for life. How does that make you feel, Mrs. Woodley?"

Paula Woodley looked straight into the camera. "Numb. Now, if you'll excuse me, I have to go to my husband. He *needs* me."

The first reporter leaned forward. "Mrs. Woodley, what's the first thing you're going to say to your husband?"

Paula Woodley took a few seconds to digest the question. Then she smiled from ear to ear. "You don't really want to know, do you?"

Nikki burst out laughing, gasping for breath. "Tell me that isn't divine justice. Oh, revenge is so sweet!"

"Any regrets, Nik?" Jack asked curiously.

"Mrs. Woodley would have died if Maddie hadn't gotten to her in time, Jack. If you're asking me if my conscience bothers me, the answer is no. Oh, yes, we got her safely away. You did notice it was her decision to come back? He deserved what he got. Any man who beats a woman because he's bigger, stronger, tougher deserves a taste of his own medicine. I won't lose any sleep over it and Paula Woodley is going to sleep like a baby from here on in. We gave her back her life."

The muffins in the toaster popped up. Jack spread the butter, Nikki spread the jam.

"What if he had died?"

Nikki bit into the muffin. "He didn't. Don't go there, darling Jack."

"OK!" Jack ripped at the cotton-candy-pink towel. Nikki squealed as she ran from the room, up the stairs, down the hall to her bedroom where she dived into the bed, her arms held out.

"Come to Mama, you sweet little daredevil!"

Jack was stepping out of the elevator in the courthouse when Ted Robinson appeared out of nowhere. It was four thirty in the afternoon.

"Let's grab a beer. I want to run something by you before I turn it in to my boss."

Jack didn't break his stride. "You buying?"

"Hell, yes, I'm buying. I'll even spring for a steak."

"You get a raise or something? I never turn down a freebie. Let's go."

Secure in a back booth five blocks from the courthouse, their orders given to the waitress, Ted pulled out two pieces of paper and slid them across the table. "I can't submit this without a source, Jack. You know the rules. You also know a good reporter—and I'm a damn good reporter—will never divulge his sources. I'll go to jail first."

Jack read all the way to the end of the two sheets of paper that would translate to a column and a half in the *Post*. He could feel his stomach muscles clench into a knot as he raised his eyes to meet Ted's. "OK, I'm your source."

"Everything I wrote is true then?"

"Yes."

"And, you know this . . . how?"

"I was there. I didn't personally lift a finger. But I made it happen."

"Did you really send those fucking shields to

the President by special messenger and sign the NSA's name to the package?"

Jack squirmed in his chair. "Now, I did do that."

Ted reached into his backpack and withdrew several photographs and another letter. "You sent me these, too?"

"I did that, too. You are a little slow on the uptake sometimes, Ted."

"I had a friend hack into the hospital records. He couldn't find anything about those three guys, but then another friend knows one of the surgeons at GW and he said the Secret Service brought in three men who needed emergency surgery. All three needed their spleens removed. They had a bunch of other injuries. How amazing is that?"

"Pretty damn amazing, if you ask me. You just buying one beer or can I order another?"

"You can drink up the whole goddamn bar and I'll go into hock paying for it. Thanks, Jack."

"Ah shucks, it was nothing. Hey, I got something for you." Jack opened his briefcase and pulled out a manila envelope. He handed it over, along with a picture of two gold shields. "The one in the envelope belongs to the guy who ruptured your spleen. I thought you might want that sucker."

Ted upended the envelope. The gold shield fell out. "Son of a bitch!"

Jack started to laugh and couldn't stop. When he had finally calmed down, Ted wiped his own eyes. "Since we're in such a good mood, is it true that a bunch of women took down the NSA?"

Jack sobered instantly. "I'm officially off duty as your source now. Beats me. All I saw was those jocks who thought they could take us on. It's the truth, Ted. I did not see any women that night. Oh, boy, here's our steak."

"You're a jerk, Jack."

"Takes one to know one. We should do this more often."

The November wind howled outside the farmhouse, reminding the residents that winter was on the way. A light snow was falling as the ladies of Pinewood made their way to the war room. Myra carried two bottles of Cristal champagne, and Charles carried the crystal flutes on a magnificent heirloom silver tray. Kathryn carried several bags of Cape Cod white Cheddar popcorn.

Myra took charge of the meeting while Charles went to his workstation to turn on his computers and the large plasma monitors. Within seconds the women were surrounded by Lady Justice. Myra looked around the table. Oh, how she adored these feisty, talented young women. "Was justice served?"

"Yes," was the resounding response.

"Do we have any loose ends? Is there anything out there that will come back to haunt us?"

"No," the women answered as one.

"Good. With the holidays fast approaching, I suggest we adjourn until the new year, when we will begin our new mission. It's time, though, to pick whose mission will be next. I'll do the honors this time." Myra reached into the shoe box that was sitting in the center of the table. She unfolded the small piece of paper and read off the name. "Isabelle."

The others cheered.

"It's time to celebrate." Myra yanked at the cork on the champagne bottle and then poured liberally. Charles joined them with a handful of printouts under his arm. He accepted his flute of champagne and held it aloft.

"To Lady Justice and to the ladies of Pinewood!" Charles said.

Now it was time to socialize. Kathryn opened the popcorn bags.

"Any news on the Barringtons, Charles?" Nikki asked.

"No, Nikki, I'm sorry. Maddie tells us Allison Banks is not suing you, your partners or the firm."

Nikki smiled. "No, she isn't. We had a . . . little talk. Actually, she's relocating. And, in case you don't know this, Judge Krackhoff is stepping down from the bench. I heard that just yesterday."

Charles smiled. "That's going to be a tremendous help in locating the Barringtons. I'll get right on that. You must be patient, Nikki."

"I am. We also had two new clients yesterday. Both referrals from Judge Easter. We'll make our way out of the misery Allison caused us."

"Charles, have you spoken to Mrs. Woodley since her return?" Yoko asked quietly.

"As a matter of fact, I did, last night when she returned home after spending some time at the hospital. She asked me to convey her thanks for all you did. She told me her husband started to scream when she walked into his hospital room. No mean feat, you understand, since his jaw is wired shut. She said she spent an hour with him, telling him how it was going to be when he returned home from the hospital. The lady was in quite good spirits."

"I'll drink to that!" Kathryn said. The others raised their glasses. Myra refilled them from a second bottle of Cristal.

Charles took that moment to hand out copies of an article written by Ted Robinson that had appeared in the morning *Post*. The women read the article, their eyes full of questions.

"Is this true?" Alexis asked.

"The *Post* is not known for printing falsehoods. Obviously the reporter had a very reliable source. It will be interesting to see how the White House responds to the article. What I find incredibly interesting is that the three agents found in the National Security Advisor's backyard had to have their spleens removed. The reporter who wrote this story had his spleen removed many weeks ago. Before any of you can ask, the man has an airtight alibi; he was in a movie theater where hundreds of people saw him. Actually, I think he was on a . . . ah . . . date."

Kathryn pointed a finger at a line in the article where it said only two of the special shields had been returned to the White House. "Where's the third one?"

"Excellent question. We'll probably never know, nor do I think we want to know," Charles said, walking back to his position behind his bank of computers.

The women made small talk as Myra gathered up the glasses and the champagne bottles.

"What are you all going to be doing for the next few weeks, aside from your jobs?" Alexis asked.

"I'm taking a vacation," Kathryn said. "The first one since Alan died. I . . . I have to go somewhere."

The others agreed they all had *somewhere* they'd like to go, too.

"Perhaps this will help you all make up your minds," Charles said as he stepped down from his perch above them. "Don't think you're fooling me for a moment. Here!" he said, handing out five airline tickets to Switzerland. "You'll be going alone. Myra and I will go over in the spring. You'd better get busy, your flight leaves in five hours. A car service will pick you up. I wrote the time on the folder. Myra and I will happily dog-sit. Have a good trip, ladies. You've earned it."

The women scattered to make their phone calls and to pack.

Kathryn was the last to leave the kitchen. She walked over to the windowsill to look at Julia's plant. It was thriving, the leaves emerald green and glossy despite everything it had been through. She carried it over to the back door and set it down on the floor so she wouldn't forget it.

It didn't look like a hospital or even a private clinic. It looked like a high-end Swiss chalet in a fancy resort. It looked cozy, warm and inviting.

The women trooped through the massive front door into a lobby that was colorful and comfortable with a fireplace massive enough for a dozen people to stand in. A fire of bonfire proportions blazed.

A man in a white coat approached, his arms extended. "I've been expecting you. Come, come, I'll show you around. I'm Dr. Stuben. Please, call me Henry. Julia did."

Kathryn took the lead, the plant in a little canvas book bag.

He was tall and fatherly-looking, with gray hair, rosy cheeks and a gentle manner. "First, I'd like to show you where Julia spent her time while she was here. She loved her little suite. Ah, here we are. None of her things are here because we needed the room. I personally packed up all of her possessions. She said you would come here but she wasn't sure when that would be. She loved you all very much. Even on her bad days she would talk about you all. She said you were the sisters she never had. Is that the plant she talked about so much?"

Kathryn didn't trust herself to speak. She nodded and handed over the little canvas bag.

"We have a wonderful atrium here. I would like to personally plant it myself, if that's all right with you. All of our plants have names with little markers. We'll call this one "the Julia." She said you would be bringing it and even picked out the spot in the atrium. She asked me to ask you all not to be sad and not to cry. She said you all need to get on with it. I'm going to leave you alone for now. When you're ready, meet me back in the lobby and I'll give you a tour of the facility. Julia was happy here. That's what I want you to remember."

When the door closed behind the doctor, the women started to cry.

Kathryn bit down on her lower lip. "I could be happy in this place, too, if I wasn't dying. How could she expect us not to be sad and not to cry?"

"We weren't wrong to come here, were we?" Alexis asked.

"No, not at all. You heard the doctor; Julia knew we'd come and even knew Kathryn would bring the plant. She knew us all so well. We were sisters and she took that literally. We should say our goodbyes and get on with it like she wanted," Nikki said.

"I can't say goodbye. That's too final," Kathryn said adamantly.

"Then we won't say goodbye. We'll just leave and wave," Nikki said as she took Kathryn's arm in hers. "Wherever she is, Julia knows we're here. Let's see some happy faces. Think what Julia would say if she knew what we just pulled off right under the nose of the President of the United States! She'd say, 'You kicked ass, ladies, and I'm damn proud of you.'"

Nikki's words had the desired effect. The women linked arms as they strode down the richly carpeted hallway to the lobby where Dr. Stuben waited for them.

If you love Fern Michaels,
don't miss her new novel,
available now!

Turn the page for a special preview of
FOOL ME ONCE,
an exhilarating story of a mother's
secrets, a father's love, and a woman who finds
romance when she least expects it. . . .

He was her client.

A superrich paying client.

And, said client was ticked off, big-time.

A murderous glint in her eyes, Olivia Lowell took one step backward, then another. "I refuse to tolerate this type of behavior, Cecil. I will not be intimidated. I was told you were a gentleman. Ha!"

Alice, the West Highland Terrier at Olivia's feet, barked shrilly and showed her teeth. "She's a killer, Cecil, so it might behoove you to rethink your actions. Now, what's it going to be? Be aware that I am a woman whose biggest failing in life is my lack of patience."

Cecil eyed the woman standing in front of him, then at the yapper at her feet. He then did what any red-blooded Yorkshire Terrier would do. He lay down, rolled over, and barked. Happily. He bounded back up on all fours immediately and raced across the studio. Then he whirled and twirled and did a hind leg jig. His one and only trick. Alice ran after him and somehow managed to swat his rear end with one furry paw. They ended up tussling on the studio floor.

"Now look at you, Cecil! The executors of your owner's estate are not going to like this. I need to take your picture, so let's get with it. You're big news, Cecil. You just inherited the Manning fortune. You're going to live a life of luxury. Don't you want to get your due? It isn't every day a fortune lands in a dog's lap. C'mon, let me take your picture. I promise it will be painless," Olivia pleaded.

Cecil hopped up on a stool, did his jig again, to Alice's dismay. Olivia resigned herself to the fact that she wasn't going to get a portrait of the famous dog but would have to go with action shots, which probably wasn't a bad thing at all. She'd tried to explain to the dog's handler, a lawyer named Jeff Bannerman, that Cecil had a mind of his own, but he refused to listen. What Bannerman had said was something to the effect that you're supposed to be the best of the best. Now prove it.

Like that was going to happen. If Cecil was an ordinary dog, maybe. She'd met Cecil two years before, when Lillian Manning had commissioned her to do a sitting portrait of the dog. The picture, while nice, reflected Cecil's more or less placid puppyhood. The moneymen responsible for Mrs. Manning's estate wanted a grown-up picture, and they were willing to pay ten thousand dollars for that picture. After all, it was going to be shown around the world, and it would aid her career, they said.

Olivia reached into her pocket and withdrew a whistle, the kind that emitted a loud, piercing sound that only dogs could hear. She blew it three times and shouted at the top of her lungs, "Cecil, get on that bench and pose! *Now!* Or . . . or you are going back home with that stiff who brought you here.

Cecil stopped pawing through the wastebasket, turned to look at the object of his torment, then pranced over to the bench and hopped up. He posed, he preened, he looked haughty, he looked devilish, then he lay down. Alice barked her approval as Olivia's Nikon clicked and clicked. Then, ham that he was, Cecil stood up on all fours and bowed. He actually bowed. Olivia burst out laughing—until Cecil showed his teeth, which meant the gig was over. He hopped down and chased Alice around the room until Alice collapsed. The Yorkie pounced on her and barked shrilly. Alice ignored him. With nothing else to entertain him, Cecil lifted his leg and defiantly peed on the legs of a tripod. Then he walked back to Alice. He lay down and was asleep within seconds.

Olivia smiled as she looked at the two sleeping dogs. She adored Cecil but felt sorry for him. He was now destined to live out his life in a fancy mansion with servants catering to his every whim. The servants wouldn't love him or play with him the way Lillian Manning had. Poor, poor

Cecil. Maybe the money people would allow Cecil to have play dates with Alice. How silly was that. How silly was leaving a hundred-and-fifty-million-dollar estate to a dog? Pretty damn silly in her opinion.

Olivia Lowell, photographer to the canine world, looked at her watch. Lunchtime. Yogurt, a banana, and a cup of coffee, and she'd be ready to photograph a seven-year-old English Whippet named Sasha for his owner's Christmas card. Christmas was ten months away, but the owner said she didn't want to have to wait till the last minute.

It was a lucrative living, and Olivia enjoyed every minute of it because she was a devout animal lover.

As Olivia spooned the yogurt into her mouth, she thought about her father. She missed him but understood when he said he wanted to retire to the islands and rent out his fishing boat to tourists. He was happier these days than she'd ever seen him. Of course that might have something to do with his new love, Lea. Maybe she would call him later in the day to ask him how things were going.

Tears pricked Olivia's deep-green eyes when she thought of her father and how he's raised her on his own. He'd sacrificed so much for her, even giving up his accounting practice and going to night school to learn photography, so he could open a studio in their home just so he could be with her. A studio that he himself built on the side of the house with its own entrance, it own bath, and a minikitchen. The studio even had a plaque beside the door that said, LOWELL AND LOWELL, and underneath their names, the word, PHOTOGRAPHY.

Her father had never remarried, despite her urging as she grew older. Not that he didn't, as he called it, keep company with various and sundry ladies. Some of those ladies were to her liking and some weren't, but she kept her own counsel where they were concerned. Until Lea came along five years ago. Lea was the mother she never had. They were friends, good friends. Maybe now that both her father and Lea were in a less stressful atmosphere and retired, they might think about getting married. At least she hoped so for her father's sake.

Three things happened simultaneously when Olivia tossed her empty yogurt container in the trash. Cecil and Alice raced into the kitchen, Sasha, the English Whippet, arrived wearing a huge red-and-white Santa hat, granny glasses that were tied to his ears, and a Christmas neckerchief, and a distinguished-looking gentleman carrying a briefcase rang her front doorbell.

Olivia strode to the front door. She really needed to make some rules around here. The least Sasha's owner could have done was take the dog to the studio door instead of the kitchen door. Now she had to contend with some door-to-door salesman, the barking, howling dogs, and her own frustrations. Her father would have had the situation under control in a heartbeat. All he ever had to do was look a dog in the eye, wag his finger, and he was rewarded with instant obedience. Her clients walked all over her.

"What?" she snapped irritably. "Whatever you're

selling, I'm not interested." She was about to shut the front door when the man held up a small white business card that said he was Prentice O'Brien from the law firm of O'Brien, O'Malley and O'Shaughnessy. A nice Irish firm, Olivia surmised. Or else it was some kind of song-and-dance act, and the man standing in front of her was a scam artist.

"What?" Olivia screamed to be heard over the din. "Is someone suing me?" Sasha's body slammed against the locked storm door. Prentice O'Brien stepped back, his face full of apprehension.

"No!" the lawyer bellowed in return. "Can we go somewhere to talk where it's a little more quiet?"

Olivia brushed at her blond curls. "I'm afraid not," she bellowed as loud as the lawyer had. "I'm running late, and, as you can see, I seem to have lost control here. Why don't you call me later, around five."

The lawyer frowned. "Ms. Lowell, this *really* is important, urgent even. We need to talk!"

Olivia turned around when she heard a sound reminiscent of a waterfall. Sasha was peeing on the hall carpet runner. Damn. She noted the look of disgust on the lawyer's face.

"Some other time. *This* situation is *really* urgent. Good-bye, Mr."—she looked down at the card in her hand—"Mr. O'Brien." She shut the door in the man's face and raced to the kitchen for a roll of paper towels.

Thirty minutes later she was still searching for Sasha's glasses and Santa Claus hat. *My father would have this under control, too. Damn.*

At three o'clock Sasha and all her gear were gone. Cecil's handler still hadn't picked him up. Anna Logan, the owner of Logan's bakery, arrived with a basket of new kittens. She wanted pictures to put up on the bakery bulletin board in the hopes some of her customers would adopt them.

It was ten after five when Anna and the kittens pulled out of Olivia's driveway. Cecil's handler still hadn't arrived to pick him up, which probably meant he'd forgotten about him. Just the way Alice's owners had forgotten to pick her up three years ago. That had been her lucky day. She loved Alice the way mothers loved their children.

At five-thirty the doorbell and the phone pealed at the same time. Olivia ignored the doorbell and answered the phone. However, Alice and Cecil raced to the front door and barked. It was Cecil's handler calling to ask if Olivia could possibly keep Cecil overnight, and he would be picked up in the morning by *someone*.

"Well, sure, for fifty dollars an hour, Mr. Bannerman. I don't operate a dog-sitting service. This is a photography studio." She was told the fee would be no problem. After all, Cecil was the richest dog in the United States. She hung up the phone wondering what she was going to prepare for dinner as she made her way to the front door. She opened it. Prentice O'Brien.

"What is it, Mr. O'Brien? It's the end of the day, I'm tired, and if no one is suing me, I can't imagine what you want to talk to me about. Make it quick."

"Can I at least come in, Ms. Lowell. It's rather cold out here, and it is snowing."

It was *snowing*. How had she missed that? Maybe she'd build a fire later, snuggle with the dogs, and think about Clarence De Witt's marriage proposal. Then again, maybe she wouldn't think about Clarence De Witt's marriage proposal. She didn't want to be Mrs. Clarence De Witt. She didn't want to be Mrs. *Anybody*. She liked her life just the way it was, thank you very much. "All right. This better be good and quick. Come in. Just so you know, Mr. O'Brien, I hate lawyers."

"Until you need us," O'Brien quipped. "Nice house," he said, looking around as Olivia led him to the great room that ran the entire length of the house.

"Thank you. My dad did all the work, even this addition and the entire studio. He can do anything," she said proudly. "This used to be just a two-bedroom ranch house, but Dad added two bathrooms, a third bedroom, and this great room. He remodeled the kitchen, too. He build the playhouse in the back for me when I was little."

"Your father sounds like an extraordinary man, Ms. Lowell."

"Oh, he is. He raised me when my mother died. If I had a mother, I can't imagine her doing a better job. Now, tell me why you're here and what I can do for you."

The attorney removed his overcoat and laid it on the side of the sofa. He looked puzzled. "Did I hear you right just now? Did you say your mother died?"

"Yes, the day I was born. Thirty-four years

ago. That's her picture on the mantel. It's the only one we have. Her name was Allison. Why are you here, Mr. O'Brien? Does this visit have something to do with my dad?"

"Not directly."

While O'Brien walked over to the fireplace and studied the picture on the mantel, she eyed the briefcase on the sturdy pine coffee table. It looked old and well used, with scuff marks and gouges in the cowhide. She wondered how many lawsuits it represented. She waited, her gaze taking in the room, while the lawyer, who had returned to stand by the coffee table, riffled through his case for whatever it was he was going to show her.

She loved this room, she really did. One wall was her own personal rogue's gallery as her father called it. Every inch of space on the wall was covered with pictures of her from the day she was born. The massive stone fireplace, with a hearth so wide and deep she could have positioned a sofa on it, took up another wall. Her father had allowed her to carry the irregular fieldstones in from outside, making building it a joint effort. In the winter they made roaring fires, popped corn, and toasted marshmallows. They even grilled weenies on sticks on occasion. The green plants and fica trees were her contribution. She trimmed and watered them weekly. All were lush and green, thanks to the three skylights that graced the ceiling.

She'd had sleepovers in this very room when she was young. She wondered where all those old friends were these days.

Olivia was jolted from her thoughts when the lawyer cleared his throat. "What I have here in my hand is the last will and testament of your mother, whom you probably know as Allison Matthews Lowell, although she changed her name to Adrian Ames soon after divorcing your father. I can read it to you, or you can read it yourself."

Olivia threw her hands in the air. "See! See! I knew this was a mistake. You have the wrong person. My mother died when I was born. I guess there's some other Olivia Lowell out there. I'm sorry you wasted your time, Mr. O'Brien."

The attorney cleared his throat again. "I didn't waste my time, Ms. Lowell. I'm sorry to be the one to tell you this, but your mother did not die thirty-four years ago. She died two weeks ago and left her entire estate to you. And whoever that is in the picture on the mantel, it's not Adrian Ames."

Olivia's heart thundered in her chest. She reached out to grasp the arm of the chair she was sitting on, only to see Cecil perched there. She picked up and brought him close to her chest. She was so light-headed she couldn't think. "No! No! Don't tell me that. My father . . . my father . . . would never . . . he wouldn't lie . . . this must be some land of cruel jokes, and I don't appreciate it. No, you're wrong."

Prentice O'Brien inched the will in its sky-blue cover across the coffee table. It glared up at Olivia like an obscene blue eye. She made no move to reach for it. She struggled with her voice. "I think you should leave now, Mr. O'Brien."

"Ms. Lowell, I'm sorry about this, but my firm

represented your mother for many, many years. This is not a mistake. Once you know the story behind all this, I'm sure you'll understand it is not some cruel hoax. I understand your being upset, so I'm going to leave. I suggest you contact your father and talk with him. After you've done that, please feel free to call me."

Olivia watched in a daze as the attorney stood up and put on his overcoat. Faster than a lightning bolt, both dogs chased him to the door. Olivia heard the little pinging sound made by the alarm system when the door opened and closed.

She burst into tears.

If what the attorney said was true, her whole life was a lie. A big, fat lie!

She cried harder. She had a mother. *Had* had a mother. A mother she never knew. A real, live, flesh-and-blood mother like all her friends had, like Dee Dee Pepper's mother. Olivia bolted from the chair and raced to the powder room off the great room. The dogs huddled and whimpered at the strange sounds emanating from behind the closed door.

Ten minutes later, Olivia literally crawled out of the powder room on her hands and knees, her face splotchy and red. She crawled across the slick hardwood floors she'd helped her father install. Tongue and groove. She'd thought that phrase so funny as a child. Her father had allowed her to hand him the pieces of wood and showed her how to lay them down. She'd been so proud that he allowed her to help. *It's just you and me, kid,* he always said after they finished a project. *Just you and me, kid.* Yeah, right. I think you left someone out, Daddy.

It wasn't until she was back in her favorite chair that she saw that the will was still on the coffee table. Well, she certainly wasn't going to touch *that.* No way was she ever going to touch *that.* Absolutely, she was never, ever going to touch *that.*

Alice pawed her leg for attention before she ran to the kitchen for her food bowl. She carried it back and dropped it at Olivia's feet. Cecil barked. Olivia looked at her watch. It was time for Alice's supper. Cecil's, too, since she was dogsitting. She felt a hundred years old when she heaved herself to her feet and made her way to the kitchen.

Olivia reached into the cabinet for the dog food. Her father had allowed her to screw the knobs into the cabinets. *Just you and me, kid.* A duo instead of a trio. She started to cry again, the tears rolling down her cheeks like a waterfall. She sniffed as she scooped out the food into two bowls and watched as both dogs gobbled it down. She let them outside. It was snowing harder. It always snowed in February. Her father was probably basking on the deck of his boat, sharing a glass of wine with Lea at this hour. It was probably warm and balmy, and they were probably both wearing shorts and tee shirts.

She needed to call her father. What should she say? How should she say it? *Just you and me, kid.* Now it was her father and Lea. And, she wasn't a kid anymore.

* * *

Nothing was what it seemed. Not even the picture of "her mother" on the mantel.

Alice scratched against the door as Cecil tried to nip her ear. Olivia opened the door, towel-dried the dogs, handed each of them a treat. She should think about her own dinner. She reached for a box of Cheerios and carried it back to the great room. She set the box down and made a fire.

Olivia was a little girl again as she hugged her knees to her chest and watched the flames dance behind the ornate grate. She picked at the dry cereal, sharing it with the two dogs sitting next to her. She had to think, but her brain suddenly wasn't working.

Just you and me, kid.

Liar! Liar!

Both dogs crawled into Olivia's lap and snuggled with her. How warm and comforting they felt. Suddenly, a red-hot streak of rage, hotter than the fire she was looking at, ripped through her. What kind of mother would . . . would . . . ignore her daughter for thirty-four years? Who was the woman who left her entire estate to a daughter she'd ignored all her life?

Well, the only person who could answer those questions, other than possibly the attorney, was her father. And only he could tell her who was in the picture on the mantel.

Just you and me, kid.

Olivia got to her feet and rummaged between the sofa cushions for the portable phone. For some reason she always stuck it between the cushion and the arm. Most times the battery was dead and she had to recharge it or use her cell phone. She took a mighty, deep breath and dialed her father's cell phone. She wasn't surprised when Lea answered, sounding happy and relaxed. Well, why the hell shouldn't she sound happy and relaxed with her father and all that warm sunshine?

"Lea, it's Ollie," she said, using her father's favorite nickname for her. "Is he there?"

"Honey, you sound . . . funny. Are you all right?" Do you have a cold or something? If you do, you need to start taking care of it. I saw on the news that it's very cold and snowing in Winchester."

"Or something," Olivia responded. "Is Dad there?"

"He was until about ten minutes ago. He's down on the pier watching some fisherman haul in a huge marlin. Can I have him return your call, or would you like me to go get him? I don't think he'll be too long. Let's face it, how long can you stare at a dead fish."

Olivia knew she was supposed to laugh at Lea's little joke. She didn't. She wondered if she would ever laugh again about anything. "No, that's okay. Tell him to call me when he gets in. It's important, Lea."

"Is there anything I can do, honey?"

"No. But thanks for asking." Olivia clicked the OFF button and replaced the phone in its stand instead of letting it slide down between the cushions. She walked back to the fire, carrying an armful of pillows. She was so cold she ached. The dogs curled up next to her, eating the crunchy cereal, she fed them one morsel at a time.

Just you and me, kid.

If you enjoyed *The Jury,* learn how the
Sisterhood got their start in

WEEKEND WARRIORS.

Turn the page for a special excerpt . . .

A Zebra mass-market paperback, on sale now!

Prologue

The traffic was horrendous on Massachusetts Avenue, but then it was always horrendous at this time of day. Rush hour. God, how she hated those words. Especially today. She slapped the palm of her hand on the horn and muttered under her breath, "C'mon, you jerk, move!"

"Take it easy, Nik," Barbara Rutledge said, her eyes on the slow-moving traffic. "One more block and we're there. Mom won't mind if we're a few minutes late. She hates it that she turned sixty today so the longer she has to wait for the celebration, the better she'll feel. I don't think she looks sixty, do you, Nik?"

"Are you kidding! She looks better than we do and we're only thirty-six." She leaned on the horn again even though it was an exercise in futility. "Just tell me one thing. Why did your mother pick the Jockey Club for dinner?"

"The first crab cakes of the season, that's why. President Reagan made this restaurant famous and all her political friends come here. If you want my opinion, thirty bucks for two crab cakes is obscene. I can eat lunch all week on thirty bucks if I'm careful. Mom pitched a fit last week when I took her to Taco Bell for lunch. We both ate for five bucks. She was a good sport about it but she can't understand why I don't tap into the trust fund. I keep telling her I want to make it on my own. Some days she understands, some days she doesn't. I know she's proud of me, you, too, Nik. She tells everyone about her two crime-fighting girls who are lawyers."

"I love her as much as you do, Barb. I can't imagine growing up without a mother. I would have if she hadn't stepped in and taken over when my parents died. Okay, we're here and we're only thirty minutes late. This isn't the best parking spot in the world but it will have to do and we're under a streetlight. In this city it doesn't get any better than that."

"We really should hit the powder room before we head for the table. Mom does like spit and polish, not to mention perfume and lipstick," Barbara said, trying to smooth the wrinkles out of her suit. Nik did the same thing.

"I spent the day in court and so did you. We're supposed to look wrinkled, messy, and harried. Myra will understand. Oops, almost forgot my present," Nik said, reaching into the backseat for a small silver-wrapped package. She handed

Barbara a long cylinder tied with a bright red ribbon. "Your brain must be as tired as mine. You almost forgot yours, too. What about this pile of books, Barb?"

"They're for Mom. I picked them up today at lunchtime. You know how she loves reading about murder and mayhem. I'll give them to her when we leave."

Myra Rutledge was waiting, a beautiful woman whose smile and open arms welcomed them. "My girls are here. We're ready to be seated now, Franklin," Myra said.

"Certainly, madam. Your usual table, or would you prefer the smoking section with a window view?"

"The window, Franklin," Barbara said. "I think tonight in honor of my mother's birthday you two can have a cigarette. Just one cigarette after dinner for both of you. I will of course abstain. Yes, yes, yes, I know we all quit but this is Mom's birthday and I say why not."

Myra smiled as she reached for her daughter's hand. "Why not indeed."

"This is so wonderful," Myra said, sitting down and leaning across the table. "My two favorite girls. I couldn't ask for a better finale to my birthday."

"Finale, Mom! Does that mean when you go home, you and Charles won't celebrate?"

"Well . . . I . . . perhaps a glass of sherry. I did ask Charles to come but he said this was a mother-daughter dinner and he would feel out of place. No comments, girls."

"Mom, when are you going to marry the guy? You've been together for twenty years. Nik and I know all about the birds and the bees so stop blushing," Barbara teased.

"Yes and it was Charles who told you two about the birds and the bees," Myra smiled.

Charles Martin was Myra's companion slash houseman. When his cover was blown as an MI-6 agent his government had relocated him to the United States where he'd signed on as head of security for Myra's Fortune 500 candy business. His sole goal in life was to take care of Myra, a job he took seriously and did well. Both girls were grateful for his attention to Myra, lessening her loneliness when they went off on their own.

Myra's eyes sparkled. "Now, tell me everything. Your latest cases, who you're dating at the moment, how our softball team is doing. Don't leave anything out. Will I be planning a wedding any time soon?"

It was what Nikki loved about Myra the most, her genuine interest in their lives. She'd never invaded their privacy, always content to stand on the sidelines, offer motherly support and aid when needed but she never interfered, or gave advice unless asked. Nikki knew Myra enjoyed the times the three of them spent together, loved the twice-monthly dinners in town and the occasional lunches with her daughter or perhaps a short stroll along the Tidal Basin.

Yes, Myra had a life, a busy life, a life of her own beyond her girls. She sat on various charitable boards, worked tirelessly for both political parties, did numerous good deeds every day, was active in the Historical Society and still managed to have time for Charles, Barbara, and herself.

"You staying in town tonight, Mom?"

A rosy hue marched across Myra's face. "No, Barbara, I'm going home. No, I didn't drive myself. I took a car service so don't fret about the trip to McLean. Charles is waiting for me. I told you, we'll have a glass of sherry together."

"No birthday cake!" Nik said.

The rosy hue crept down Myra's neck. "We had the cake at lunchtime. Charles needed a blowtorch to light all the candles. All sixty of them. It was very . . . festive."

"How does it feel to be sixty, Mom?" Barbara asked, reaching for her mother's hand across the table. "You told me you were dreading the day."

"It's just a number, just a day. I don't feel any different than I did yesterday. People always talk about 'the moments' in their lives. The special times they never forget. I guess this day is one of those moments. The day I married your father was a special moment. The day you were born was an extra special moment, the day Nikki came to us was another special moment and then of course when the candy company went 500. Don't laugh at me now when I tell you the other special moment was when Charles said he would take care of me for the rest of my life. All wonderful moments. I hope I have years and years of special moments. If you would get married and give me a grandchild I would run up the flag, Barbara. I don't want to be so old I dodder when you give birth."

Nikki poked Barbara's arm, a huge smile on her face. "Go on, tell her. Make your mother happy on her sixtieth birthday."

"I'm pregnant, Mom. You can start planning the wedding, but you better make it quick or I'll be showing before you know it."

Myra looked first at Nikki to see if they were teasing her or not. Nikki's head bobbed up and down. "I'm going to be the maid of honor and the godmother! She's not teasing, Myra."

"Oh, honey. Are you happy? Of course you are. All I have to do is look at you. Oh, there is so much to do. You want the reception at home in the garden, right?"

"Absolutely, Mom. I want to be married in the living room. I want to slide down the bannister in my wedding gown. I'm going to do that, Mom. Nik will be right behind me. If I can't do that, the wedding is off."

"Anything you want, honey. Anything. You have made me the happiest woman in the whole world. Promise that you will allow Charles and me to babysit."

"She promised me first," Nikki grinned.

"This is definitely 'a moment.' Do either of you have a camera?"

"Mom, a camera is not something I carry around in my purse. However, all is not lost. Nik has one in her car. I'll scoot over there and get it."

Nikki fished in her pocket and tossed her the keys.

"I'm going to be a mother. Me! Do you believe it? You'll be Auntie Nik," Barbara said, bending over to tweak Nikki's cheek. "I'll ask Franklin to take our picture when I get back. See ya," she said, flashing them both an ear-to-ear grin.

"I hope you had a good day today, Myra. Birthdays are always special," Nikki said, her gaze on the window opposite her chair. "Knowing you're going to be a grandmother has to be the most wonderful thing in the world. I'm pretty excited myself." She could see Barbara running across the street, her jacket flapping in the spring breeze. "Do you remember the time Barbara and I made you a birthday cake out of cornflakes, crackers, and pancake syrup?"

"I'll never forget it. I don't think the cook ever forgot it either. I did eat it, though."

Nikki laughed. "Yes, you did." She was glad now she had parked under the streetlight. She could see several couples walking down the street, saw Barbara open the back door of the car, saw her reach for the camera, saw her sling it over her shoulder, saw her lock the door. She turned her attention to Myra, who was also staring out the window. Nikki's gaze swiveled back to the window to see Barbara look both ways for oncoming traffic, ready to sprint across the street at the first break. The three couples were almost upon her when she stepped off the curb.

Nikki was aware of the dark car that came out of nowhere, the sound of horns blowing and the sudden screech of brakes. Myra was moving off her seat almost in slow motion, her face a mask of disbelief as they both ran out of the restaurant. The scream when it came was so tortured, so animal-like, Nikki stopped in her tracks to reach for Myra's arm.

The awkward position of her friend's body was a picture that would stay with Nikki forever. She bent down, afraid to touch her friend, the friend she called sister. "Did anyone call an ambulance?" she shouted. She heard a loud, jittery response. "Yes."

"No! No! No!" Myra screamed over and over as she dropped to the ground to cradle her daughter's body in her arms. From somewhere off in the distance, a siren could be heard. Nikki's trembling fingers fumbled for a pulse. Her whole body started to shake when she couldn't find even a faint beat. Maybe she wasn't doing it right. She pressed harder with her third and fourth fingers the way she'd seen nurses do. A wave of dizziness riveted through her just as the ambulance crew hit the ground running. Tears burned her eyes as she watched the paramedics check Barbara's vital signs.

Time lost all meaning as the medical crew did what they were trained to do. A young woman with long, curly hair raised her head to look straight at Nikki. Her eyes were sad when she shook her head.

It couldn't be. She wanted to shout, to scream, to stamp her feet. Instead, she knuckled her eyes and stifled her sobs.

"She'll be all right, won't she, Nikki? Broken bones heal. She was just knocked unconscious. Tell me she'll be all right. Please, tell me that. Please, Nikki."

The lump in Nikki's throat was so large she thought she would choke. She tried not to look at the still body, tried not to see them straighten out Barbara's arms and legs. When they lifted her onto the stretcher, she closed her eyes. She thought she would lose it when the young woman with the long, curly hair pulled a sheet up over her best friend's face. Not Barbara. Not her best friend in the whole world. Not the girl she played with in a sandbox, gone to kindergarten with. Not the girl she'd gone through high school, college, and law school with. She was going to be her maid of honor, babysit her baby. How could she be dead? "I saw her look both ways before she stepped onto the curb. She had a clear path to cross the street," she mumbled.

"Nikki, should we ride in the ambulance with Barbara? Will they let us?" Myra asked tearfully.

She doesn't know. She doesn't know what the sheet means. How was she going to tell Myra her daughter was dead?

The ambulance doors closed. It drove off. The siren silent.

"It's too late. They left. You'll have to drive, Nikki. They'll need all sorts of information when they admit her to the hospital. I want to be there. Barbara needs to know I'm there. She needs to know her mother is there. Can we go now, Nikki?" Myra pleaded.

"Ma'am?"

"Yes, officer," Nikki said. She loosened her hold on Myra's shoulders.

His voice was not unkind. He was too young to be this kind. She could see the compassion on his face.

"I need to take a statement. You are . . ."

"Nicole Quinn. This is Myra Rutledge. She's

the mother . . ." She almost said "of the deceased," but bit her tongue in time.

"Officer, can we do this later?" Myra interjected. "I have to get to the hospital. There will be so much paperwork to take care of. Do you know which hospital they took my daughter to? Was it George Washington or Georgetown Hospital?" Myra begged. Tears rolled down her wrinkled cheeks.

Nikki looked away. She knew she was being cowardly, but there was just no way she could get the words past her lips to tell Myra her only daughter was dead. She watched as police officers dispersed the crowd of onlookers until only the three couples remained. Where was the car that hit Barbara? Did they take it away already? Where was the driver? She wanted to voice the questions aloud but remained silent because of Myra.

Nikki watched as the young officer steeled himself for what he had to do. He worked his thin neck around the starched collar of his shirt, cleared his throat once, and then again. "Ma'am, your daughter was taken to the morgue at George Washington Hospital. There's no hurry on the paperwork. I can have one of the officers take you to the hospital if you like. I'm . . . I'm sorry for your loss, ma'am."

Myra's scream was primal as she slipped to the ground. The young cop dropped to his knees. "I thought she knew. I didn't . . . Jesus . . ."

"We need to get her to a doctor right away. Will you stay with her for a minute, officer? I need to get my cell phone out of the car to make some calls." Her first call was to Myra's doctor and then she called Charles. Both promised to meet her at the emergency entrance to GW Hospital.

When she returned, Myra was sitting up, supported by the young officer. She looked dazed and her speech was incoherent. "She doesn't weigh much. I can easily carry her to the cruiser," the officer said. Nikki nodded gratefully.

"Can you tell me what happened, officer? Did you get the car that hit Barbara? Those couples standing over there must have seen everything. We even saw it from the restaurant window. Did they get the license plate number? I saw a dark car, but it came out of nowhere. She had a clear path to cross the street. He must have peeled away from the curb at ninety miles an hour."

"I ran the license plate one of the couples gave us, but it isn't going to do any good."

"Why is that?" Nikki rubbed at her temples as a hammer pounded away inside her head.

"Because it was a diplomat's car. That means the driver has diplomatic immunity, ma'am."

Nikki's knees buckled. The young cop reached out to steady her.

"That means he can't be prosecuted," Nikki said in a choked voice.

"Yes, ma'am, that's exactly what it means."

One

Sixteen months later

It was dusk when Nikki Quinn stopped her
cobalt blue BMW in front of the massive iron
gates of Myra Rutledge's McLean estate. She
pressed the remote control attached to the visor
and waited for the lumbering gates to slide open.
She knew Charles was watching her on the closed-
circuit television screen. The security here at the
estate was sophisticated, high-tech, impregnable.
The only thing missing was concertina wire along
the top of the electrified fence.

Nikki sailed up the half mile of cobblestones
to the driveway that led around to the back of
the McLean mansion. When she was younger,
she and Barbara referred to the house as Myra's
Fortress. She'd loved growing up here, loved
riding across the fields on Barbara's horse Starlite,

loved playing with Barbara in the tunnels underneath the old house that had once been used to aid runaway slaves.

The engine idling, Nikki made no move to get out of the car. She hated coming here these days, hated seeing the empty shell her beloved Myra had turned into. All the life, all the spark had gone out of her. According to Charles, Myra sat in the living room, drinking tea, staring at old photo albums, the television tuned to CNN twenty-four hours a day. She hadn't left the house once since Barbara's funeral.

She finally turned off the engine, gathered her briefcase, weekend bag, and purse. Should she put the top up or leave it down? The sky was clear. She shrugged. If it looked like rain, Charles would put the top up.

"Any change?" she asked, walking into the kitchen.

Charles shook his head before he hugged her. "She's gone downhill even more these last two weeks. I hate saying this, but I don't think she even noticed you weren't here, Nikki."

Nikki flinched. "I couldn't get here, Charles. I had to wait for a court verdict. I must have called a hundred times," Nikki said, tossing her gear on the countertop. Her eyes pleaded with Myra's houseman for understanding.

Charles Martin was a tall man with clear crystal blue eyes and a shock of white hair that was thick and full. Once he'd been heavier but this past year had taken a toll on him, too. She noticed the tremor in his hand when he handed her a cup of coffee.

"Is she at least talking, Charles?"

"She responds if I ask her a direct question. Earlier in the week she fired me. She said she didn't need me anymore."

"My God!" Nikki sat down at the old oak table with the claw feet. Myra said the table was over three hundred years old and hand-hewn. As a child, she'd loved eating in the kitchen. Loved sitting at the table drinking cold milk and eating fat sugar cookies. She looked around. There didn't seem to be much life in the kitchen these days. The plants didn't seem as green, the summer dishes were still in the pantry, the winter place mats were still on the table. Even the braided winter rugs were still on the old pine floors. In the spring, Myra always changed them. She blinked. "This kitchen looks like an institution kitchen, Charles. The house is too quiet. Doesn't Myra play her music anymore?"

"No. She doesn't do anything anymore. I tried to get her to go for a walk today. She told me to get out of her face. I have to fight with her to take a shower. I'm at my wit's end. I don't know what to do anymore. This is no way to live, Nikki."

"Maybe it's time for some tough love. Let me see if she responds to me this evening. By the way, what's for dinner?"

"Rack of lamb. Those little red potatoes you like, and fresh garden peas. I made a blackberry cobbler just for you. But when you're not here, I end up throwing it all away. Myra nibbled on a piece of toast today." Charles threw his hands in the air and stomped over to the stove to open the oven door.

Nikki sighed. She straightened her shoulders before she marched into the living room where Myra was sitting on the sofa. She bent down to kiss the wrinkled cheek. "Did you miss me, Myra?"

"Nikki! It's nice to see you. Of course, I missed you. Sit down, dear. Tell me how you are. Is the law firm doing nicely? How's our softball team doing? Are you still seeing that assistant district attorney?" Her voice trailed off to nothing as she stared at the television set whose sound was on mute.

Nikki sat down and reached for the remote control. "I hope you don't mind if I switch to the local station. I want to see the news." She turned the volume up slightly.

"Let's see. Yes, I'm still seeing Jack, and the firm is doing wonderfully. We have more cases than we can handle. The team is in fourth place. I'm fine but I worry about you, Myra. Charles is worried about you, too."

"I fired Charles."

"I know, but he's still here. He has nowhere to go, Myra. You have to snap out of this depression. I can arrange some grief counseling sessions for you. You need a medical checkup. You have to let it go, Myra. You can't bring Barbara back. I can't stand seeing you like this. Barbara wouldn't approve of the way you're grieving. She always said life is for the living."

"I never heard her say any such thing. I can't let it go. She's with me every minute of every day. There's nothing to live for. The bastard who killed my daughter robbed my life as well. He's out there somewhere living a good life. If I could just get my hands on him for five minutes, I would . . ."

"Myra, he's back in his own country. Shh, listen. That man," Nikki said, pointing to the screen, "was set free today because of a technicality. He killed a young girl and he's walking away a free man. Jack prosecuted the case and lost."

"He must not be a very good district attorney if he lost the case," Myra snapped. Nikki's eyebrows shot upward. Was that a spark of interest? Childishly, she crossed her fingers.

"He's an excellent district attorney, Myra, but the law is the law. The judge let things go because they weren't legal. Oh, look, there's the mother of the girl. God, I feel so sorry for her. She was in court every single day. The papers said she never took her eyes off the accused, not even for a minute. The reporters marveled at the woman's steadfast intensity. Every day they did an article about her. Jack said she fainted when the verdict came in."

"I know just how she feels," Myra said, leaning forward to see the screen better. "What's she doing, Nikki? Look, there's Jack! He's very photogenic."

Nikki watched as the scene played out in front of her. She saw Jack's lips move, knew he was saying something but she couldn't hear over the voices of the excited news reporters. She saw his arm reach out but he was too late. Marie Lewellen fired the gun in her hand point-blank at the man who killed her daughter.

The television screen turned black and then came to life again.

Barnes looked directly into the camera, his eyes wide with shocked disbelief. Blood bubbled from his mouth. "I . . . should have . . . killed . . . you, too . . . you bitch!"

"You killed my little girl. You don't deserve to live. I'm glad I killed you. Glad!" Marie Lewellen screamed.

Barnes fell face forward onto the concrete steps of the courthouse.